# Something True

# Something True

## KARELIA STETZ-WATERS

New York   Boston

Copyright © 2014 by Karelia Stetz-Waters
Cover design by Brigid Pearson
Cover copyright © 2014 by Hachette Book Group, Inc.

Forever Yours
Hachette Book Group
1290 Avenue of the Americas
New York, NY 10104
hachettebookgroup.com
twitter.com/foreverromance

First published as an ebook and as a print on demand: January 2015

Forever Yours is an imprint of Grand Central Publishing.
The Forever Yours name and logo are trademarks of Hachette Book Group, Inc.

The publisher is not responsible for websites (or their content) that are not owned by the publisher.

The Hachette Speakers Bureau provides a wide range of authors for speaking events. To find out more, go to www.hachettespeakersbureau.com or call (866) 376-6591.

ISBN: 978-1-4555-6054-7 (ebook edition)
ISBN: 978-1-4555-6056-1 (print on demand edition)

*For Fay*

# Acknowledgments

Thank you to all my friends and colleagues at Linn-Benton Community College and to all the friends, near and far, who make my life so rich. Thank you to Jane Dystel and Miriam Goderich for opening the doors of the publishing world for me. Thank you to Scott Rosenfeld for believing in this manuscript and polishing it so that it shines. Thank you to my parents, Elin and Albert Stetz, for supporting me and supporting my love of writing since I was a little girl. Thank you to my wife, Fay Stetz-Waters. Because of you, I get to live the best romance ever. Finally, thank you to Portland for being as magical in reality as it is in this story.

# *Something True*

# Chapter 1

It was late June, the kind of warm summer evening when hopeless romantics make bad choices about beautiful women. The twilight was all watery, yellow-blue brightness, and Portland glowed with the promise of warm pavement and cool moonlight. It was, as it turned out, a dangerous mix for Tate Grafton, who stood at the till of Out in Portland Coffee trying to make out what her boss had done to the change drawer.

"How is it possible," she called without looking up, "that you are eight dollars over, but it's all in nickels?"

Just then, the wind chime on the door tinkled. It was because of that evening light that came from nowhere and everywhere at the same time and filled the city with a sense of possibility that Tate did not say, "Sorry, we're closed."

The woman who had just walked in wore her hair pulled back in a low ponytail and had the kind of sleek magazine blondness that Tate was required, as a feminist, to say she did not like. And she did not like it in magazines. But in real life, and in the dangerous twilight that filtered through the front window, the woman was very pretty. She did not carry anything. No laptop. No purse. Not even a wallet and cell phone clutched in one hand. Nor did she have room in the pockets of her tight jeans for more than a credit card. Tate noticed.

The woman stood in the doorway surveying the coffee shop, from the exposed pipes, to the performance space, to the mural of Gertrude Stein. Right down to the cracked linoleum floor. Then she strode up to the counter and asked for a skinny, tall latte with Sweet'N Low.

"I'll, um…" Tate ran her hand through her hair, as if to push it off her face, although the clippers had already done that for her. "I'll have to warm up the machines. It'll be a minute."

"I'll just take what's in the airpot," the woman said, still surveying the shop.

Tate filled a paper cup and squeezed a biodegradable corn-plastic lid on it. The woman drew a bill from the pocket of her crisp, white shirt. Tate shook her head.

"On the house. It's probably stale."

She was about to go back to counting the till when the woman asked, "How long has this been a coffee shop?"

Tate considered. "It opened as a bookstore in 1979. Then it closed for a few years in the early '80s, opened back up as a coffee shop in 1988, and it's been running since then. I think. I've been here for nine years."

*Too long.*

"'Out in Portland Coffee.'" The woman read the side of her cup.

"Out Coffee," Tate said. "That's what everyone calls it."

"Any other businesses in the area?"

"There's Ron's Reptiles, the AM/PM, the Oregon Adult Theater."

Across the street, the theater's yellow letter board advertised HD FILM! STRIPPER SPANK-A-THON WEDNESDAYS!

From the back room, Maggie, the boss, called out, "They're all perverts."

The woman nodded and turned as if to leave. Then she seemed to reconsider.

"Are there any women's bars in the area?" She glanced around the shop again, her eyes sliding past Tate's, resting everywhere but in Tate's direction.

"There's the Mirage." Tate gave her directions.

"Is it safe to walk?"

"As safe as anywhere in the city."

As soon as the woman left, twenty-year-old Krystal—Maggie's surrogate daughter or pet project depending on who you asked—popped out of the back room, where she had ostensibly been studying.

"I heard that," she said. "As safe as anywhere in the city." She hopped up onto the counter next to Tate.

"Get off the counter." Tate ruffled Krystal's short, pink hair.

"Is my butt a health code violation?"

"Yes."

"Well, anyway," Krystal said, swinging her legs and kicking the cupboard behind her, "I heard that. She practically asked you to walk her. *Is it safe?*" Krystal imitated a woman's soprano with an added whine. *"Hold me in your big, strong arms you sexy butch."*

"Ugh." Tate rolled her eyes. "Why is she still here?" she called to Maggie in the back room.

"She's part of our family, Tate!"

Kindhearted Maggie; something had happened in utero, and she had been born without the ability to understand sarcasm.

"Some family," Tate said, winking at Krystal and pulling her into a hug.

"Did you like her?" Krystal asked, pulling away from Tate.

"Who?"

"The woman who was just here."

"No." Tate turned back to the cash register and rolled a stack of nickels into a paper sleeve.

"Why didn't you go after her, like in the movies? She probably thought you were cute."

*Like in the movies.* That was always Krystal's question: Why isn't it like the movies?

"I'm *working*," Tate said with feigned annoyance. "She just wanted a coffee. Anyway, I just got dumped, remember?"

"So?"

In the quiet minutes between customers, Tate had been reading *The Sociology of Lesbian Sexual Experience*. Now Krystal pulled the book from behind the counter and flipped it open.

" 'The Alpha Butch,' " she read. " 'In this paradigm' "—she pronounced it par-i-di-gum—" 'the femme lesbian is looking for a strong, masculine—but not manly—woman who can protect her against the perceived threat of straight society.' That's you!" Krystal sounded like a shopper who had just found the perfect accessory. "I bet that's why she came in here. She saw you through the window and she was like, 'I've got to meet this woman.'" Krystal closed the book and examined the woman on the cover. "You're way cuter than this girl."

It wasn't hard; the woman on the cover looked like a haggard truck driver from 1950.

"Aren't you supposed to be studying for the GED?" Tate asked.

"My dad taught me most of that stuff already, when I was, like, a little kid."

"Then take the test and go to college," Tate said.

"I don't need to, 'cause my dad and I are going to start a club, and I don't need a degree for that."

"Right."

"She was pretty," Krystal said. "Like Hillary Clinton if Hillary Clinton was, like, a million years younger."

Tate took the book from Krystal's hands and pretended to swat her with it.

"I am not 'Alpha Butch.'"

Nonetheless, Tate did steal a glance at her face in the bathroom mirror before leaving the coffee shop. The woman's perfect good looks made her aware of her own dark eyebrows and her nose, which jutted out and then took a hook-like dive. She looked older than her thirty-five years. She looked tired after the long shift. And she did not feel alpha anything, even with her steel-toed Red Wings and her leather jacket. She did not even feel beta, or whatever letter came next in Krystal's alphabet.

Still, a spring spent rebuilding the network of railroad-tie stair steps in the Mount Tabor Community Garden had defined the muscles beneath her labrys tattoo. She was tanned from the work. Her head was freshly shaved. And it was summer, one of those perfect summer nights that Portlanders live for, so warm, so unambiguously beautiful it made up for ten months of steady rain.

When Tate sidled up to the bar at the Mirage, her friend Vita, the bartender, leaned over.

"She's here," Vita said.

For a second, Tate thought of the woman.

"Who?" she asked.

Vita shot her a look that said, *Don't pretend not to know when you've asked me about her every day for six months.*

Abigail. Tate could see her legs wrapped around the body of the cello, her hips splayed, her black concert skirt riding up, her orange hair falling over the cello's orange wood.

Vita plunked a shot in front of Tate.

"On the house. She's with someone."

Tate knocked the shot back, nearly choking as her brain registered the taste a split second after it hit the back of her throat.

"What the hell was that?" She wiped her mouth.

"Frat Boy's Revenge. Jägermeister and grape vodka. I made one too many for the baby dykes in the corner."

Tate grimaced and cleared her mouth with a swig of beer. Then she noticed something: that indefinable feeling of being watched. She turned. At a table by the door, the woman from

Out Coffee sat, one hand resting on the base of a martini glass, as though she feared it might fly away. She caught Tate's eye for a second, smiled, and then looked away with a shake of her head. When she looked up again, Tate raised her beer with a slight smile.

"God, you have it so easy!" Vita said, punching Tate on the arm.

Tate turned back to the bar. "She's not interested in me. Look at her."

"*You* look at her," Vita said, raising both eyebrows.

In the mirror behind the bar, Tate saw the woman picking her way through the tables, hesitating, looking from side to side as though puzzling her way through a maze.

"She's cute. Don't blow it," Vita said in a whisper the whole bar could hear.

"Hello." The woman took the stool next to Tate's. She sat on the very edge, as though ready to flee.

Vita leaned in. She looked predatory. Her hair was teased into a rocker bouffant, and she had on more leopard print than Tate thought was appropriate work attire, even at a bar.

"Will you be buying this lady a drink?" Vita asked Tate.

"I'm fine," the woman said. "I was just leaving."

At that moment, Abigail appeared. Tate took in the sight: Abigail on the arm of Duke Bryce, drag king extraordinaire. Duke grinned, a big toothy grin, like an Elvis impersonator on steroids. Abigail clung to Duke's arm, a romance heroine hanging off the lesbian Fabio.

"Someone you know?" the woman asked.

"Knew."

A moment later, Abigail released her lover and came over, an apologetic look on her face.

"I'm sorry. I didn't think I'd see you here. I mean, I was going to tell you about me and Duke, you know, earlier."

Tate shrugged. The music had dropped a decibel, and a few of the other patrons turned to listen.

"I mean, I know you're still really upset about the breakup. About us. Really, I wasn't looking for anything. I just saw Duke one day and presto!" Abigail's giggle made it sound like she had suddenly been transported back to seventh grade. "I thought I wanted someone who understood my music."

That had been the explanation when Abigail cheated on Tate with the oboist.

"But then I met Duke, and she's just so...brava."

Duke was an alpha butch, Tate thought. She could take a picture and show Krystal.

"I just know it all happened for a reason, Tate."

Tate was trying to think of a response to this when she was startled by a touch. The woman from the coffee shop had touched the back of her head. She ran her hand across Tate's cropped hair, then slid her fingertips down the back of Tate's neck. Then she withdrew her hand quickly.

"Who is she?" The woman's voice was much softer than it had been in the coffee shop, almost frightened.

Tate was still concentrating on the woman's touch, which seemed to linger on her skin. It had been six months since Abigail officially dumped her, but much longer since she had been touched like that. Abigail had never caressed her. Abigail seduced her cello, everyone in the orchestra agreed, but she had squeezed Tate. Tate had always come away from their love-making feeling rather like rising bread dough: kneaded and punched down.

Now Tate stumbled over her words. "This is…this is Abby. She's a cellist."

The woman leaned closer to Tate, and Tate could smell a sweet perfume, like citrus blossoms, rising from her hair.

"What seat?" the woman asked Abigail.

This had been an important distinction that had always been lost on Tate.

"Third," Abigail answered defensively.

"Oh. Only third." The woman turned and, with a gesture even more fleeting than her fingers on Tate's neck, she pressed her lips to Tate's cheek.

Abigail mumbled something Tate did not catch and walked away, disappearing down the hallway that led from the bar to the dance floor. The woman straightened and crossed her legs.

"I'm sorry," the woman said. She took a large sip of her drink. "I don't do things like that. I just don't like all those freckles."

"Freckles?"

Tate had loved the beige-on-white-lace of Abigail's freckles. Plus, one couldn't hold someone's freckles against them. Or maybe, if one looked like this woman, one could.

"She reminds me of my sister." The woman spoke quickly. "The freckles and that whole 'I'm going to be nice to you, but I'm actually sticking the fork in' thing. 'You can't tell me to piss off because that would make you look like a jerk, even though I'm the one who's ruined your life.' I know that routine." The woman finished the rest of her martini in one sip.

Tate was still trying to figure out what to do with the feeling that suffused her body. The woman's touch, offered unexpectedly after months of abstinence and then just as quickly withdrawn, left her dizzy. She felt like she had just swallowed a bowl of warm moonlight. But she recovered her manners and held out her hand.

"My name is..."

The woman cut her off. "I don't want to know."

Tate withdrew her hand, the moonlight cooling. But as soon as she withdrew her hand, the woman grabbed it, holding on as though she were going to shake hands but lingering much longer than any handshake.

"I didn't mean it like that," she said.

She leaned forward, her perfect good looks furrowed by worry.

Behind the woman's head, Vita flicked her tongue between the V of her two raised fingers.

Tate widened her eyes, the only nonverbal cue she could flash Vita. *Embarrass me, and I will strangle you*, her eyes said. But she wasn't sure Vita was listening.

"It's not that I don't want to know you." The woman still held Tate's hand, now stroking the back of Tate's knuckles with her thumb. "It's just...I don't live here. I live a thousand miles away." The woman raised Tate's knuckles to her lips and kissed them. "Right now I don't want to be me."

"You're straight," Tate said.

Behind the woman's head, Vita mouthed, *So?!*

The woman said nothing.

"You've got a husband and two kids at home." Tate extracted her hand. "A husband with a shotgun and two kids who will spend thousands of dollars on therapy when they realize you weren't going to the PTA meetings at all."

The woman bowed her head and laughed. Tate could only see her dimples, suddenly apparent in the smooth face. *All right*, Tate thought. *I'll take it.* It was the first time in months that she had sat at the Mirage and not thought about Abigail. She hadn't even looked up to see if Abigail had come back in the room.

"I don't have any kids," the woman said. "I can promise you that. I was married once, but we divorced years ago, and I'm not straight. I just wanted one night where I'm not what I do or where I work or who I know, but that's silly, isn't it?"

Tate thought about Out Coffee. About Maggie, Krystal, Vita, and the Mount Tabor Community Garden Association. About her studio apartment off northeast Firline and the old Hungarian couple who lived in the unit below hers. She thought about Portland, with its mossy side streets and its glorious summers.

"If you're not who you know, where you work, where you live, who are you?" she asked.

"I'm this," the woman said and took Tate's face in her hands and kissed her.

At first it was just a soft kiss, lip to lip. Then Tate felt the woman's hands tremble against her cheeks. Their lips parted. Her tongue found Tate's. Beneath the bar, their knees touched, and Tate felt the woman's legs shake as though she had run a great distance.

A second later, Tate pulled away, but only because she wanted the woman, and she felt herself going down in the annals of barroom legend. She could already hear Vita's rendition of the story: *Tate just reached over and grabbed the girl, practically swallowed her. It was like she unhinged her jaw, and the girl's head was in her mouth. Bang! Like a boa constrictor.* Friends and customers would listen attentively, waving away Tate's protests. Who wanted a story about a lonely barista longing for summer romance when they could have Vita's tale about Tate Grafton, Python Lover?

"Would you like to play a game of pool?" Tate said, to get out from under Vita's grin and to give herself a moment to think.

She was not the kind of woman who picked up girls at the bar. Vita picked up girls. Vita had picked up so many women she remembered them by taglines like "The Groaner" or "Wooly Bicycle Legs." She often told Tate that Tate could do the same, if she would only "put out some effort." According to Vita, half the girls at the Mirage were in love with Tate. But Tate did not believe her, nor did she want an assortment of half-remembered encounters.

But she wanted this woman.

They moved toward the side of the bar where two pool tables stood on a raised platform under low-hanging lights.

"Are you any good?" she asked.

"I'm all right," Tate said.

The woman rolled her pool cue on the table to see if it was true.

"None of them are straight," Tate said.

"I suppose not." The woman glanced toward the door. "Not here."

Tate laughed.

"You break then," the woman said.

Tate cracked the balls apart, sinking two solids and following with a third.

"So, if you won't tell me your name," Tate began. "Or where you live or what you do, what are we going to talk about?"

"We could talk about you."

The woman sank a high ball but missed her next shot. Her hand was unsteady, and she looked around the bar more than she looked at the table. She looked at *Tate* more than she looked around the bar—but only out of the corner of her eye.

"I already know where you work," she said, casting that glance at Tate and then looking down. "And I know that, prior to right now, you've had bad taste in women. So...what's your name? How long have you worked at the coffee shop?"

Tate took another shot and sank a ball.

"No," she said slowly. "I'll tell you what you tell me."

"Okay." The woman leaned over the pool table and her hair draped in a curtain over one side of her face. She took her shot but missed. "I learned to play pool in college with three girls who I thought would be my friends for life. We played at a sports bar called the Gator Club. And I don't know any of them now. They could be dead. They could be professional pool sharks." She leaned against the wall and surveyed the table. "How about you?"

"I learned to play here the summer I turned twenty-one," Tate said. She sank another ball and shot a smile in the woman's direction. "The table is off. It slopes. It's not fair, you being from out of town and all. I should give you a handicap."

"Tell me how it slopes and give me two out of three."

Tate had never been the kind of person who made bets or the kind of person who sidled up to beautiful women, looked down at them lustfully, and said things like, *What will you give me when I win?*

But apparently that was the kind of woman she was. Tonight. In the summer.

"What will you give me if I win?"

The woman did not step away. Or laugh. She rested one hand on Tate's chest, right over Tate's racing heart.

"I'll answer one question," she said. "About anything. I'll tell you one true thing. And if I win—it's that corner, right?—I want you to take me someplace."

"Where?"

"Someplace special. You've been playing pool here since you were twenty-one. You must know someplace no one goes. Someplace I wouldn't see otherwise. Something I'll remember."

"Okay."

They played in silence, standing closer than necessary, touching more than necessary. The woman seemed to relax, and her game got better. Tate won the first game but only just barely. The woman won the second, masterfully compensating for the uneven table. Tate was in line to win the third game but scratched on the eight ball. The woman laughed a sweet, musical laugh tinged with victory.

"Take me somewhere," the woman said.

At the bar, Vita pointed and mouthed, *You rock.* At a table near the door, Abigail leaned against Duke's leather vest and scowled. But Tate did not see them. She slipped her hand through the woman's arm and stepped out into the moonlight.

# Chapter 2

Do you mind a walk?" Tate asked as they stood outside the Mirage in the glare of a streetlight.

"I came for a walk," the woman said.

They headed up Division toward the hills that cradled the city.

"It's an interesting question," Tate said after a few blocks.

"What is?"

"What can you know about someone if you don't know the details, the stuff on their tax return?"

The woman squeezed her hand, but did not answer.

"For example, you could tell me how you feel about dogs," Tate said, "if you fight with your lovers and how clean you keep your home, how you feel about money, and what you like to eat. That would probably give me a better picture of whether or not we would be compatible than your job."

Tate paused, embarrassed. Compatible implied a future.

This was a mistake Vita's lovers made. Tate had heard Vita complain about it many times. "We made out at a Portland Timbers game," Vita would say, raising her hands in frustration. "Someone poured beer on us. What part of that says ''til death do us part'?"

But the woman just said, "I suppose."

She gazed up at the moon, tripping on the uneven sidewalk. Tate steadied her, one hand touching the woman's belly just for a second. She felt the soft flesh and beneath that the hard muscle of the woman's stomach. She thought she heard the woman take a quick breath. Then Tate pulled away shyly.

"Not that there's much on my tax return," Tate added.

"No dependents?" the woman asked.

"Not even a dog."

"Want one?"

"I live in an apartment. If I didn't, I'd have a Rottweiler. I had one as a kid. I loved that dog, but I had to give it up when…" Tate stopped herself. "Of course, if I got one, I'd have to get a rescue. My boss, Maggie, she's like a mother to me, to half of Portland really. She used to do dog rescue. With all the dogs that get put down, it would break her heart if I bought some fancy pedigree. So I'd probably get one that ate my couch."

The woman laughed.

"You'd pick a dog to make your boss happy?"

"Yeah." Tate shrugged. With all the hard facts off-limits, it was strangely easy to be honest about the rest. "I'd do anything to make her happy."

"I shouldn't laugh," the woman added, her voice going cold. "I do everything to make my bosses happy."

"And your job is...?"

Tate was just teasing. She did not expect the woman to tell her. But the woman looked at her with such apprehension.

"No. Don't tell me," Tate said.

After a moment, the woman said, "I like dogs, but I travel too much to have one. I live in a hotel room."

"And is it tidy?"

"Never."

"And to eat?"

"Sushi."

"And your lovers?"

"They're like the dogs."

"They eat your couch?" Tate teased.

"I'm not home enough to have one."

Tate indicated a change of direction, and they turned off the gritty flank of Division, with its barred windows and peeling auto repair signs, and onto a tree-lined side street.

"And you?" the woman asked. "Tell me about your life."

"That's not the game we're playing, is it?"

"All right." The woman leaned into her. "Tell me more about Portland."

And Tate told her about the markets and the coffee shops, the secret tunnels that ran beneath the city streets, the Chinese garden, the pirate-themed vegan strip club and the mausoleum that housed fifty thousand of Portland's deceased in a giant apartment complex. She told her how the high-rises looked in the rain: as though they had risen from the Willamette River, blue and green and gray. She told her how Portlanders loved to play—dodgeball, kickball, roller derby, disc golf, women's rugby, men's volleyball—and how sometimes a horde of people would dress up like zombies and go barhopping.

The farther they walked the larger the houses grew, the greener the lots, and the stronger the scent of honeysuckle and jasmine.

"What do people do where you're from?" Tate asked.

"Pilates."

"Do you?"

"Of course," the woman said.

"Like it?"

"I hate it. It's a bunch of hypercompetitive alpha females all trying to out-tone each other."

"Alpha females." Tate laughed.

"It doesn't work either. I mean they're fit, but they're not sexy."

They passed under the shadow of a particularly leafy maple. The woman slowed, raised up on tiptoes, and delivered another quick kiss to Tate's cheek.

"You are," the woman said.

Eventually, they arrived at the Mount Tabor Community Garden. The garden was built on a steep hill. Gardeners followed the network of steps Tate and her team of amateur engineers had fashioned out of railroad ties and hay bales. It had been cultivated for years and many plots had stayed in the same hands for decades. There were fruit trees that stood twenty feet tall, blueberry hedges that stretched for a quarter of an acre, and a hundred varieties of tomato. But in the darkness it was just shadows and the smell of compost and warm earth.

"Are we allowed to be here?" the woman asked.

"Sure."

"But what about the people who own it?"

"Nobody owns it," Tate said.

The woman cocked her head. "Someone owns *everything*."

"Not this."

Tate pushed open the sagging wooden gate that kept nothing out. She caught the smell of the woman's hair mixing with the smell of the garden as they walked.

"Did you love that woman at the bar?" the woman asked.

Tate stopped. "I thought we weren't asking personal questions."

"We aren't asking tax-form questions. Who, what, when, where, and how much money did you make? Those are the opposite of personal."

"Okay. Yes. I loved her very much," Tate said, offering the woman a hand as they clambered up onto a tall hay bale.

"Have you loved every person you've dated?"

"Of course."

"Of course." The woman paused beside a tree that Tate could tell, by smell, was a plum tree. She put her hand against Tate's cheek. "That's precious."

Tate drew her hand away and kissed it. Somewhere a plum released its grip on the branch and fell. Tate led the woman over another hay bale and down a long row of tomato plants.

"My friend Vita says I'm hopeless." She pulled a cherry tomato off a vine and held it out. "It's a Golden Globe."

The woman put the tomato to her mouth cautiously.

"And how did she leave you?" the woman asked after a few more steps.

"The cellist? She cheated on me."

"With that woman?"

"Duke? No." Tate sighed. "With an oboist."

She had only seen the woman once. In a rehearsal. Puffing out the space between her upper lip and her nose as she tooted a long, low note on the ridiculously narrow instrument. Then, as if dissatisfied with the sound, she had turned her instrument upside down and emptied out a pool of spit. It seemed, to Tate, like something that should be done in the privacy of a bathroom.

"I can't imagine," the woman said. "You're lovely."

*Lovely.* Tate felt herself blush.

"Come. This is what I want to show you," she said.

They had reached the top of the garden and, with it, Tate's plot. There, at the peak, stood a dark hump, like a yurt at the top of the hill. Tate led them around it to the opening, and they stepped through.

"It's a kiwi tree. I planted it nine years ago."

There was a low bench in the center of the leafy enclave, and Tate dusted it off so they could sit. Through an opening carved out of the hanging leaves, they could see the whole city spread out below. Through its midst ran the river, crisscrossed by bridges. On the other side, the city towers glittered, and behind them, the northwest hills looked like an elfin forest. Tate put her arm around the woman's shoulders.

"Have you ever been in love?" Tate asked.

"I was married once, but I didn't love him." The woman leaned against Tate's shoulder. "Did you know married people live longer? They are healthier and richer. All the studies show it. And they don't have to be particularly happy to get the benefits of marriage. That's what I was thinking about at the altar." She gave a short, sad laugh. "I was thinking marriage would lower my blood pressure. I was thinking it would ensure a comfortable retirement, and I was telling myself that in 1840 that was enough. Why not now?"

Tate touched the woman's neck.

"In 1840 people died of strep throat," she pointed out.

"I never told anyone that." The woman gazed out over the city. "You are the only person in the world who knows what I was thinking when I said 'I do.'"

"So why did you marry him?"

"I always knew I was gay," the woman said.

"Not the usual reason to marry a man."

"It was all so inconvenient. If I wanted to get ahead, if I wanted the job, the life, all that tax-return stuff." The woman leaned her elbows on her knees and rested her chin on her folded hands. "Gay just didn't fit into the picture."

The woman was even prettier worried, Tate thought. It wasn't fair. Worry brought out Tate's nose. She was not sure how it happened, but it did. And it pulled her eyebrows together in a Frida-Kahlo-ish way that had almost worked for Frida and did not work for Tate at all. But that was just a passing thought. Mostly, Tate wanted to pull the woman into her arms and kiss away her grief.

"And now?" she asked.

"*Now* is what I'm looking for. Just this moment and nothing else."

The woman stood up as if she were about to leave, but when Tate stood to follow her she took a step toward Tate and stopped, frozen.

"Now?" Tate asked.

The woman nodded.

Tate cupped her face. The woman's eyes were very wide. Her face was pale. Her expression was close to fear but closer to desire. Very gently, Tate pressed her lips to the woman's. The woman returned her kiss with a shyness that surprised Tate. Not since she was a teenager had a girl kissed her with such tentative uncertainty. But it was sweet, and they kissed like that for a long time, and slowly the woman relaxed. Her hands slid beneath Tate's T-shirt. Her hips pressed against Tate's body. Her breath quickened.

Tate felt as if all the dull longing of the past months had suddenly wound itself into a tight, hot knot below her belt. She held the woman close, resisting the urge to press herself against the woman's thigh, and then giving in, and then resisting again, until the woman said, "Come here."

The woman took a step back, positioning her back against the trunk of the kiwi tree, and then pulling Tate to her. She sighed as their bodies connected.

"Fuck," the woman whispered. Her eyes flew open.

"Are you okay?" Tate's voice was rough.

Suddenly, the woman clutched Tate's ass in her hands and moved her hips in a circle that pressed against every part of Tate's aching body. Again and again. Each rotation soothing the ache and making it more acute. Tate braced one arm against the tree. Her legs felt weak.

"Oh, God," the woman said again. "It's so much better."

Tate's body felt liquid. One more rotation of the woman's hips, and she knew she would come. A remote part of her brain thought she shouldn't. She didn't do things like this. With strangers. In public gardens. But her thoughts were no match for the warmth that was spreading through her body, and the woman seemed ready for the same climax.

"I didn't know. I..." the woman said. Then she stopped suddenly, releasing her grip on Tate's hips. "I hear something."

Voices rang out, far off in the garden.

Someone called, "Wait up."

And another voice chimed in, "We're over here."

A moment later they saw flashlight beams far off in the garden. The woman stared at them, transfixed. Her eyes were wide and dark and startled.

"We have to get out of here," she said.

Tate could barely stand for wanting the woman so much, and for a moment, she was certain the woman was about to flee. The disappointment she felt was a physical pain. Her breath came in a quick, deep gasp.

Then the woman touched her chest, fleetingly, like a forbidden lover.

"Please say you live nearby," she said. "Take me home."


Tate led the woman into the foyer of her apartment building. Pawel and Rose, the old Hungarian couple, had their front door open although it was after midnight. A talk show blared on the television. Tate glanced in the direction of the sound and motioned for the woman to be quiet.

*They'll want to talk*, she mouthed.

Once upstairs and inside her studio apartment, Tate turned on a small, fringed lamp. It was a present from Krystal. Tate would never have bought anything with so many tassels, something so purple, but the light it cast was perfect.

"Let me put on some music."

Tate opened her laptop and selected a playlist.

When she turned, prepared to offer the woman a drink, the woman was unbuttoning the last button of her shirt. As Tate watched, she let it slide to the floor. Then the woman caught Tate's gaze and held it as she unclasped her bra and let it drop, revealing a body as beautiful and lush as summer itself. She was somehow bigger unclothed, curvier. Her hips seemed wider and her breasts heavier. Her stance was commanding, yet Tate read a question in the woman's eyes as she pushed a strand of her long blond hair behind her ear. Tate had a sudden intuition: *She thinks I might say no.*

"You are very lovely," Tate said.

She stepped toward the woman and kissed her, tenderly at first and then hungrily, enjoying the feel of the woman's skin beneath her hands, enjoying the woman's hands beneath her own shirt.

"I want you," the woman said, her voice lower than a whisper.

Tate took her hand and drew her to the bed, which stood in the center of the studio.

"Lay down," she said softly.

Then she pulled off her own shirt and bra and kicked her boots off. She lay down next to the woman.

"You're beautiful," Tate said.

She cupped the woman's face in her hand. The woman watched her with wide eyes. Tate let her hand slide down the woman's body to her perfect breast. She stroked her nipple until the skin hardened, and the woman pushed her chest toward Tate's hand. Then Tate drew the woman's nipple into her mouth while her other hand explored the woman's jeans, loosening the button, and stroking the woman through her lace underwear.

"You don't know how long I've waited for this," the woman whispered.

Tate looked up.

"It has been a long time for me too."

"For you?" The woman appraised Tate with a quizzical smile. "Really?"

"Really."

The woman gave a gentle laugh. "I wouldn't have guessed."

Tate was going to say something else, but she lost her words before she could form them.

They shed the rest of their clothing in a flurry. When they were both naked, Tate lay on top of the woman, straddling her hips, certain that if she allowed their legs to intertwine, she would come helplessly and instantly. From the way the woman wrapped her legs and arms around Tate's body, holding her tightly, pressing against her, Tate guessed the woman was on the edge of the same cliff.

Then the woman slid her hand along Tate's ass until her fingertips brushed the back of Tate's naked sex. Tate had been supporting her weight on one arm. Now she felt her arm tremble. The woman gave her a gentle push, indicating that she wanted Tate on her back. Tate rolled over, and the woman leaned over her, her hair falling like a silk curtain around her face. Slowly she slid her hand across Tate's belly and down her thigh.

"You've been waiting for this?" she said quietly.

"Yes."

The woman's hand drifted across Tate's pubic hair, making her whole body shudder in anticipation.

"What did you miss? What do you want most now?" the woman asked.

Tate wanted everything. She wanted the woman's hand on her sex, the woman's lips on her body, her breath on her face. She wanted the woman on top of her and beneath her. She wanted to go slow, and her body screamed to go fast.

Tate closed her eyes. The woman's gaze was too intense.

"What do you want?" she whispered.

Abigail had often asked that question. After barking orders to Tate for half an hour, she would roll over, satiated, and frown at Tate. "What do you want?" As though Tate's desire was an inconvenience Abigail was resigned to deal with.

Now the woman asked, and Tate felt powerless to speak, prostrate with desire. Seeming to sense her distress, the woman gently dipped one finger into Tate's body. Tate felt her hips rise of their own accord.

"I'll just go slow," the woman said. "And you tell me if I get it wrong."

Very slowly and very gently, the woman slid her fingers inside Tate, then out, and around the opening of Tate's sex. Around and around until Tate thought she would faint if the woman did not touch her clitoris. But the woman explored each fold of her labia, gently massaging the engorged flesh. Finally her fingers found the hood of Tate's clit.

"There," Tate gasped.

"There?" the woman echoed. "Or there?" She slid her fingers down a fraction of an inch, massaging Tate's clit until Tate felt like the whole world had disappeared except for the place where the woman touched her, teasing her and teasing her until suddenly it wasn't a tease, and Tate felt the orgasm rock her body like an electrical current.

When she had caught her breath, she pulled the woman to her and kissed her.

"What do *you* want?" Tate whispered into their kiss. "Since it's been such a long time?"

But the woman seemed as stricken by the question as Tate had been.

"I don't know," she said. "I'm so…I haven't felt this way."

Tate kissed her forehead. Then she rolled the woman onto her side and lay behind her, cradling the woman in the curve of her body. She wrapped her hand over the woman's leg and slipped her thumb inside the woman's body so she could press the sensitive flesh behind her clitoris from the inside.

She was not sure if she should command the woman's body like this, without instructions. Abigail had always had a list of instructions. It was rather like working at Out Coffee. *Double, decaf, soy milk. A little to the left. Harder. Not like that. And two sugars.*

But the woman was wet, and Tate felt the woman's body contract as she began to massage her clit from the inside and the outside at the same time. The woman sighed. And they lay like this until the woman's every breath became a moan, and her body moved more frantically against Tate's hand.

It was wonderful holding such a beautiful creature in her arms, in her hand. Tate couldn't help it; she felt a brazen pride at the sound of the woman's moans. Some part of her animal brain crowed *I did that!* And another part of her simply longed to make the woman happy.

Finally Tate whispered, "Is there anything else?"

"It's so good." The woman's voice was almost a sob. "But I never... You don't have to keep going. I can't with other people."

But Tate did not believe her. Gently she withdrew her hand. Then she rolled onto her back and drew the woman on top of her so her legs straddled one of Tate's and their pubic bones met.

"Don't think about it," Tate said, pressing her hips up toward the woman's body.

Tate could feel the moisture of the woman's body on her thigh as the woman worked her clit against Tate's leg.

"I can't." The woman closed her eyes.

Tate put her hands on the woman's hips, urging her toward the rhythm she already knew.

"Just enjoy it," she whispered.

The woman pushed herself hard against Tate's thigh, holding Tate's hips in her hands, pulling their bodies together even as she pushed Tate deeper into the bed. She rocked back, then forward again, then her eyes flew open. Her body jerked several times, and with each convulsion she let out a cry. Then she fell back, her head on Tate's chest, her breath deep and ragged.

"I didn't know…" she began, but she did not finish the sentence, only clutched Tate to her, pressing her face into Tate's breast.

"Are you all right?" Tate asked after a moment.

The woman looked up, her face pinched, not so much with worry, Tate thought, but with grief.

"Talk to me," Tate said.

The woman's lips trembled. "It *does* matter. All that stuff on your tax return matters. It matters more than you know." The woman sat up and grabbed her bra off the floor. She fastened it hastily. "Where's my shirt?" She stood up, casting around for her clothing.

"Okay. It matters," Tate said, rising up on her elbow. "Come back to bed."

The woman fumbled with her jeans.

"Stay the night," Tate said. She was not sure if she was pleading for herself or pleading because it seemed the woman wanted to stay. It was as though some unseen hand was pulling her away. "What is it? Is someone waiting for you? Are you cheating?"

The woman shook her head vehemently.

"Do you have to be somewhere?"

Again, no.

"Did I hurt you?"

At this the woman shook her head even more vigorously.

"Then stay the night," Tate said.

"I don't even know what that means," the woman said, almost to herself, searching the floor for her shoes. "What do you *do* when you 'stay the night'? You can't 'stay' anything."

It occurred to Tate the whole scene would be terribly awkward—like one of Vita's one-night stand debacles—if it wasn't for the wave of tenderness she felt for the woman. She held out her hand. Slowly the woman took it. Tate gently pulled her to the bed and made room for her to lie down.

"I'm sorry," the woman said.

"Shh."

Tate wrapped one arm beneath the woman's neck, one over her waist, so she was encircled in Tate's arms. She pulled her close, feeling the woman's breathing return to normal.

"This is how you stay the night."

"But what happens in the morning?" the woman asked.

Tate pulled her closer.

"That's tomorrow."

# Chapter 3

But in the morning, the woman was gone. It took Tate an agonizing moment to realize she was not in the bathroom, not on the small porch overlooking the vacant lot next door. It took her another minute to search the apartment for a note, but there was none. After that, the pain of picking up her cell phone—silenced in the kitchen drawer—and seeing eight missed calls from Maggie barely registered. She was three and a half hours late to work, but it was the first time she had been late in nine years, a fact that was both reassuring and deeply depressing.

While the night before had been clear and warm, the morning was gray. Portland in the summer was like a tearful bride, radiant but given to the occasional, unexpected burst of rain. The rain lasted just long enough to soak Tate as she rode her Harley to work.

She walked through the door, feeling tired, cold, damp, and unloved—not that she had a right to expect love from a woman who would not even reveal her name. Nonetheless, she had felt loved, had at least felt the possibility of love, as she drifted off to sleep with the woman in her arms.

"You're a good person," the woman had said, just before Tate closed her eyes for the night. *A good person.*

It was a sentiment Maggie had often expressed, but not the one she shared as Tate walked into Out in Portland Coffee, pulling off her helmet and rubbing the rainwater out of her eyes.

"Where have you been?" Maggie asked. "You are three hours late! You're three hours and forty-two minutes late."

Maggie wore baggy elastic-waisted pants printed with Keith Haring figures. On top of the Haring pants, she wore a faded purple T-shirt with a cartoon mouth screaming WHAT PART OF "OFF MY BODY" DON'T YOU GET? It struck Tate that the whole outfit hung off her. Maggie was getting older. She was shrinking. She still had the same narrow, flinty eyes, the same practical chopped-off ginger hair, but it was graying, and her outspoken clothes looked deflated.

Tate rubbed her eyes.

"The cup order just came in," Maggie exclaimed. "We ran out of scones. The cash deposit has to go out. Krystal can't stock the back room. Bella Starr and the Forrest Voices are playing tonight, and we never got the microphone back from the shop."

On the counter, in flagrant violation of health code regulations, Krystal sat, swinging her legs and popping pink gum that perfectly matched her hair, lipstick, and pink Hello Kitty purse.

"I called, and you didn't answer," Maggie went on. "I want to respect your privacy and the equality of our workplace. There is no *boss*; you are not the proletariat. But you could have been killed on that motorcycle of yours, and we need someone to fix the computer. I only clicked one link. It was to save the Bolivian sea snail. They are an important part of the ecosystem of…"

Tate put her hands on Maggie's shoulders.

"Maggie, I love you, but Bolivia is landlocked. I told you; don't click anything, just…don't even look at the computer. Okay?"

Maggie straightened her shoulders. "We have to be engaged in the world," she said.

"You be engaged with the counter," Tate said. "Krystal can do the bank run. I'll get the back stocked."

At that moment, the door opened and a slender woman with two braids, one jutting out over each ear, walked in, her braids swinging energetically. It was a hairstyle Tate could not understand on a grown woman. The woman was Lill, Maggie's ex-partner and current best friend. Lill had her two adopted children in tow. She waved, releasing the hand of Sobia, the little one, who immediately ran to Krystal for a hug. Bartholomew, the eleven-year-old, headed to the sugar bar and began to glut himself on raw sugar cubes.

"Maggie!" Lill cried, opening her arms to embrace her distraught friend. "What happened?"

Little Sobia sneezed loudly behind the counter.

"Krystal!" Tate hissed, pointing at the child and at the health-code-appropriate side of the counter.

"Come on, Tate," Krystal said, picking Sobia up. "Sobia's not dirty. Are you, sweetie?"

"Let's go in the back," Lill said, steering Maggie toward the storeroom.

"I don't know how we're going to survive this onslaught," Maggie said. "I really don't. This kind of blatant disregard for the businesses that make this a community!"

After they disappeared into the back, Tate turned to Krystal.

"Is this all because I was late?"

"Yeah. Five minutes after your shift started, Maggie just broke down and cried," Krystal said.

"Shit!"

"I'm kidding, Tate," Krystal said, carrying Sobia around to the front of the counter. "It's the lease. So where were you? You're never late."

"What about the lease?"

Krystal swung Sobia around in a circle, threatening to crash into the cream and sugar station.

"They're selling the building." She put Sobia down.

"This building?"

"Yeah." Krystal knelt down and put her arms around the child. "Maggie thinks it's the end of the world. We're going to be out on the streets. It's not going to happen though, right?" Sobia squirmed and Krystal released her. "I mean, there'll be a protest and lawyers and stuff, like in the movies, right?"

"Like in the movies," Tate echoed. "I've got to talk to Maggie."

# Chapter 4

The early light coming through the open curtains of Laura Enfield's hotel room illuminated the mess. A $200 Burberry bra lay crumpled on top of the television. Yesterday's suit lay on the untouched bed like a vaporized business associate. She counted four stray coffee mugs. She unbuttoned her blouse and dropped it on the floor. It didn't matter. No one saw the room except the cleaning staff, who reordered as much as they could while maintaining the illusion that they saw nothing and touched nothing.

She walked over to the window. Below her, the push-pull of rush hour traffic had not yet begun on Naito Parkway. Beyond the four-lane road, Waterfront Park woke slowly in the early-morning light. A girl on an old-fashioned bicycle glided by, taking advantage of the wide sidewalk to avoid two homeless men who reclined on a bench watching the river. A man with a wicker basket filled with flowers paused at the intersection, then crossed against the light. Two Vespa riders waved at each other and then shuttled off in different directions.

Portland. She did not even know why her company had assigned her the small development project in east Portland. She did not do single-lot purchases. It was probably because she had told them she was taking a sabbatical to work on her father's campaign. The City Ridge Commercial Plaza project was small enough to wrap up before the Palm Springs project and then her leave. Paid leave, of course. A nice, untraceable campaign donation to the past and future Senator Enfield. Nothing flashy, just a way for the CEOs of the Clark-Vester Commercial Realty Development Group to show that they valued the American family as much as Stan Enfield did.

At her elbow, the hotel phone rang. She jumped, then touched the speaker button.

"You're up early." It was Brenda Phillips, the associate director of Clark-Vester.

"Always," Laura said wryly, although this morning she felt wide-awake in a way she could not remember feeling before: anxious, nauseated, and yet full of something bright and restless.

"Jen did your travel expenses. Apparently you're homeless." Brenda went on to inform her that she had spent 241 of the last 365 nights in one of seventy-three different hotels. "I'm sending you an itemized expense sheet. It's just FYI. I thought you might be curious now that you're going home for a while."

*Homeless.* That was just Brenda's sense of humor, but the word struck a chord.

"Brenda, I have a question." The words came out too fast.

"What's up?" It sounded like Brenda was typing on the other end of the line.

"Tomorrow I have a purchase convocation with the City Ridge Commercial Plaza property," Laura said.

The term always grated on her. A *purchase convocation* was the twenty-minute meeting she had with the small-business owner the Clark-Vester Group was about to destroy, a twenty-minute meeting so that she and Brenda could check the box labeled "fostered positive relationships with all development stakeholders." But this was different, and Laura felt her stomach contract.

This was something Laura did not do: make mistakes. She often wondered about other people's mistakes. The secretary who got abducted on a bargain-basement cruise to Cambodia. The coworker who left Clark-Vester to start a restaurant that served only macaroni and cheese. What possessed these people? she wondered. Wasn't there a moment before they set forth when they stopped and thought, *This is the worst idea I've ever had*? But apparently they didn't have that moment, or if they did, it didn't stick, because they ordered the macaroni and boarded the ship. And she had too.

"Do we really need to meet with them?" Laura asked, trying to affect the blasé tone she and Brenda always used with each other, as though their jobs were a minor inconvenience they shared the pleasure of disliking.

"Clark-Vester fosters…" Brenda began.

"I know. Positive relationships."

She and Brenda both saw through the rhetoric.

"We're putting this coffee shop out of business," Laura said.

"Immediately. A week ago, it was business as usual. In a month, they won't even recognize their street corner. Is an informational session going to make them feel better?"

"If you don't want to go, send Dayton or Craig," Brenda said. "They're there to do your dirty work for you. That's their job."

"Dayton and Craig have the emotional intelligence of sponges."

"Then do it yourself." Brenda paused. Laura could almost hear her remembering Senator Stan Enfield, Laura's father, Laura's shield and armor. Brenda's tone softened. "Is everything all right?"

"Of course."

"How's the campaign?"

It was the only thing that could trouble an Enfield in June of an election year.

"To hear my family talk about it, all is lost." Laura laughed without any real humor. "Dad's got a strong majority with registered Republicans. More Democrats on board than any other republican senator in Alabama history. Independents up a bit." It was an easy recitation, the native language of the Enfield family. Although, at her parents' huge mahogany dinner table the statistics were more precise. Fractions of a point. Incremental rates of increase. Statistical abnormalities examined and reexamined. "They'll still manage to act surprised when he wins. And it's still early," Laura added, more realistically.

"Still time for a major scandal?" Brenda chuckled. "This will be his sixth term?"

"Yes."

"Your father is a good man."

Everyone said that.

"He is," Laura said reflexively, still gazing out at the street, winding the phone cord around her fingers. She paused, then said, "Brenda. One more thing. Who is going to the purchase convocation? Do we have names?"

She pressed the phone to her ear, holding her breath.

"One woman. Margaret Davidson, store manager. She holds the business license. There used to be a Lillian Whitaker, listed as co-owner. She used to hold some sort of majority share in the place, but she dumped that about nine years ago. Why do you ask? Do you expect trouble?"

At the woman's apartment, the night before, Laura had glanced at a stack of mail on the kitchen table. She had broken her own rule. She had read the name: Tatum Grafton. Laura exhaled. The convocation attendee was not the tall, masculine-looking woman who had held her so gently the night before.

"You still there?" Brenda asked.

"I'm here, and I'll be at the convocation."

Laura put the phone down and dropped into a chair. That was it. She would meet with the coffee shop manager, share the bad news using a tone that conveyed sympathy but left no room for argument. Then she would pack her bags, fly to Palm Springs, and then back to the house she owned in Alabama to remedy her absence from the Enfield campaign.

The woman from the bar would become a distant memory, an untraceable one—as Laura had intended. Tatum Grafton with the jutting nose, high cheekbones, and deep eyes that combined gave her a face that was not beautiful but was more than beautiful. It was that face, and her look of patience tinged with sadness, that had drawn Laura to her when every other woman in the bar would have been a safer choice. But now it was over. She would never see the woman again.

It should have felt like a relief. Disaster averted. She had learned her lesson. But as she opened her laptop to check on the Palm Springs project, she felt a weight settle on her shoulders. It was the weight of knowing there was not one person in the whole world she could call and ask, *Guess what I did last night?* Not one person to whom she could explain how she felt, the mix of shock at what she had done and sadness at everything it could not mean. That beautiful night. The perfect tomato. The woman's strong hands trembling slightly as she touched Laura's face. The woman's confession: "It's been a long time." And Laura's mind reeling, *I can't!*

"Tatum Grafton," Laura said to the empty hotel room. It took her a moment to figure out why she felt like she had been punched in the stomach. She touched her face. *Oh*, she thought, surprised. This was something else she never did: cry.

# Chapter 5

In the back room, Lill and Maggie were sitting at the card table, on which were spread an ominous quantity of legal-looking documents.

"Maggie, is this true? They're selling the building?"

Tate pulled up a chair without waiting for an invitation.

"They're selling, and the new owner doesn't have to honor our lease. We could be out on the streets in a month if they want." Maggie took a breath. "I can't start over. I'm sixty-five. And that's what these people don't get. This isn't just a business. This is a piece of history."

Lill patted Maggie's hand.

"Sixty is the new fifty."

Lill was fifty-four, with two beautiful children, a wealthy and conveniently emasculated husband, and a top management position at Namaste Yoga in the Pearl District. It didn't seem fair. When Lill was in her twenties Maggie had been the cool, older woman. A real dyke. An original. With broad shoulders, a crew cut, and a pink triangle ring, large enough to break a man's jaw. Tate had seen pictures. Maggie had looked like a woman who could change the world, and Lill had looked like a little girl. A couple of decades later, Lill had a new life, and Maggie had Out Coffee, a bunch of T-shirts that said WE CAN SAVE THE WORLD, and a world that still needed saving.

"When the goddess closes a door, she opens a window," Lill said. "Maybe we can sue for breach of contract. Where's the lease?"

Tate thought for a moment.

"We can move," she suggested. "We could find another shop, maybe on a busier street."

Lill pulled a small stick out of a pocket in her shirt and offered it to Maggie. "Lemongrass. It's an antioxidant."

Maggie shook her head.

"Tate, do you want one?" she asked.

"No."

Lill held the twig of lemongrass under her nose, inhaled deeply, then set it on the table.

"The eviction process itself could take several months. By then, Tate's right, you could have a new space."

"We rent all the fixtures," Maggie said glumly. "They came with the building."

"You could buy them off the landlord or buy new," Tate suggested.

Maggie rested her chin on her knuckles. Her hands were big, competent, but Tate could see the arthritis starting to swell her joints. She was like the old bull elk police found wandering the Northwest Industrial District: graceful and powerful and lost.

"It will be okay," Tate said. "The store has assets, right? We'll pull through."

Maggie had been resting her elbows on a ledger book, which she now turned toward Tate. Tate flipped through the spreadsheets. The numbers were all in the negative.

Lill pulled the book away from Tate.

"Maggie!" she exclaimed.

"For how long?" Tate asked.

"A year at least."

"How is that possible?" Lill asked. "You can't run a business like this. How did you pay for inventory?"

"The bank said...with interest rates where they were...I put a second mortgage on my house," Maggie said.

"Oh, Maggie," Tate said. "And you've been using the money to float the shop?"

Maggie nodded.

"Why?" Tate asked.

But she knew why. She had known why since she was fifteen, when the only place she felt safe in the world was nestled in an easy chair underneath the mural of Gertrude Stein, even if the artist's rendition had left Gertrude looking cross-eyed and a bit psychotic. There had been a dog-eared copy of *Oranges Are Not the Only Fruit* floating around the shop, and it was possible, Tate thought, that it had saved her life.

"You can't run a business like this, Mags. It's not a charity," Lill said.

Maggie's lips tightened.

"I am not going to run some profit-driven factory farm."

"Who's farming, Maggie?" Lill asked.

Tate shot Lill a warning look.

"I'll figure something out," Tate said.

"I know you will." Maggie clasped Tate's hand. "You're so good, Tate. You're such a good person. I don't know what I'd do without you. The buyer wants to meet with us tomorrow," Maggie added. "They said they'd send a 'commercial real estate development consultant,' whatever that is, to explain the sale to us. Laura something. She wants me to meet her in Beaverton. Say you'll come." She looked back and forth between Lill and Tate. "Will you come?"

"Of course," they answered together.

"You won't be late?" Maggie looked at Tate.

"Late?" A voice chimed in from the doorway behind them. It was Vita, in for her morning coffee. "Was Tate Grafton actually late to work?"

Vita ambled behind the counter like a coworker. But not so much like a coworker that she felt inclined to wait on the three people lined up for coffee. Krystal followed her.

"Krystal," Tate said. "There are customers."

"But I need to know what's happening," Krystal said plaintively. "Maggie, they're not going to close down Out Coffee, are they?"

Vita threw an arm around Krystal's shoulder, her massive faux-gold bracelets clanging.

"One more year and you can work for me, kiddo," she said.

"But I work *here*," Krystal complained.

"Yes you do," Tate said. "And there are customers out there

right now. Vita, you too. No one behind the counter except staff. Krystal, I promise I'll tell you everything, just get back to work," Tate pleaded, heading to the register to help the neglected patrons herself.

"It was that girl!" Vita exclaimed, following Tate to the counter. "That's why you were late. You spent the night with that girl, didn't you?"

"The girl who looked like Hillary Clinton?" Krystal asked, following behind them. "Did you talk to her?" To Vita she added, "I told Tate that woman liked her."

"Good eye, kid." Vita pretended to punch Krystal on the shoulder.

"Did you meet a nice woman?" Maggie followed after them. A look of hope crossed her face. It was a kind of your-lesbian-love-will-save-the-capitalist-world-from-ruin look, and it made Tate angry at the woman from the bar. *See*, she wanted to say, *you ruined Maggie's day too.* But she did not have time to rue her recent disappointment or fume about the present crisis. She had to get Lill's children out of the sugar cubes, Krystal back at the counter, and Lill out of the shop before she did something to remind Maggie of their breakup, which was many years past but came quickly to Maggie's mind anytime something went wrong in her life.

Tate shot Vita a look that said, *If you want to spend another minute as my best friend, you will drop it.*

For once, Vita complied.

At home after her shift, Tate dropped wearily onto her bed. She was so disappointed. She couldn't help it; she had spent the whole day hoping the woman would appear in the coffee shop doorway. She had forgone her breaks so that she would not miss the appearance. But the woman had not shown up. Now Tate felt foolish for wishing. The woman had not been willing to reveal her first name. That heralded a second date about as much as a card reading SHOVE OFF.

Tate wandered into the bathroom and stared in the mirror. There were circles under her eyes, and the hook in her nose was getting more pronounced. An aggressive nose. A square jaw. A little bit too much muscle where her neck joined her shoulders. Not a lot of anything for her sports bra to contain. Maybe it all worked in Portland where skinny boys in glasses were the Brad Pitts of the city, and even the straight girls grew their leg hair. But the woman, if she was a lesbian at all, was probably some slick LA dyke with a pool and a closet full of Prada.

Tate sighed. And then she looked down at the bathroom counter. She had not noticed it before: a necklace, made of such a fine silver thread it looked like a crack in the porcelain. At the end of the chain was a white jewel. A diamond or, guessing by its size, a cubic zirconium grown in a lab by chemists. The whole thing was arranged in the shape of a heart. For a moment she wondered if the woman had snuck back into her apartment. Then she remembered how bleary-eyed and rushed she had been in the morning. She had simply missed it. A little good-bye present. A token to soften the blow.

She called Vita.

* * *

An hour later they were sitting at Tate's kitchen table, and Tate was finishing the story of her brief encounter with the woman at the bar.

"And she just left. No good-bye. Not a note. No number," Tate finished.

Outside, the twilight had finally given way to night, and a cool breeze blew through the open window.

"Just this." Tate pulled the necklace out of a bowl on the table. "She left it in the shape of a heart on the bathroom sink."

"That's quite a rock."

"It's not real," Tate said.

Vita took the necklace and held it up to the lamp above the table. It moved in the breeze. Tate caught specks of light reflected in its center.

"You sure?" Vita asked.

"It's huge," Tate said.

"I don't know." Vita examined the necklace. "Remember when I was seeing Susan? She was all into the rocks. After six months with her, I knew my diamonds."

Vita picked up the beer she had been drinking. She pinched the rock between her fingers and dragged it along the glass bottle.

"See?" She held the bottle out to Tate. "It scratched."

"So?"

"Diamonds scratch glass. The fakes don't."

Vita leaned back in her chair and swigged her beer with a satisfied smile, the hardworking detective finishing a difficult case. But she hadn't solved anything for Tate.

"She wouldn't even give me her name," Tate said.

"Did you check her wallet?"

"Of course not. I wouldn't!"

"I would," Vita said.

Tate could tell Vita was honing in on one of her favorite subjects: Tate the Boy Scout, Tate the upstanding. Vita had a lot of theories about how much better Tate's life would be if she just compromised all her principles all the time.

"You're awful," Tate said.

"Look, Tatum. I always check IDs."

"You work at a bar. You check everyone's ID."

"I mean before I sleep with someone." Vita rolled her eyes. "I know it's a violation of privacy or whatever, but what if some girl says she's twenty-one and she's really seventeen?"

"I'm not going to sleep with any girl who looks like she is twenty-one *or* seventeen."

"But what if she's a man!" Vita clinked her beer bottle down on the table as though this settled the matter. "You just can't tell these days."

Tate stared out the kitchen window at the weedy lot next door. It would make a wonderful garden, she thought, but the landowner was forever threatening to build an apartment building on the lot.

"You just wait until she goes to the bathroom," Vita went on. "Then take a quick look at the card. Name. Age. If you get her driver's license number, I know a girl who works at the police department. She could run it for you. See if she has any convictions."

"Anyway, she's gone now," Tate said.

Vita grinned. "If you love her, you got to do what you got to do."

"I hardly know her."

The breeze carried a whiff of honeysuckle through the window. Downstairs, Rose and Pawel, the old Hungarian couple, turned on their television and Lawrence Welk called out his greeting from beyond the grave.

Vita pushed her beer aside and folded her hands on the table, her face suddenly serious.

"I've been studying you for a long time," she said. "Since I was fifteen and crazy in love with you. And don't look nervous. That ship sailed a long time ago, and, sadly for you, you missed it. But what I'm saying is, I *know* you. You don't take every girl home with you. God knows why not. The whole Mirage is hot for you. If I had that butch appeal..."

"Why does everyone keep saying that?" Tate asked.

"See? You don't even know it. That's half the appeal. And you don't take girls home. You're a romantic. But you like this woman. I can see that. And that's worth fighting for."

"How? I don't know anything about her. She doesn't even live here."

"Start by putting this on." Vita held up the necklace.

"That?" Tate took it and dangled the impossibly delicate chain across her T-shirt. "On me?"

"That way, when she sees you again..."

"If she sees me again."

"...she'll know you care."

\* \* \*

The meeting with the "commercial real estate development consultant" took place the following day. Tate tapped the address into her GPS, secured it between the handlebars of her Harley, and headed toward Beaverton on the Sunset Highway. As soon as she got out of Portland and into the suburbs, she regretted not riding with Lill and Maggie. Beaverton was, as far as she could tell, one giant strip-mall parking lot fed on all sides by freeway arteries. Traffic wasn't fast, but it was congested and erratic, and there was no room for motorcycles.

When Tate's GPS finally signaled her destination, she found it looked exactly like every other corner she had passed: a large parking lot in front of an office park. CORPORATE SOLUTIONS, the sign on the building read. Inside, she was greeted by a receptionist who looked about twelve but dressed like a CEO on a soap opera.

"Your party has arrived," the girl said before Tate had a chance to speak.

She stood and led Tate down a windowless hall to a small conference room. Maggie and Lill were already seated at the long table. "Your other associates will be here shortly."

"They are not our associates," Maggie said. "They are the corporate…monsters who are trying to take over our business."

*Monsters.* Tate looked at Maggie, whose face was set like something carved in stone—the kind of stone that gets worn away by rain…or tears. *Go ahead and say "assholes,"* she thought. But she said nothing, resting her hand on Maggie's shoulder for a moment before sitting down at the table.

"Why wouldn't they just meet us at Out in Portland?" Maggie asked no one in particular. "How can they close it down without even seeing it? They don't even know what they're doing. They don't know who we are."

Lill put a hand on Maggie's arm.

"Your energy feels unstable."

Lill was dressed in loose-fitting yoga pants and a green sweatshirt embroidered with hummingbirds. Her gray-brown hair was plaited into her signature braids, like the ears of a donkey. It was a fine outfit for an athletic mom about to take her children for a picnic in Forest Park, but not right for a business meeting. Even Maggie had put on a rather misshapen suit, and Tate had starched a white shirt for the occasion.

"You need to meet love with love," Lill went on. "And tell them you've hired Simon, Bristen, and Curtis."

Tate and Maggie looked at each other and then at Lill.

"Portland's biggest law firm," Lill said, as though every coffee shop owner had them on speed dial. "The bulldogs of the West."

"They just won't join us in our space," Maggie said.

"They're probably afraid we'll knife them," Tate said.

"You wouldn't!" Maggie looked up.

"Of course, I'm not going to knife anyone," Tate said.

Behind her, someone cleared their throat. A young man in a shiny gray suit and purple tie had appeared in the doorway. A second later, he was joined by an older man with a mustache and a suit that looked like it had been borrowed from his grandfather's funeral.

"Dayton." The man in the shiny suit stuck out his hand.

Maggie remained motionless, her arms crossed.

Lill said, "I'm sorry. I don't shake hands. It disrupts the chi."
Reluctantly, Tate shook his hand.

"Craig Bryant." The older man shook Tate's hand. "Ms. En-field, our commercial real estate development consultant, will be just a moment."

They sat in uncomfortable silence. Craig flipped through a binder of spreadsheets. Dayton tapped his phone, glared at the screen, and then scrolled quickly through screen after screen of text, shaking his head as though he could actually read the words flying beneath his thumb.

"So, how y'all doing?" Dayton said finally, as though silence might literally kill him.

"Seeing as you're trying to destroy one of the great community resources in Portland and ruin a business that's been flourishing since 1950…" Maggie said.

Tate noted a bit of exaggeration—both the "1950" part and the "flourishing" part—but she kept quiet.

"You haven't even heard our plans," the older man grumbled.

"I read the paperwork," Maggie added. "I know you want to destroy a lesbian-owned, woman-centered business in favor of some corporate big-box store."

Dayton laughed. "Sandwich Station is boutique fast food." The fluorescent light rippled off the arms of his suit as he fidgeted with his phone.

"It's a male-owned, male-dominated corporate scam that's filling the pockets of the richest rich!" Maggie's voice trembled.

"You can hardly call Out in Portland Coffee woman-owned." Craig sounded as somber as his suit, but it didn't sound like grief—certainly not grief for Out in Portland. He sounded more like a bored funeral director. "I've looked at your books. The landlord owns the space, the fixtures. You owe him money. I'd say that building owns you."

"You're right. It owns me because I care about the people in it," Maggie said, then glanced at the door behind Tate. The men too had fallen silent. Dayton put down his phone. The commercial real estate development consultant had arrived. Tate turned.

"Good morning. I'm Laura Enfield," the woman said.

Tate did not know if her jaw literally hit the ground or if the connection between her brain and her body simply short-circuited, leaving her frozen in place, unable to feel either her body or the floor beneath her feet.

The woman had looked pretty and polished at the Mirage, but now she looked like a first lady, impeccably dressed in a cream-colored suit and high, sharp heels. Apparently she could afford to leave diamond necklaces in the apartments of her one-night stands because her neck was now adorned with an opal so large if filled the hollow at the base of her throat. A similar jewel adorned each ear, visible before the upsweep of her blond hair.

For one second, Tate thought she saw a look of terror cross the woman's face. Then she was certain she had imagined it, as the woman shook Tate's hand, her face devoid of recognition. In the corner of her mind, Tate wondered if her life was about to become one of those action films in which everyone had an evil doppelganger or perhaps an indie film in which the well-meaning barista descends into madness, realizing, at the end, that all her friends were figments of her imagination. She glanced at Maggie and Lill, but they were still there.

"Ladies, shall we begin?" Laura Enfield said. She pulled up a chair and placed a leather portfolio on the table.

"Mrs. Davidson here seems to think this is some kind of hostile corporate takeover," Craig said, pointing his thumb at Maggie. "She thinks…"

The woman, Laura, lifted two fingers off her pen, and he stopped in mid-sentence. She was clearly the boss. It was hot. Tate did not want to admit that. She did not want to admit that her eyes had just followed the curve of Laura's neck, down to the opal, to the swell of her breasts beneath the lapels of her suit, all the way down to the tips of her, now, French-manicured nails. She was glad that Maggie and Lill did not have Vita's mind-reading powers. What kind of lesbian feminist met the corporate overlord and thought, *I'd like a piece of that*?

Laura explained the sale in clear, concise terms. The building would be sold. An outside company would handle the sale of fixtures, probably at auction. Everyone working at the coffee shop would be given an interview at Sandwich Station, the anchor store that would turn their dusty brick building into the City Ridge Commercial Plaza. The men listened, folding their hands and watching her attentively. Even Maggie and Lill seemed drawn in by her authority.

"We have contacted a few other businesses," Laura went on. "Cell phone retailers, a tanning salon, a dental clinic. After renovations, we will be able to use four thousand square feet of ground floor for commercial real estate. The upstairs, we'll convert to lofts and flex space."

"It's an awesome project," Dayton added, snapping his phone closed to punctuate the remark. "You can be right in the front line working at Sandwich Station. Most people get promoted to lead worker within six months."

"You're wasting your time," Craig droned. "They think we're corporate bastards."

Laura made a slight gesture of her head that seemed to say, *I didn't give you permission to talk.*

"We are the corporate bastards," she said. "From their perspective, that's absolutely right." She faced Tate, her eyes resting just to the left of Tate's forehead. Tate thought she caught a hint of the sad, faraway look she had seen in Laura's face the night they had spent together. "I realize you are not going to be happy about this. None of you are." She looked at Maggie and Lill. "But keep our offer in mind. Sandwich Station has a three-tiered management structure which allows for significant professional growth. They offer full benefits, including health, dental, and 401(k) to anyone who works 20 hours or more. And this isn't the kind of shop where managers are instructed to keep their employees at 19.5 hours. They want to contribute to the community. They want to strengthen the job base of the communities they work with."

"By closing down a business that's been serving Portland for years?" Maggie asked.

"Since 1920," Lill added. "We're going to contact the historical registry, by the way."

At this rate, Tate thought, they'd be serving Jesus coffee by the end of the meeting.

"Out Coffee is a landmark," Tate said. "People came to Out with their parents, and now they're coming with their kids or grandkids. It's not *just* a coffee shop."

"I'm sorry," Laura said.

"Are we done here?" Craig asked. He sounded like he had been doing this for decades.

"Wait," Tate said.

She had to buy time. Out Coffee was on the line. Maggie was on the line. Her own livelihood was on the line. And the woman…the woman was so hard and cold and beautiful and yet, when her eyes did finally meet Tate's, Tate saw something soft and lost.

"Where is your company from?" Tate asked.

"Alabama."

"Do you do a lot of business in Portland?"

"This is our first Portland acquisition."

"Do you spend a lot of time in Portland?" Tate pressed.

"No. Not a lot."

"So you don't know Portland." Tate put her elbows on the table, leaning in, trying to hold Laura's gaze.

"We've done all the market research you need," Craig said.

"I don't think market research from Alabama is enough," Tate said, still watching Laura.

"Thank you, barista, but I think we know our business," Craig said.

Laura turned to her subordinate.

"That's enough, Craig. And I'm not going to say that again. I'm sorry, Ms. Grafton. Go on."

"Portland is unique," Tate began. "It's not every city in America. And I don't think a chain of sandwich shops, boutique or not, is going to be the anchor you want. Right now the hottest restaurant in Portland is Pok Pok. It's four tents attached to a Victorian house and heated with propane lamps. They serve boar's collar. People wait for hours in the rain to get in. See, Portland doesn't want Pok Pok cleaned up. That's what your market research isn't going to show you. Put that restaurant in a nice building with good lighting, and Portland will lose interest."

"What are you suggesting?" Laura asked.

"Keep Out in Portland Coffee. Out Coffee is your anchor store. Out Coffee is the kind of place Portland loves. Gritty. Imperfect. Human."

"I'm not at liberty to make any decisions about what stays or goes in the City Ridge Commercial Plaza," Laura said, but she seemed to be considering something.

"Who is?" Tate pressed.

"Our corporate office. The board."

Tate was aware of Maggie and Lill watching her intently.

"Give me a week." Tate held Laura's eyes. "Let me show you Portland. Let me show you everything your market research can't tell you." She didn't know if she was pleading for Out Coffee or herself. Either way, she felt the adrenaline rise in her blood. "I'll show you the underside. The B-side. Everything that Portland loves. And if you agree, if you see what I'm saying..." *If you see me*, she thought. "Talk to your corporate office. That's all I'm asking. Just talk to them."

Dayton and Craig protested, but Laura rose in one smooth motion, extending her hand to Tate, holding on for just a second longer than dictated by business necessity.

"All right. One week," she said.

Tate had just mounted her bike when she caught sight of Laura hurrying across the parking lot of the Corporate Solutions building. She waited, the bike rumbling beneath her. A sensible woman would tear off in a cloud of exhaust, she thought. She did not move.

"Tatum Grafton?" Laura peered at the opaque surface of Tate's helmet visor.

Tate said nothing.

"Tatum, is that you?"

Reluctantly, Tate removed the helmet.

"Thank you." Laura exhaled.

"For what?"

"You could have given me hell in there, and you didn't."

Up close, and in the bright light, Laura looked older, closer to forty than the twenty-seven or twenty-eight Tate had guessed initially. A few fine lines creased the skin around her eyes, making her even more beautiful in Tate's estimation. Tate did not know what to say.

"I don't expect you to forgive me for all this." Laura gestured vaguely toward the office park behind them, then ran her hand over her face, brushing away an invisible strand of hair. "You have every right to hate me. I'm not going to pull that 'please see me as a person, I'm only doing my job' crap, because that *is* crap. We are our jobs. I am my job. But just in case you don't despise me entirely, I have to be clear with you. What happened..." She paused as though English had suddenly become a second language, and she was searching for words. "...the other night...that can never happen again."

The hope that had previously kept Tate from roaring off in a cloud of exhaust died. *Of course* "what happened" could never happen again. Hadn't Abigail taught her that? Whatever seemed good and special to Tate would seem paltry and inferior to the women she liked.

"I can't...do that again. I can't ever." Laura paused as if waiting for Tate to speak.

Tate said nothing. She was thinking about Abigail and the oboist. Abigail and Duke. Laura and her perfect first-lady face.

"It wouldn't be ethical," Laura added. "You need to know, if you're doing this Portland thing because..." She glanced over her shoulder again. "If you are doing this because...I can't ever do that again. Do you understand me, Ms. Grafton?"

"It's just Tate," Tate said.

# Chapter 6

And then what?" Vita asked.

It was four in the afternoon. Behind Tate, the door to the Mirage stood ajar, letting in a beam of sunlight that illuminated features of the bar Tate preferred not to think about.

"This place is filthy," Tate said, running her hand over one of the stools.

Vita waved the comment away. "It's patina."

"I think it's grenadine." She wiped the seat with a cocktail napkin.

"You're evading." Vita leaned her elbows on the bar directly across from Tate. She had given up the pretense of preparing the Mirage for the night's drinkers. "Talk. You go to this meeting. You find out your mystery girl is Maggie's nemesis. Does Maggie know?"

"No. And you can't tell her!"

"Your secret's safe." Vita winked, fake eyelashes flicking

through her rocker bangs. "Just tell me everything. So after the meeting, she runs to you saying, 'Tate, I can't. I can't.' And you say?"

"I told her I still thought Out Coffee could be the anchor store she's looking for."

"What about the sex?" Vita threw up her hands. "What about 'that thing we did'?"

"I said okay."

"Okay what?" Vita leaned in. Today's animal pattern was a purple leopard print that looked a little bit like eyeballs.

Tate tugged Vita's sleeve. "Nice. Colorful."

Vita pulled her sleeve away. "You said okay to what?"

"She said she couldn't sleep with me again," Tate said, "and I said okay. Then we arranged to meet at Out Coffee tomorrow, and I said okay."

"You're hopeless." Vita pretended to bang her head against the bar. "Are you not my best friend? Have I not tried to educate you about women?"

*Educate.* It wasn't quite the word Tate would have chosen.

Vita leapt off the stool. "Cairo!" she called to the line cook, who was also her latest fling.

The beautiful, Egyptian-looking woman appeared from the back. Tate wondered again if she was actually Egyptian or if "Cairo" was just an apt nickname and she was, in fact, a Latina girl from Gresham or Lincoln City. It did not seem polite to ask, but Tate always found the thought vaguely distracting. It made her wonder if the quintessential New Yorker might earn the nickname Nyc. The perfect Californian, Callie. Or the perfect Portlander, Portlandra. Perhaps she herself was Portlandra. She glanced down at her scuffed boots, cargo jeans, and leather jacket. What made her think she could woo a woman like Laura Enfield?

"Cairo, if you had a hot, one-night stand with a woman…" Vita began.

"I did, and then she put me to work in the kitchen stuffing jalapeno poppers," Cairo teased.

"Well imagine she disappeared while you were sleeping and left nothing behind except a giant diamond."

"Oh, Tate's girl," Cairo said.

Tate put her chin on her hands. That was Vita for you. She didn't let anyone suffer in isolation. Maggie called it the "solidarity of the lesbian community."

"Thanks, Vita." Tate shook her head without any real ire.

Vita ignored her. "Let's say, the girl shows up again at a business meeting. Then afterward she runs across a parking lot."

"She didn't run," Tate said.

"She probably ran. She was running in her heart," Vita said, as though she had been there to witness it. "Then she says, 'Tate, I can't. I can't.' What does that mean?"

Cairo giggled. "It means 'I want to.'"

Tate frowned at Vita. "Didn't you drag me to a rally once and make me chant 'No means no' for two hours?"

"Of course no means no." Vita crossed her arms, bracelets jangling. "But 'Oh Tate, I can't' means something entirely different."

"What does it mean?" Tate sighed.

"I'd say it means 'Please.'"

Vita grabbed Cairo, who was heading back toward the

kitchen, and pulled her close. "Please kiss me and throw me over that monster of a Harley you sexy butch thing." She kissed Cairo. Then, still holding Cairo around the waist, she glanced back at Tate. "You could have done that or you could have thrown the diamond at her and told her to call you when she came out. But I wouldn't do that because if it all tanks, you can always pawn the rock."

Tate turned to stare out the door at the slice of sunlight pouring in off Division Street. *With friends like these*, she thought.

The next day, Tate slipped into work quietly, trying to listen for any snippet of conversation that suggested that gossip from the Mirage had reached the coffee shop. Thankfully, all seemed calm in the shop even if her heart was racing. It was bad enough that she had only one week to convince Laura to save Out Coffee. She had one week—she barely dared to hope—to see if there was some truth to Vita's theatrics. And one week in which she absolutely could not let Maggie find out that the commercial real estate developer who was trying to ruin her life had been, for one strange, magical night, Tate's lover.

Tate busied about the stockroom, still listening, then served the morning rush. Then, in a lull between customers, she rounded up Maggie and Krystal. They stood in a huddle beside the espresso machine. Tate put her hands on both their shoulders as she imagined a coach would when preparing her star players for the big game...or imminent death.

"We're not just selling Portland," Tate said. "We're selling Out in Portland Coffee. We need Laura Enfield..."

"That horrible woman."

Tate guessed Maggie wanted to say "bitch," but several decades of feminist consciousness-raising stopped her.

"Laura Enfield," Tate said, "whether we like her or not, needs to see that this is an amazing, productive, profitable business. It's like her sandwich shop only better. She's coming by at one p.m. I want us to be ready. First, I want to take down the Mariah Lesbioma dioramas."

"We just put her show up," Maggie protested. "She'll be devastated if we take it down. She's worked on it for years."

"Years she spent in the loony bin," Krystal said, readjusting one of the pigtails she had put in her short, pink hair.

"Mariah is emotionally vulnerable," Maggie said.

"We'll put it back up when Laura leaves, but we can't have it here now." Tate looked at the collage pieces on the wall. "They look like vaginas."

"They're *supposed* to look like vaginas," Maggie protested. "Mariah is reclaiming the gynic power, the female symbol. Every capitol building in America is a phallus. Mariah's art says it is time for the female form to take its true place in art."

The shellac that held the collages together glistened. Inside *Vagina Denta #13*, Mariah had glued a plastic ball from a gumball machine. Inside it, a photo of George Bush leered out.

"They're terrifying," Tate said. "Krystal, be careful when you take them down. Maggie, you call your women's group and see how many people we can get in here around one p.m. I want every seat occupied. I want the coffee pouring. Let's show Laura she would be crazy to close Out in Portland."

* * *

At twelve thirty, Tate had never loved Out in Portland more. Maggie knew everyone in Portland, and half of everyone had filed into the store. By the window, a group of graduate students spread their books out. In the corner, Lill's husband plucked a gentle tune on his acoustic guitar while Sobia and Bartholomew sat listening and munching on flaxseed biscuits. Every two minutes, the door chime announced a new customer. Meanwhile Lill and Maggie swirled chocolate hearts on every mocha, a graceful, four-armed, two-headed, bighearted coffee-making machine—just like they had been when they were a couple and had run Out Coffee together.

Tate smiled. It might not work out. Laura might not be moved. Out Coffee might close. Laura would probably never again press her sumptuous body against Tate's. But at least she would see this. Portland at its best. Out Coffee at its best. People at their best. Tate stepped into the bathroom to collect herself so she too could be at her best. She took a quick look in the mirror. It wasn't a gorgeous face, but it was the face of a good woman.

Then she heard the sound of metal breaking, followed by Krystal's scream.

Stepping out of the bathroom, Tate froze. Krystal was sitting on the floor behind the counter, waving a book in one hand and a wrench in the other and swearing prodigiously. Maggie stood above her, her arms wrapped around herself protectively, saying, "I appreciate that you are trying." From beneath the sink, a torrent of water poured onto the floor. A cataract. Much more water than ever escaped the sluggish faucet above.

"What happened?" Tate ran over. She plunged her hand into the stream of water, reaching for the shutoff valve, just as Krystal yelled, "Don't, it's hot!"

It was scalding. Tate pulled her hand back.

"Get a bucket. What did you do, Krystal?"

Krystal shoved the book at Tate and ran for the back room. Tate looked at the cover. *A Woman's Guide to Home Repair.* It was her book, purchased months ago when she had come up short for rent, and her landlord had asked her to fix the splintered molding in Pawel and Rose's apartment in exchange for the shortfall.

"Krystal!" Tate yelled.

The line of coffee customers had bunched up at the counter. Several were leaning over to get a better look at the deluge.

"Can I help the next person in line?" Maggie called, waving her hands as though she could distract the customers from the disaster behind the counter. "I can still get you a cup of brewed coffee."

No one was listening except Lill.

"It'll be fine. It's nothing. Just get a bucket," Lill said.

"Don't tell me what to do." Maggie was starting to pace, which was never a good thing. "You always tell me what to do, but you're not here when it all falls apart."

"I'm present now," Lill said, with a huff. "I am here with you, but your anger is separating us."

"Lill!" Tate shot her a look. She mouthed, *Go away.*

"She asked me to help," Lill snapped. "I could have told her not to let that girl back there."

"Krystal is not 'that girl.' She's family," Maggie protested.

"Yeah. I'm family." Krystal had returned with a coffee mug instead of a bucket.

Tate plunged her hand into the scalding water again and felt for the valve. It was gone. She had to agree with Lill on this one. Krystal should never have been allowed behind the counter with a wrench.

"Krystal," Tate called. "What happened to the valve?"

"It broke." Krystal knelt at her side, pink pigtails sticking out of her head like antennas.

"What broke it?"

"You fix things." Krystal's lip was trembling. "You told me I should take responsibility for myself and learn new skills and…" A tear slid down her cheek, taking a stream of black mascara with it. "…it was your book and Maggie says it's empowering."

"What is?" Tate's hand stung from the hot water.

The customers had moved away from the counter as the water began to run in rivulets across the floor.

"Plumbing," Krystal said. "The book said I'd be more self-confident if I maintained my own home. It said feminists should clean their own sink traps."

"Krystal, you're supposed to be studying for the GED, and this is not a sink trap, and this is not your house, and you've seen the Pink Pages, you just hire a lesbian plumber. That's all the empowerment you need."

"I just thought I could do it on my own." Krystal's eyes were going puffy. "I just wanted to help you! My dad would show me how to fix it. My dad would have wanted me to do it."

"Your dad is doing twenty to life. Your dad could turn this

wrench into a switchblade." Tate felt bad as soon as she spoke. It was only the pain in her scalded hand that made her honest. The mascara streamed from both Krystal's eyes now. "I'm sorry, Krystal. Please, don't cry. I know you were trying to help. Now, just get a real bucket. We'll fix it. Find the Pink Pages. I think there's a copy by the front door."

Krystal disappeared again. Tate grabbed her wrench and made one more go at the deluge. This time she was able to pinch the metal and turn the valve, reducing the torrent to a drip and then to nothing. She was soaking.

The customers who knew Maggie were filing to the edges of the store, trying to look engaged in the seascape photographs that Tate had hung in place of Mariah Lesbioma's vagina art. The customers who did not know Maggie were heading for the exit. Maggie had begun to dab at her eyes with a napkin.

Lill was following her around behind the counter saying, "Maggie, Namaste. Namaste!" It sounded like something one might yell at a terrier.

On the other side of the counter, young Bartholomew had taken advantage of his parents' distraction and was emptying the sugar canister into his mouth. And right in front of the counter, little Sobia had taken off her pants, walked up to a stranger, grabbed the woman's hand, and said, in a shrill voice, "Bartholomew has a pee-pee because he's a boy, and if he doesn't want a baby, he's going to put a condo on his pee-pee." She pointed at her pink underwear. "But I don't have a pee-pee because I'm a girl."

Only it wasn't a stranger. No. It was Laura who knelt down

in the water so she could face Sobia directly and say, "That's very interesting. Is your mommy or daddy here?"

The rest of the afternoon was less disastrous but no more profitable. For one thing, Tate had envisioned spending the day alone with Laura, but Laura had brought her entourage. Laura, Tate, Dayton, and Craig piled into Laura's rental car, a large, cream-colored Sebring.

Tate had decided the first day should be a tour of Portland's most eccentric coffee shops as well as a few empty strip-mall Starbucks. She wanted to show Laura that Portland loved its locally owned shops and that the big national chains did not have the same pull.

Laura followed Tate from shop to shop, silent and incredibly poised. It was a little unnerving in fact; Tate had never seen anyone have such good posture for such a prolonged period of time. Meanwhile, Dayton complained like a boy on a dull field trip, and Craig pointed out a dozen flaws in every café they visited.

Finally, around six p.m., as they sat in Rimsky-Korsakoffee House, Craig said, "I appreciate your effort." He did not sound like he appreciated it at all. "But we have studied the Portland food and beverage market. That's what we *do*. We wouldn't move forward on a project like this without understanding the city. We know there are 493 independent coffee shops and kiosks, and 615 chain-operated and franchise coffee purveyors. Coffee amounts to 12 percent of the food profits. We also know that there are only 91 dedicated sandwich shops and those bring in an average of $49,000 a year profit, but we know the chains are the leaders by far, pulling the average up by almost 200 percent."

"Yeah. We know all this already," Dayton chimed in, looking up from his phone.

Tate glanced at Laura. She said nothing, but her eyes concurred. Tate had wasted their time.

"Okay," Tate said. "One more stop, and then I'll let you go for tonight."

Tate was pleased when she paused in front of the Pied Cow, and Craig and Dayton looked confused. Laura looked up at the vine-covered Victorian house.

"In here?" Laura asked.

Tate nodded.

Inside they were greeted by an entryway lined with Elvis busts, baby-doll heads, and glowing religious art from all faiths but particularly those that featured gods with extra extremities. Tate led them through the house and into the garden out back. The ground was covered in damp Persian rugs. Cold fire pits dotted the area, waiting for the fall days when customers would cluster around their warmth. That night, the only smoke came from an ornate hookah smoked, simultaneously, by three old men, each connected to the hookah by a pipe stem on a flexible tube. Craig coughed.

"Here, sit." Tate smiled at the waitress who was clearing a table. "Could we have four bowls of kava?"

The waitress returned her smile, and, a moment later, came back with a tray balanced on her shoulder. She placed four mismatched bowls before them.

"This looks like dishwater," Dayton complained. "There's a twig in mine."

"That's the kava," the waitress said. "We start by pulping the roots, then we steep them in water until they form the milk. It's a Polynesian tradition. You're supposed to drink it with friends. It relaxes you."

Again, the waitress smiled at Tate. She was cute, Tate thought, in a fresh, wholesome way that suggested she biked everywhere and ate vegan. Tate recalled all Vita's outrageous encouragement. *You've got that butch magnetism. Do you know who I would kill for your jawline?*

Tate flashed a smile at the girl. It felt awkward, but the girl put her hand on Tate's shoulder.

"Some people even say it's an aphrodisiac," the waitress added.

Tate wasn't sure, but she thought she saw Laura's excellent posture stiffen.

"What's your name?" Tate asked the waitress.

"Leaf."

Of course it was.

"Do you have any books here, Leaf? A couple of books you could loan us to read while we enjoy our kava?"

"There's a box of books customers left behind."

"That would be perfect."

Dayton lifted the kava to his lips, then spat it on the dirt.

"It's warm, and it tastes like sawdust," he protested. "Is this like some reality TV show? Like where's the fucking camera?"

Craig pushed his away.

Laura took her bowl in both hands and took a deep gulp.

Her face said *skim milk and sawdust*, but she said, "It's a cultural experience. Drink it."

Leaf reappeared with a cardboard box and put it on the table.

"*Collected Works of Hegel*," she read as she lifted the first book out of the box. "*The Homesteader's Guide to Compost. Fight Club.*" She read out a few more titles. "Will these do?"

"Perfect," Tate said. She passed Jeanette Winterson's *Sexing the Cherry* to Laura. "This is good." For herself, she took *A Supposedly Fun Thing I'll Never Do Again*. She opened it, took a swig of her kava—it really was disgusting—and pretended to read.

Apparently bored after fifteen seconds of silence, Dayton said, "What are we doing?"

Tate glanced over the top of her book.

"I'm showing you Portland."

"Where?"

"Here," Tate said. "Your friend made it very clear you've done your research, so I'm going to show you something you can't get from a spreadsheet."

Out of the corner of her eye, she glanced at Laura. A slight smiled pulled at the corner of her eyes. She was curious.

"We are going to sit here until this place closes," Tate went on. "We're going to sit and listen and read these books and drink this kava and *just be*. Because that's part of Portland. Sure there are people getting ahead and working overtime and going balls to the wall every day, but those guys over there..." Tate pointed to the hookah smokers. "Fifty bucks says they've been here all day, and they'll be here all night. People here know how to live, or at least they know there is a difference between living and working. And you can't see it on a spreadsheet, and you can't see it if you don't slow down."

Craig sighed.

"Are we really going to do this?" he asked Laura.

Laura took another sip of her kava.

"I am," Laura said.

Laura opened the book Tate had given her, and Dayton and Craig fell into disgruntled silence. She was the boss. Tate saw it again. The men could not move without her permission—and they weren't happy about it. Dayton flipped through book after book, sighing as though each page personally offended him with its dullness. Craig folded his arms and glared at the bowl of kava.

Then suddenly, Dayton said, "My lips." He poked his lips. "My lips are numb. I can't feel my lips. My tongue is all fuzzy. Is your tongue fuzzy?"

"Don't," Laura said without looking up from her book.

"No, I'm serious. Something's wrong. I'm going all numb."

Tate glanced from Laura to Dayton.

"It's probably an allergic reaction," Laura said.

"You don't feel it?" Dayton asked. "Aw shit, man, this is messed up!"

Laura shook her head.

"I need a Benadryl. Do my lips look swollen?" He stuck his tongue out. "My tongue?"

"It's still there," Laura said, deadpan.

"I'm not kidding!" Dayton started tapping his phone. "I've got to get help."

"Craig," Laura said with utter indifference. "Why don't you take Dayton back to the hotel? Get him some Benadryl before the inflammation gets into his brain."

When they were gone, Laura turned to Tate.

"My lips *are* numb," she said.

"You were messing with him!" Tate did not expect someone with such good posture to be devilish. Tate reached out and touched two fingers to Laura's lips. Her hand trembled.

"Can you feel that?" Tate asked.

She expected Laura to flinch, but she didn't. She just looked scared. Tate withdrew her touch.

"Yes, but it doesn't feel right." Laura touched her own lips.

"You didn't read the menu, did you?"

"No."

"You better text Dayton," Tate said. "It's supposed to do that. It's got a mild anesthetic in it."

"Milky anesthetic water with twigs in it?" Laura asked.

"It's what's for dinner." Tate winked.

Laura looked relieved. She wrote Dayton a text.

"They are not going to come back, are they?" Tate asked.

"I don't think I could get them back here if their jobs depended on it."

Tate sipped her kava. "It really is awful, isn't it?"

Laura nodded.

"They serve a nice port. Can I order you one?" Tate paused. She thought about the flood at Out Coffee and Craig's litany of statistics. "You don't have to stay, if you don't want to. Craig is probably right. I can't show you anything you don't already know. This is your business. I guess people on the ground floor are always doing that. They think they understand the big picture just because they work somewhere."

"Sometimes," Laura said. "And sometimes big companies with lots of analysts make mistakes because they don't ask the people they're actually trying to serve or the people who actually do the work. And yes, I'd like a port."

Leaf took the kava away and brought the port. Another table ordered a hookah and the cherry-scented smoke thickened. The sound of traffic died down and conversation filled the air, lending a cover of privacy to their talk.

"Now that I know your name," Tate ventured, not sure if she should even reference the night they had spent together, "can I ask about the stuff on your tax return? Where are you from? How did you become a commercial real estate developer?"

Laura sipped her port and surveyed the garden.

"I live in Alabama," Laura said, then paused. "No, that's not right. My name is on a four-bedroom house in Alabama and on a Prius that I never drive because I'm never home. I've worked for the Clark-Vester Group for four years. My father would like me to work for him, but I can't do it."

"What does your father do?"

Laura hesitated. "He's in policy making."

"And you are the boss of Craig and Dayton?" Tate asked.

"And I am the boss of Craig and Dayton, which they both hate. Craig because he's older than me and thinks he knows more than me, which he probably does."

"And Dayton?"

"He hates me because he's younger than me and doesn't understand why he doesn't have my job yet."

Laura had a clipped, matter-of-fact way of speaking and everything she said seemed to be tinged with a bit of wry humor. *Look what I've gotten myself into*, she seemed to be saying.

Somewhere, someone plugged in an extension cord and a string of white lights sparkled from the hedge surrounding the garden. A band had arrived and was setting up their equipment. The guitarist struck a single chord.

"They're going to be loud," Tate said. "Would you like to take a walk?"

They walked on Southeast Belmont Street for a few blocks, then Tate gestured toward a side street lined with mossy bungalows.

"What about you?" Laura asked. "How long did you say you've worked at Out in Portland?"

"Nine years."

"Nine years! I don't know anyone who has worked anywhere for nine years."

Laura was right. It was too long.

"What about your parents? What do they do?" Laura asked.

"My stepfather sold insurance," Tate said.

Around them, the street was quiet and dark, like a Thomas Kinkade painting that had gone to sleep for the night.

"Nine years," Laura said again. "That's a long time."

"I get to work with my friends. The hours are good. I can sleep in or garden in the mornings, close the shop at night, and still get to the Mirage." Tate's hand brushed against Laura's. "I don't go to bed at night and worry about work. Not until recently."

"I'm just doing my job," Laura spat out. Then she said, "I'm sorry. I promised myself I wouldn't say things like that. That's not an excuse. Just because it's your job doesn't mean it's right. But I believe in the Clark-Vester Group. I really do. At least, I've been impressed with their developments…"

Tate touched Laura's wrist. She thought she could feel Laura's pulse.

"Shh," Tate whispered. "It's okay."

Then she leaned forward and kissed Laura.

Down the block, a motion-sensitive streetlight turned off. The moonlight grew bluer and brighter. From somewhere far away, a saxophone played. Then Laura's hands were on Tate's neck and running through her cropped hair. And she was pulling Laura's hips to hers. Their lips pressed together in a hard, deep kiss that Tate felt all the way through her body. Her very bones longed for Laura's weight on top of her. Laura sighed and clung to her. And Tate felt each star in the sky spin on its axis.

Then a car turned down the lane. The streetlight flicked on.

"Whoo-hoo! You go, girls!" someone in the car yelled.

Laura stepped back.

"I have to go. I'm sorry. I can't do this," she said.

"Yes you can." Tate caught her hand. Her body ached for Laura's touch. Between her legs she felt a wet heat, so much more intense than the tedious longing of the months before, sharper than any frustration she had ever felt with Abigail. As she gazed at Laura, she was certain Laura felt the same desire.

"No. I can't." Laura pulled away reluctantly. "I misled you. I'm just sorry. Please don't. Don't try. Don't ask me again." She stared at Tate as if she expected Tate to pounce on her.

"Did I do something?" Tate asked.

"No. Yes. You're...wonderful, but I can't."

"Are you sure?"

"I'm sure." Laura's voice trembled, but her stance was certain.

Tate clasped the diamond that she had worn beneath her T-shirt and pulled on the delicate chain. It resisted for a second, then broke without a sound.

"You better take this." She held the jewel out to Laura. "My friend says it's a real diamond."

"It is."

"She said if it didn't work out, I should hock it. But I think you should probably just take it back."

"I like your friend," Laura said, sadly. There was that wry smile again. "She's probably right. You should hock it. But I'd like you to keep it." Suddenly Laura was right in front of her, her hands clasping Tate's arms, her face tilted toward Tate. "Because you're right. I do want to. I want you. And that night that I spent with you, that was wonderful in a way that nothing in my life is wonderful. And I want to think that a little piece of something I owned, I touched, stayed with you, like I could leave a little tiny piece of myself in that night forever."

She looked at Tate's lips as though she was going to kiss her again, then backed up quickly.

"So come home with me tonight," Tate said with a smile.

"No." This time Laura's voice was fierce, her face set. "I can't do that and be the person I am and do the things I need to do."

"Is this about your job?"

"It's about everything," Laura said.

Tate sighed, gazing beyond Laura down the lane of quiet houses to the faint glow of sunset at the end of the road.

"I don't know who you are. Or what you do. Not really," Tate said. "But here in Portland, if something is fun and good we do it twice. We do it a hundred times. We make a festival out of it and sell beer and T-shirts. We don't worry about rules or trajectories or balance sheets."

"And that's why you've been working at a coffee shop for nine years, a coffee shop that is so far in the red it's amazing they haven't repossessed the sugar cubes." The words flew out of Laura's mouth. "And you want to show me what's great about Portland, so you show me some old guys who sit around smoking all day. And they have done what? Achieved enlightenment? Found their inner chi? That's not a life. *This* is not a life."

Her gesture seemed to encompass the whole street, which was unfair since the houses in that neighborhood went for half a million at least. Their occupants might not be spiritually fulfilled, but they were certainly high achievers.

"Working at a coffee shop in your thirties isn't a life. It's a mistake." Laura said it so matter-of-factly that neither of them registered the comment for a second. Then Laura covered her mouth. "Oh, Tate, I'm sorry. I didn't mean that."

Tate stepped back. She felt her throat tighten and she looked away before Laura could see into her eyes.

"Yes, you do," she said.

It was clear what Laura thought, even if she didn't want to think it.

"I just meant it wouldn't be the right choice for me," Laura said. "Don't you see, I can't be part of this city, this life, your life. None of this is possible for me."

Tate held out the diamond again, but Laura kept her hands at her sides.

"Fine." Tate opened her hand and let the stone fall to the sidewalk.

She could already hear Vita's protest: *Do you know what that thing is worth?!*

"Good night, Laura." Tate turned her back on Laura. Over her shoulder she added, "I presume you can find your way back to your car."

"How will you get home?" Laura called after her.

"It's Portland," Tate said, striding into the fading twilight. "I am home."

# Chapter 7

Laura picked up the diamond and clutched it in her hand. Then she hurried away. She had almost reached the street where her car was parked when she heard footsteps behind her. They weren't pounding, but they were hurrying. She could hear her sister's voice in the back of her mind.

"You don't know what those people are like."

They had been sitting at the mahogany dinner table—the "think tank," as her father called it—the first time Natalie had made that pronouncement.

"Do you think it's a culture?" their brother had asked.

"It's biological," Natalie had asserted.

"Strategy!" their father had declared. "It doesn't matter what they are. It's what the voters think that matters."

Now, Laura prepared her strategy, as she quickened her step. When she reached the safety of the main road, she would turn. *I said no.* She practiced her speech, silently mouthing the words. *I'm sorry that's not the answer you want to hear, but I think we can both agree that you need to respect it.*

The steps grew nearer. She could hear the breath, fast and deep. She stepped into the artificial light of the main road and spun around, Tate's name on her lips.

But it was a jogger: a young, overweight man, his hair held back by an orange headband. He nodded to her as he passed. Tate was nowhere in sight. And Laura realized it was hope, more than fear, that had quickened her pulse. She had hoped that Tate would follow her. Wasn't that what Natalie implied when she talked about "those people"? They were ruthless seducers, relentless in pursuit of their prey. Wasn't that what her sister's words had...promised?

Tate had no intention of chasing her down, Laura realized. Laura had said no, and Tate had walked home.

Laura tried to maintain some righteous indignation as she drove back to the hotel. Spare books and hookahs and port and wet Persian rugs; it was all ludicrous. Who carpeted an outdoor garden with area rugs? And what was she supposed to learn from the evening, if she did enjoy drinking mildly anesthetic water with twigs in it? Was she supposed to emulate Tate Grafton? Burn up her 401(k) and serve coffee all day? Did Tate even know who paid for the unemployment benefits she would get when Out in Portland went under?

"Taxpayers," Laura said out loud. "Like me." She jerked the car from one lane to another. "That's who'll pay. That's who always pays."

She headed toward the artery that led to downtown Portland and then made a sharp merge onto the freeway. A purple VW bus veered away like a startled hippo. She slammed the heel of her hand into the center of the steering wheel to honk but hit the steering wheel radio controls instead. The radio blared to life.

*"Into the cataclysm with your pig's head on, just one more raver in the storm, singing, give me a cigarette and a streetlight love. Give me a cigarette and a hard, fast glove."* The DJ cut in. "And that's a song we can all relate to, another tune we love here at 94.7. That one just doesn't get old, does it?"

"Portland!" Laura cursed. It was as close to the end of the world she had ever gone, a mossy promontory at the edge of commerce. A nut fringe. A green space on the political map of Oregon, always throwing off the electoral vote with its half-million Teva-wearing, chai-drinking, urban subsistence-farming baristas, all celebrating the simple life while listening to opaque music.

"This is not the real world," she complained to the highway. "You can't just spend your life doing what you want because it's fun."

And with that thought, her anger began, inexorably, to shift. She tried to hold it on Tate, press it to Tate's face, but it wouldn't stick. A quiet life, surrounded by friends—that was the life Tate had described. Laura did not dare form the thought: That was the life Tate offered.

By the time she slammed her car into park in the basement beneath her hotel, she was just as angry, but it had all turned inward. She leaned her forehead on the steering wheel, remembering Tate's warm, strong hand on her wrist.

She had looked up at Tate then. The moonlight had caught a slight roughness in Tate's cheeks, but the imperfection just made her more handsome. *Weathered,* that was the word people would use if she were a man. And it would be a compliment. Tate had been in the world. She had worked and gardened and rode her motorcycle and gotten her hands dirty and her heart scuffed. Laura had seen that in her face. Tate's eyes said she was not afraid of heartbreak; she expected it. She was walking knowingly into it, sad and open-eyed.

"And you dished it up," Laura muttered to herself.

She felt the same punched-in-the-gut feeling she had felt the morning she draped her diamond necklace across Tate's bathroom counter, but this time she didn't cry.

Instead she wandered into the faux atmosphere of the hotel bar. Craig and Dayton were already there, enjoying their faux friendship. Above their heads, a television blared a reality TV show. As she entered, the man on the screen dropped a live beetle into his open mouth. Dayton let out a roar of applause. Craig glared at him and then at Laura.

"Hi, boss," Craig grumbled.

"Tell me we're not going to do that again," Dayton said. "What was that? High school show-and-tell? *These are my ten favorite coffee shops. Aren't I cool?*"

Laura sighed and signaled the bartender to pour her a drink.

"What would you like?" the bartender asked.

"I don't know," she said. "Whatever. A scotch."

"Seriously," Dayton said. "We're not going to do that again, right? What was that stuff she made us drink? Dude. I don't get paid enough for that." His phone blinked, and he picked it up, grunted, and put it back down.

Laura considered pulling rank—Craig and Dayton did what she told them; that was their job description. But she didn't. She twirled the scotch around in its glass, staring into the golden liquid.

Why had she brought them at all? Just to shield her from Tate Grafton. Then she waited them out. She wanted them to go. If she were honest with herself, she had to admit they were there to keep her from giving in to her own temptations. She hadn't really thought Tate would attack her. She would not have met her if she believed that.

"No," she said. "We're not going to see her again."

The sadness must have sounded in her voice because Craig said, "Don't take it too hard. It's rough being the one who always shuts something down. My father owned a grocery store. Twenty years he ran that store, then one day Walmart comes into town. Poof. His whole life ended that day. I know what you were thinking."

*Probably not*, Laura thought.

"You wanted to be the good guy for once. You thought maybe we could save the underdog. But you know, we're not the bad guys. We're just…"

"Change?" Laura suggested.

"Yeah. Change," Craig said.

"That's nice of you to say," Laura said.

"Anyway," Craig added. "They're all a bunch of dykes."

"They could open a carpet store." Dayton guffawed. "Carpet munchers! They'd never have to go out to eat. They'd only have to eat out. Am I right?"

Dayton tried to give Craig a fist bump. The older man stared at him.

Laura stood, her stool screeching against the floor.

"That is inappropriate. I should not have to remind you that you represent the Clark-Vester Group for the duration of this trip, and derogatory language is never acceptable."

"Whoa." Craig held up his hands.

Dayton covered his snigger with the lip of his beer.

"Don't get all PC," Craig added. "With your dad being who he is, I didn't think you'd mind."

"I am not my father's…" Laura stopped. What hadn't she been for Stan Enfield? She was his beaming poster child at age eight, the founding member of High Schoolers for Enfield at sixteen, college campaigner at twenty, financial manager at twenty-five. "My father is not a homophobe."

"We're not hating on your dad," Dayton said. "I don't want those people getting married either."

"It's a campaign strategy," Laura said. "He doesn't care about gay marriage or gay anything."

"Don't tell me that. I voted for him," Craig said.

"I'm going upstairs," Laura said.

With that she slammed the scotch back in one shot. She didn't like scotch, didn't know why she had ordered it, but she knew it was the kind of gesture that would impress Dayton, and maybe even Craig. The satisfaction of doing it lasted all the way to the elevator. Then the liquor hit her stomach.

*What the hell am I doing?* She punched the button for the

elevator. Her mind bounded back and forth between Craig and Dayton, her father, and the vision of Tate's naked shoulders bathed in moonlight. The combination, on top of a shot of scotch, was unsettling.

"Are you all right?" An elderly woman with a floral-printed cane had just entered the elevator beside her.

"Yes," Laura said. "No." Then the door opened on her floor, and she hurried to the privacy of her room.

# Chapter 8

Maggie and Krystal were still at Out Coffee when Tate arrived to collect her motorcycle. They were waiting; Tate could tell. All the counters were wiped. The floor was mopped. The to-go cups were stacked in neat rows. Between them steamed two cups of chamomile tea, the same tea Maggie had brewed for Tate when she was a teenager, home sick with the flu. The tea Maggie brewed for breakups and deaths and HIV diagnoses and miscarriages and lost jobs. Comfort tea. Can't-do-anything-else-but-be-with-you tea.

Maggie's face was a question mark.

"I'm sorry," Tate said.

Maggie cupped her hands over her cup and lowered her head. Tate sat across from her. Krystal edged her chair closer to Tate and leaned her head on Tate's shoulder.

"No. I'm sorry," Maggie said. "You told us to make a good impression. Then me, Lill, and Krystal, we tore the place up."

She ran a hand through her short, ginger-gray hair. Her hands looked swollen, and she had taken off the friendship ring that she and Lill had exchanged after their breakup.

"It was my fault," Krystal added. "I kinda knew I shouldn't try to fix that sink, but the book just made it look so easy, and I knew you were busy, and you…"

Tate gave an infinitesimal shake of her head just in case Krystal was going to say something about Laura.

"You just always know what to do," Krystal finished.

Tate thought about Abigail and Duke, Laura, Out in Portland, her own unfinished bachelor's degree. She sighed.

"I wish."

"I should have kept an eye on everything," Maggie said. "I just forgot. With Lill there and all those people, it was like back in the day."

"Complete with disaster," Tate said. "Remember the time the coffee grinder caught fire?"

"Or the time the delivery man brought us an ounce of cocaine in the fair-trade coffee beans?"

"Or when I was Krystal's age and you let me close the store by myself. I thought the meter reader was trying to rob us."

Maggie laughed, but the smile quickly faded from her face. "We blew it this time. That corporate harpy…"—it was a clever work-around for *bitch*. "She doesn't want a good story. She wants to see things run right."

"I don't know what she wants," Tate said truthfully. "But I don't think she's going to be coming back tomorrow. And I don't think it's your fault or Lill's or Krystal's. If it's anyone's fault, it's mine for thinking I could pull some sort of heroic save. She's got a company. They've done research. This thing is settled, and they're not going to change their minds because I show her a good time."

"Then what happens?" Maggie asked. "What happens to us?"

"I don't know," Tate said. "We go home. We go to bed. We figure something out. Krystal, you want a ride on my bike? I'll take you home."

Maggie grumbled that she could take Krystal home. After all, they were going to the same place. But Krystal had already leapt up and run outside to the weathered Harley. Tate followed her.

"She'll be fine, Maggie. I'll take her straight back to your place," Tate said.

She fastened her full-face helmet onto Krystal's head and retrieved a spare half-helmet from her saddlebag. Krystal mounted the seat behind her, wrapping her arms around Tate's waist and squeezing like a boa constrictor. Tate pried Krystal's fingers apart, loosening her grip a little bit.

"I still have to breathe," she teased.

"What about the girl?" Krystal asked, laying her helmeted head on Tate's shoulder.

Tate revved the engine, hoping to lose Krystal's question in the noise.

"You liked her," Krystal yelled.

Tate longed for the privacy of a full-face helmet. She didn't want Krystal to see her face, even in profile.

"I don't like her," she lied.

Krystal said nothing more until they reached Maggie's

squat, white cinder-block house in southeast Portland. Maggie was already inside. Tate could see her moving about the kitchen.

"I won't tell her," Krystal said, glancing at the kitchen window.

"Tell her what?" Tate asked, but she knew. She took the helmet from Krystal, and tucked the small half-shell helmet back in her bag. "It'd break Maggie's heart," Tate added, as though Krystal had answered her question. "And plus, nothing is going to happen."

When she looked up, Krystal was staring at her like an anime drawing of innocent confusion. Her pink ponytails stuck out at odd angles, half-crushed by the helmet. Her eyes were wide in the darkness.

"But she likes you," Krystal said, as though it were a fact, as though it were enough.

"No she doesn't," Tate said wearily.

"But she does! She *loves* you."

Tate pulled Krystal into a motherly hug.

"Like in the movies?" Tate asked.

"Yes!" Krystal said. Apparently she was developing Maggie's lack of irony. "Like in the movies!"

# Chapter 9

The phone in Laura's hotel room rang as she walked in the door.

"Hello?" she answered tentatively.

"You sound like someone's stalking you." It was her mother with a voice like sunshine, although it might just have been gin.

"How are you, Mom?"

"We just got out of a planning session. Inspirational. Just inspirational. Your father has some brilliant campaign advisors this time. That's what I want to talk to you about."

"Now?"

"Oh, hon, are you tired? Are you all right?" The sunshine in her voice dimmed.

For a moment Laura considered an honest answer.

"I'm fine," she said. "Just tired."

"You work so hard." Her mother was on the road almost

as much as she was, but somehow the campaign travel never seemed to dampen her spirits or deflate her blond bouffant. "We're looking forward to having you home."

*Home?* Laura thought. The word seemed to have a permanent question mark attached to it.

"You know your father can hire a lot of talent, but he only has two daughters. He's only got one *you.*"

"Of course. I just have to finish up some things in Portland, then Palm Springs, then I'll be home." Laura sat on the bed, slipped off her Jimmy Choos, and dropped them beside the end table. Her feet ached, and her Achilles tendons burned as they stretched back to their proper length.

"Oh, Laura." Her mother's voice had returned to its original sunny sweetness. "You know Brenda would let you come home early."

Laura rubbed her calf.

"I don't know. I haven't asked her."

"No, love, she would. I talked to her."

Of course she had. Laura sighed.

"She and Doug Vester are very excited about this campaign," her mother said. "The whole Clark-Vester Group is behind us. And that job has you running ragged. You're in a different city every day and doing what? There are hundreds of people who can sell property."

"I buy property."

"I'm sorry. I'm just so excited about the prospects. Think about what your father can do for Alabama. You could be on a flight tomorrow, and then we'd all be together."

Laura hesitated. There had been a time when nothing had

felt quite as good as sitting around the "think tank" with her mother, father, sister, and brother. Before any of the children were married, before Stan Enfield could afford an army of advisors, when it was just "the fabulous five" as her father called them, sitting under the scattered light of the Waterford crystal, late at night, a bottle of gin half-empty on the table. Before them, between them, in the very air they breathed, there had been the dream of a better America. An America where everyone worked, where industries expanded, where investments grew. But most of all, Laura remembered being together.

"I'll be home soon," she said.

"But why not now? Your father has built his whole campaign on the American family. What is it going to look like if you're not there? And there's that lovely house you bought in Montgomery."

*Home.*

"That house still has the fake flowers the house stagers set up," Laura said. "I barely remember what it looks like." She knew she should not go down this path with her mother, not when everything was settled. She *was* going home. She *would* work on the campaign. It did not matter if 8420 Euclid Lane did not feel like the Platonic ideal of "home"; neither did a messy hotel room. But her interaction with Tate had left her angry and resentful, with nowhere to push her ire. "I don't even know if I own that house. Johnny bought it as an investment. I think he put my name on it to spread out the tax liability. I hadn't even seen it when he bought it."

"It's a lovely house."

"I don't remember."

"That's my point exactly." Her mother really was a politician's wife. "Your brother cares about you. We all do. And your job is making you a visitor in your own home, a nomad."

Laura closed her eyes. Again, she saw Tate's muscular shoulders, bare in the moonlight. Again she traced the dark symbol inked into Tate's arm. She had never been that close to a tattoo, never touched one, had always imagined there would be something diseased about the skin, but it had been as smooth as Tate's whole body.

"Why won't you just come home now?" her mother urged.

And Laura knew that anything she could say in reply would be a lie.

# Chapter 10

Back at her apartment, Tate wanted nothing more than to throw herself onto the bed and pull the blankets over her head, but Rose was standing in the foyer, leaning on her cane. She was so small, she barely reached Tate's waist.

"What is it, Rose?" Tate sighed.

"We have document in the mail. Pawel says don't trouble you. Busy girl, you have so much to do, but I tried and I tried. My English is not so good. My eyes!" She pressed a hand to her heart. "So old. I will be eight-four. Eighty-four! You know when I was sixty, my sisters all say I look twenty. I bake cookies. Come in. One minute."

Reluctantly, Tate followed Rose into her apartment. Once again, she took in the profusion of decorative plates that lined every exposed wall, commemorating American presidents, pop stars of the 1950s, and members of the British royal family. Why a Hungarian couple would want the "Elvis Through the Ages" plate set was a mystery to Tate. Luckily, the document—a letter from the landlord explaining that he would be checking on the water heater—was not. Tate translated, ate her cookie, and excused herself under a rain of protests from Pawel and Rose.

"You are so busy. Busy girl. You don't eat enough. So thin."

In her own apartment, Tate surveyed the contents of her refrigerator: kale, soy milk, and cheese curds. What was she thinking? She slammed the door.

On her phone, Vita had texted: *soooo?*

*No*, she wrote back. Then she shut off the phone and booted up her laptop.

*Laura Enfield*, she typed into the search bar. She felt like a spy, a bad spy who had already lost the war and was now trying to learn a few things about the victor. Her ship sunk, her troops captured; it wasn't even damage control at this point. It was just the wrong thing to do at the end of an awful day. She kept searching.

Several dozen entries came up. She typed in *Alabama*. The findings diminished. Laura C. Enfield of the Clark-Vester Group. She looked at the company portrait of Laura grinning out at the camera, her hair fluffed up like a prom queen, her eyes empty. Tate scanned the results again. The next link took her to a news article.

*Republican senator Stan Enfield appeared at a symposium on affordable housing along with his daughter, commercial real estate development consultant Laura Enfield.*

In the foreground of the photo, a cheerful barrel-shaped man shook hands with an old woman. In the background,

Laura sat at a table, deep in conversation with a young black man, her face concerned, her pen poised over a notebook.

"I get it," Tate said staring at her computer. Of course, the girl she fell for would be the closeted daughter of a Southern politician. Of course, Laura's father worked in "policy." Of course. But it was over now.

Tomorrow was her day off. She would walk up to the Mount Tabor Community Garden and climb the steps she had built with her own hands, eat the fruit she had grown, and watch, from afar, the city that she loved.

Tate had been working in her garden for about an hour when she spotted Vita's familiar silhouette moving between rows of green beans.

"How do you get up here every day?" Vita asked when she arrived at Tate's plot.

Tate surveyed Vita's outfit: high heels, slashes of neon, a lot of vinyl. It was too much to take first thing in the morning. She held her fingers to imitate a viewfinder.

"You look like Stevie Nicks." She pretended to take a picture.

"You're dirty," Vita said. She really did look like Stevie Nicks. Stevie Nicks circa 1995. A bit too old for the outfit. Not quite pretty enough for the makeup. "Why aren't you answering your phone so I could talk you into going to Dots and buying me jalapeno cheese fries?"

"I'm gardening."

Vita surveyed the small pile of weeds Tate had collected beside her Sunny Jubilee tomatoes. She pointed to Tate's boot.

"You're stepping on one."

It was true. A stalk had bent over, heavy with tomatoes. The fruit now squished out around Tate's boot. Tate kicked the plant out of the way.

"So, do you want to buy me jalapeno cheese fries, or what?"

"Now?" Tate checked her watch. It was barely ten.

"Ha! I worked until three last night, so in my world, it's like ten p.m."

"And that does not make me want cheese fries," Tate said.

Vita squatted down beside Tate, an impressive feat given her spike-heeled boots.

"You're sulking," she said.

"I'm weeding," Tate said.

"It's *that woman*."

"That's what Maggie calls her. 'That woman.'"

"Walk with me," Vita said. "I can't sit here smelling compost all morning."

"I just want to get some stuff done around here." Tate cast around for something that needed doing.

"Give it up. You should just buy that shit at the store like everyone else. Come on. Do you think I just *happened* to be walking through the urban farmstead? I'm going to cheer you up whether you like it or not."

Tate pulled off her gloves and tossed them in a basket hidden in the kiwi arbor.

"Come on, babe." Vita linked her arm through Tate's. "It cannot possibly be as bad as you think."

Together they walked through the garden, Tate pausing to

haul Vita over the hay bales, Vita mincing along in black pleather boots.

The community garden bordered Mount Tabor Park, and soon they were walking through the paths that crisscrossed the wooded hillside. Eventually, they rounded a bend in the trail and the trees thinned. To their right they could look down on the Hawthorne district. To their left, the Mount Tabor reservoir stood behind its wrought iron fence.

"So? You going to tell me about 'that woman'?" Vita sat down on a bench, looking up at Tate through glittery, fake eyelashes.

Tate picked up a pebble and tossed it into the water, sending ripples that reached the farthest edge of the pool. She waited until every trace of the pebble had disappeared, then said, "How long have you been going out with Cairo?"

"Three glorious weeks."

"Do you love her?"

"I do." Vita folded her arms over her chest. "I think she's the one."

Tate took a seat beside her friend. "You *do* realize how many times you've said that, right?"

"Yes." Vita drew the word out. "But this is different."

"Do you realize how many times you've said *that*?"

"Yes," Vita drawled again. "But this time it really is different."

Tate plucked a sprig of boxwood from the hedge behind her. She held it to her nose. It smelled of travel, of truck stops, of something lonely.

"I know," Vita added. "You can know after three hours."

"Do you really think that's true? Or is that just something we tell ourselves later?"

Vita paused. "Do you love that girl?"

Tate rested her elbows on her knees, her chin on her folded hands, and released a sigh that told the whole sad story.

Only it didn't.

"Well?" Vita asked.

Tate told her about her night, about Dayton and Craig, and her failed attempt at promoting Out Coffee, the passion with which Laura spoke to her, and the venom with which Laura decried her life in Portland.

"She thinks I'm a loser," Tate said.

"You never did love that job," Vita said.

"I like my job."

"You're only doing it to save Maggie's ass, and you know it."

Tate began to protest, but Vita stopped her.

"That's what? Nine years of saving Maggie's ass? Weren't you supposed to go back to college in there somewhere?"

"Maybe I am a loser."

The punch to her arm came hard and fast.

"Ow!"

"If that's how you want to think…fine," Vita said. "You're her bit of rough stuff. You're just some dumb working-class dyke. Why don't you strap on, get some grease under your fingernails, and put on a hard hat? Just show up at her doorstep, drop your pants, and say, 'Come to Daddy, Princess.' Carpe fucking diem. That's what I say."

Tate needed all the advice she could get; she readily admitted that. And she got plenty. But like other things that came in bulk for free it wasn't particularly high quality. She was just gearing up to tell Vita why it was all a lot more complicated than "carpe fucking diem" when her phone rang.

"Where are you?" It was Krystal.

"At the park, with Vita."

"Guess what." Krystal did not wait for Tate to guess. "I got a letter from my father today. He said he might get out. He says they might give him something called 'compassionate release.' Isn't that, like, the most awesome thing ever?"

"Oh, Krystal." Tate sighed. "Every time he writes to you he thinks he's getting out."

"But that's not why I called." Krystal dropped her voice to a conspiratorial whisper. "I called because Hillary Clinton is here."

Vita mouthed, *Is it her?*

"Laura?" Tate's eyes met Vita's.

"Yeah, I told her you were working today so she wouldn't think you came in *just* to see her, so you can be, like, 'Oh, I didn't know you were going to be here.' You know, so you can act all cool and butch and stuff. But you gotta get in here fast. Maggie just started showing her those vagina collages. You know the one where the rubber centipede is getting eaten by the purple vagina? Remember it?"

It was a hard thing to forget.

"I'll be there in ten."


Tate wanted to be angry at Laura. She was angry. And hurt. It was just that the tableau before her was so perfect. Maggie had retrieved all the Vagina Denta collages and arranged them on a long table by the front window of Out Coffee. She was holding one up and lecturing Laura, her fingers in the vagina's toothy mouth. She looked like some stern, butch art teacher.

"This captures the universal female experience of penetration," Maggie was saying.

Behind Maggie, Krystal was shaking her head and mouthing the words, *It doesn't.*

Meanwhile, Laura sat in white slacks, blouse, and blazer, her head tilted.

"It's very unique," she was saying. "I do like the purple."

"Purple represents the menstrual blood and the body starved of oxygen."

The rubber centipede dangled out of the vagina's mouth.

"It's...vivid," Laura said.

Catching sight of Tate, Laura rose. Tate took in her cream-colored heels, the curve of her thigh, the low-cut V of her blouse. Around her neck Laura wore a white ascot with a pale, nautical pattern printed on it or, more likely, woven in gold. No one Tate had ever known wore an ascot with anchors.

*The perfect politician*, Tate thought, and anger surged up in her chest, flushing her cheeks. Laura had wanted her. She had felt her desire like the crackle around high-tension wires. And it wasn't just sexual. There had been tenderness in the way Laura begged her to keep the necklace and sadness in Laura's eyes when Tate refused. That was what made Tate angry. It wasn't even the accusation about working in a coffee shop; it was that she was sure Laura felt the same attraction she did, and yet it wasn't enough.

"Ready?" Tate said brusquely.

Laura's face said *You are my savior.*

"It's art," Tate said, as though Laura had voiced an opinion to the contrary. "It's progressive."

"I'll watch the counter," Krystal called after them. "Like, all night. Don't worry about anything. Don't even come back tonight. Maggie and I will close up."

"She's very helpful," Laura said, putting her key in the rented Sebring parked out front.

Tate ignored the comment. "Not traveling with your minions today?" she asked.

"They're doing some market research."

"So they can ruin some other small business."

"Thank you for meeting me," Laura said.

"I didn't think you'd come back."

"Well, I did." Laura slid into the driver's seat. "You still want to show me around?"

*Not really.* Tate took her place in the passenger seat. She considered her options.

"We'll start with the velvet painting museum. I think the exhibit is naked black women. You'll have to get it vetted by the senator first. Make sure no one sees you going in."

It was a challenge.

"You did your research," Laura said, starting up the car without looking at Tate.

"*My father is in 'policy,*'" Tate said, echoing Laura's evasion of the night before. "Of course he is."

"Which way?" Laura said.

Her hands were tight on the steering wheel as she followed Tate's directions. When they reached the small museum, Laura marched in and began at one end of the room as though she was getting paid for spending exactly 1.3 minutes looking at each painting. As it turned out, this month's exhibit was lonesome cowboys.

Tate followed behind her wearily. At the fourteenth cowboy she stopped.

From the front desk, the curator called out, "That's a really interesting one. Look how the lasso could also be a noose dropping over his head. It's subtle."

"Nothing about velvet cowboys is subtle," Laura said dryly.

"You don't have to do this," Tate shot back.

"I said I'd give you a week. I'm giving you a week."

It was ridiculous, dragging some senator's daughter to the velvet painting museum because she thought...what? This would win her over? She could hear Vita: *You want to bed her, and you want to go into business with her, and the best you can come up with is velvet cowboys?*

"Look, Laura." Tate touched her elbow lightly, but Laura did not turn. "This is a waste of your time and mine. You work for a big company. They're going to do what they're going to do. You're right. Out Coffee is in trouble. Maggie is so far in debt she can't see out. I'm done with the heroics. You can go back to your hotel and get back to your real life."

Laura continued staring at the lasso-noose.

Tate tried again, her voice gentler this time.

"I appreciate whatever you are trying to do here—fulfilling your commitments—but you don't have to. And honestly, I've got to start looking for a new job, and I've got to figure out what's going to happen to Maggie."

Laura lifted a finger and hovered it an inch above the velvet. "I'm sorry," she said.

"It's just business," Tate said, stepping away from her. "Your business and my business at opposite ends. And there's no point in us going through this charade. You're buying the building. I'm not going to hang myself with my lasso."

Laura turned, a sharp authoritative turn like a prosecutor spinning to face the jury, but then she stopped and stood clasping and unclasping her hands.

"There is nothing wrong with working at a coffee shop."

"No. There's not," Tate said.

"I am sorry about what I said last night."

Tate waited for the caveat.

"It's nice," Laura said, almost to herself. "I got there early. Some woman sat with me for half an hour and told me how she was trying to make a 'didgeridoo' out of pine trees thinned from timberland. I'm not exactly sure what she was talking about, but it was nice. She cared. She thought she could do her part to change the world, and she wanted to share that with me. Then Maggie and Krystal showed me the artwork." She shrugged. "It's very…"

"Postmodern American primitive?" Tate suggested.

Laura looked surprised.

"I took an art class my last term at PSU." Tate stared over Laura's shoulder at the street outside. "Though I think 'postmodern' might be a little bit grandiose for the Vagina Denta series." She turned away to hide her smile.

"If you have other things you need to do, I understand," Laura said. "But if you still want to show me around Portland,

I want to see it. Nothing is set in stone yet. I could still talk to the board about Out Coffee."

Tate looked at Laura. Her brow was furrowed and her lips turned down in an expression Tate could only read as hope.

In the car on the way to their next stop, the Grotto, Laura broke the cautious silence that had fallen between them.

"I hate it," she said, staring ahead at the paint wholesalers and used-tire shops that lined Sandy Boulevard.

"The velvet cowboys?"

"Being a senator's daughter." The words were like coins pushed across a counter, an offer. "I want you to know that. I hate it."

"Why?" Tate asked.

"I think you know."

Laura pulled to a stop at a red light and looked over at Tate. *No*, Tate thought, *not* at, *into*. She felt like Laura looked right into her soul, into her past and her future, into everything that she was and could be. It was distinctly uncomfortable, even if the stare came from a beautiful woman, and Tate kept her eyes fixed on the red light. When it turned, she was quick to say, "It's green."

The Grotto was more than the name promised. There was, indeed, a mossy grotto at the foot of a cliff where a few Catholic women clustered in prayer. But beside the actual grotto stood an equally mossy elevator that carried visitors up to a meditation garden and a glass-fronted prayer room perched on a cliff 110 feet above the city. Inside the glass room, pews sat in three rows and a wax statue of the Virgin Mary stood in a plexiglass case, presiding over the city below.

Here Tate and Laura sat, facing the window that looked out over northeast Portland. In front of them, a toddler pressed his sticky hands against the window. A young woman looked at the drop and turned pale. Two Chinese teenagers flashed the peace sign while their friends photographed them against the Portland skyline. But eventually, the tourists filed out.

"It's beautiful up here," Laura said.

Tate ran her hand along the smooth surface of the pew. "I slept up here once. At night, it's amazing."

"You slept here?"

"When I was homeless." She hadn't meant to reveal anything. Every important person in her life knew her story and had always known it. Now she felt suddenly self-conscious. She shrugged and looked away. "It was only for a week. Then Maggie rescued me."

"Why were you homeless?"

The concern in Laura's voice touched her.

"It was all a long time ago. I was only sixteen."

She meant to explain it away. Sixteen was a lifetime ago.

Laura exhaled carefully. "Sixteen."

Tate could not tell if it was tenderness or pity that pulled Laura's lips into a frown.

"What happened?" Laura asked.

"My mother is something of a lost soul."

Tate meant to leave it at that, shrug it off and return to some safe topic. But it was so unexplainably easy to talk to Laura, much easier than it should have been given that Laura was poised to crush Maggie's dreams. The woman who had, only the night before, told her she was a miserable underachiever. The woman who had left her breathless and then left her entirely.

Still the story poured out of her, as if of its own volition: the hot motel rooms she shared with her mother, Debby-Lynn, Debby-Lynn's on-and-off jobs, the equally transitory boyfriends. Then there was *the* job, the temporary filing job that put Debby-Lynn in the path of Jared Spaeth.

"He was everything my mother wanted. He was a State Farm agent, which to my mother was like being the prince of England. He had a little ranch house in Gresham and a boy about my age. He told my mother he would take care of us."

"And then?"

Laura rested her hand on Tate's, and Tate felt like a rare bird had landed on her. She was afraid to move lest it fly away. But a second later Laura withdrew her touch and folded her hands in her lap.

"My stepbrother was three years older than me," Tate went on. "Tommy. When I was fourteen he started touching me. I told my mother."

"But she wouldn't help you?" Laura asked.

"She did not want to, and it kept happening, so I told one of my teachers at school." Tate shrugged. "After that, Mother took away my house key. One night after I was out late with my friend Vita, my mom wouldn't answer the door. I thought she was just punishing me for staying out late, but the next day she sent Tommy out to school, and he told me to get lost. He said I wasn't part of the family anymore. He said if I told anyone else, he'd kill me."

"I'm so sorry," Laura murmured.

"I would have run away anyway. I wasn't going to let him touch me again."

Tate glanced over at Laura. Her face was pale.

"It was all a long time ago," Tate said, because the story felt both too big and too small for the glass-fronted room where they sat. Beneath them, Tate could see airplanes rising off a distant tarmac. In her peripheral vision she felt Laura's gaze on her face.

"The other night." Laura stumbled over her words. "I...I wouldn't have done that to you if I had known."

Tate cocked her head, trying to discern what vile, clammy-handed Tommy Spaeth had to do with the other night.

"I mean..." Laura's eyes darted to the tourists who had just walked in and then down to the floor. Her pale cheeks flushed scarlet. "Does it remind you of him?"

"You mean sex?" Tate realized a second after it should have been obvious. "I like sex." She tried to catch Laura's gaze, but Laura stared at the tiles beneath her feet. "I wouldn't let Tommy Spaeth take that away from me."

"Is that why you prefer women? Because of him?"

Laura's voice was still hushed, and Tate lowered her own to match.

"I've been kissing on girls since I was six years old. I like women because I'm gay," Tate said. "Is that why you...?"

Another wave of tourists came in, snapping photographs and ogling the wax museum Mary. When the room emptied, Laura said, quietly, "No. But that was always the party line in my father's campaign. Homosexuality was the result of childhood trauma. 'Protect the child; heal the victim.' Sounds good, doesn't it?" Laura had regained her composure and now stared out the window like an executive waiting for her flight in the skycap lounge. "Say no to that, and you're saying yes to child abuse. Reframe the question, and you're supporting pedophiles and molesters." Her voice had taken on a dry, bitter edge. "He has a whole team of people who think these things up for him."

"I can see why you would hate that," Tate said.

Laura stood and strode to the window.

"What happened after your mother kicked you out?" she asked.

"I slept at my girlfriend's house until her mother kicked me out too. That was my friend Vita. We only dated for three months, but when she found out what Tommy had done to me she tried to burn their house down. She got the whole porch on fire before it started to rain, and the fire department showed up. You can imagine why her mother didn't let me back in the house after that." Tate smiled. "That was the last time *I* was a bad influence on *Vita.*"

Laura stood, backlit by the window, and Tate could not read anything in the shadows of her eyes. Still it felt good to tell her the story, to lay it out like the bony surface of the cliff on which the Grotto garden perched. The foundation. The beginning.

"I spent the first night after that in a bus station," Tate said. "I spent the next three nights here, one night in a club called the City Nightclub, and one night in an abandoned RV. I started showing up at Out Coffee in the morning and staying until closing. That's when Maggie realized something was wrong."

The sightseers ambled out, leaving the quiet more potent than when they entered.

"I remember the day after the RV, I went to Out," Tate continued. "I didn't have money for coffee, and I was sure Maggie was going to bust me for being there. She was tough, or she seemed tough to me, but she gave me a cookie and a coffee and she said, 'You better come home with me tonight.' I think she spent the rest of the day triaging her relationship with Lill. Or the rest of her life."

It made Tate sad to think of that first night at Maggie's, how she had lain on the couch and listened to them fight.

Laura listened, neither sympathizing nor interrupting. When Tate was done, she said simply, "You're strong."

Tate stood, shaking off the compliment.

"You do what you have to do. And that was twenty years ago. It felt like the end of the world then, but it wasn't."

"Are Lill and Maggie a couple?" Laura asked.

"Come. I'll tell you the whole sordid story on the road."

Without thinking Tate reached her hand out to Laura. To her surprise, and perhaps to Laura's own, she took it.

Their next stop was Powell's Books, the largest independent bookstore in the world. Then they took a tour through the seedy red gates of Chinatown, past Darcelle XV's drag club, and through a few avant-garde art galleries. As they strolled, Tate regaled Laura with tales from Out Coffee, the Mirage, and all the other venues she frequented, each a strange, troubled, loving family unto itself.

She told her how Lill and Maggie met when Lill first worked for her. How Lill said she wasn't gay but fell hard for Maggie. And how they had fought the night Maggie brought Tate home, because Lill didn't want another problem child sleeping on their sofa. Then how, after what seemed like a lifetime together, Lill left Maggie and a year later was married to Stephen. They adopted Bartholomew and some years later adopted little Sobia. Their family looked as well-established as if they had been together forever. And she told Laura how Maggie found Krystal when she aged out of foster care and ended up in the shelter of Out in Portland Coffee, cold and hungry and full of Hollywood dreams.

"She is like the kid sister I never had." Tate dropped her head back and stared up at the vaulted ceiling in one of the galleries. "I see all the mistakes she's going to make, and I can't stop her…"

"She seems like a bright girl."

"She'll do great if she can stay away from her father. He's in jail right now. I'm just worried one of these days he'll get out and convince her to go away with him, and we'll never see her again. She thinks he's getting out. I just hope it's not true."

"Do you think he will?" Laura asked.

"Every year or so he writes to her and tells her he's getting out. He's got an appeal. Nothing ever comes of it, but I'm still worried. He's got a history of violence against women."

Laura laid a gentle hand on Tate's lower back. Tate jumped slightly at the unexpected touch.

"I can't talk to Maggie about this," Tate said, shaking her

head. "She's already worried enough about Krystal. But if Krystal's father gets out, I'm afraid he's not going to see her as a daughter. He's just going to see a pretty, young girl, and that's who he's preyed on in the past. Krystal doesn't understand that. She still thinks he's 'Daddy.' And he's been in prison for so long all she's got, really, are dreams."

"Families have such a tight hold on us," Laura said, turning away from the ink prints to the window and the leafy street outside the gallery. "There's no way to get out, is there?"

It was almost five, and Tate had promised to get Laura back to her hotel. They were just getting in the Sebring when Laura asked suddenly, "Why did you drop out of PSU?"

"What?"

It had been almost nine years since Tate had walked into the registrar's office and withdrawn from her courses. The man at the counter had looked at her transcript. "Remember," he had said. "Your credits are good for ten years. If you don't finish your degree in ten years these credits will disappear and you'll have to begin all over." Ten years. She had laughed. Ten years was a lifetime. "I'll be back next quarter," she had told him. Nine years ago.

"You only had a term left," Laura added.

"You did your research."

The Sebring glided down a shady side street. Tate allowed herself just a minute to consider what it would be like to live in one of the stately houses, set behind sweeping maples, with a woman who loved her.

"What would I do with a BA in physics?" she asked finally.

"You'd been accepted into a graduate program. You had loans, and your second year you were going to get a teaching fellowship."

Tate's surprise ran deeper.

"Nobody knows that. Not even Maggie."

*Especially not Maggie*, Tate thought.

"So why?" Laura drove on, her eyes on the road, but Tate felt her attention focused on her.

"I was never that good," Tate said.

"You must have been good enough."

"Maggie needed me."

It was all in the past and, like the mansions, so far beyond her reach now that longing for it was like longing for a dream.

"To run the shop?" Laura asked.

"Lill left her," Tate said. "It wasn't entirely my fault. I was one of many charity cases Maggie took in. Poor Mags. She was heartbroken, but more than that she finally realized how much Lill did for Out Coffee. Lill may go on about recalibrating the chakra, but she can balance a checkbook. She found fair-trade merchants they could actually afford. She hired employees who would actually show up. She fired people who stole. People came to the shop because they loved Maggie, but the shop survived because of Lill."

"So when Lill left her," Laura finished for her, "you dropped out of school and filled in? You took the place of her wife?"

"Not romantically."

They had arrived at Laura's hotel. Laura turned into the underground parking garage and circled down a story. Then she parked, turning off the car but not getting out.

"In every other way?"

Vita teased Tate about saving Maggie's ass, about keeping Out Coffee afloat, but Laura's questions felt different. They felt inescapable.

"I help her because she helped me," Tate said.

"You never wanted to finish your degree?"

"I like my job."

"And that's enough?"

"You think everyone with a degree is happy?" Tate countered, even though she was certain that was not what Laura meant.

"I'm not saying. I'm asking." Laura's gaze met Tate's. "Are you happy?"

Tate looked away and shrugged.

"My girlfriend dumped me for an oboist because she said she needed someone who understood her art. Then she took up with the biggest player in the Portland lesbian scene, who, I am sure, could not identify an oboe if it was up her ass. My coffee shop is being bought out, and the woman I think of as a mother is too old to work on her feet anyway. I haven't had sex in months except for one marvelous night with a woman who said it could never happen again."

Laura reached for her purse as though she suddenly needed something, but once she had it, she just clasped it in her lap.

"I'd like to be in love," Tate went on. "With someone who loved me back. I'd like to have enough money so that I didn't worry about my bike breaking down or cracking a filling. I'd like to be able to take care of Maggie, and maybe take in my own Krystal someday. But you know, it's summer. It's so beautiful out there." She gestured up at the ceiling. "And tonight my friend Vita, who I've known since we were kids, who once tried to kill my family in a house fire because she cared so much about me, she is going to make risotto, and we're going to sit outside and eat and talk. And, yeah, I'll be happy."

"Okay," Laura said. It sounded like good-bye.

Tate got out of the car. She was a few steps away when she heard Laura open her door. She turned. Laura leaned one elbow on the roof of the car. Tate waited for her to speak, but she said nothing, so Tate asked, "How did you know I got into graduate school? No one knows that."

"I asked my father's research analysts to run a background check on you." There was a flash of that wry smile again.

Tate shook her head to hide her own grin.

"And what did they say when you told them you wanted to know all about some dyke barista in Portland, Oregon?" she asked.

"I told them I was looking into a business partnership."

Out Coffee was quiet when Tate returned.

"It's your day off," Maggie said. "You should relax. But how did it go?"

Krystal sat on a back counter, swinging her legs.

"How was the girl?" Krystal asked.

"Better," Tate said, not meeting Krystal's eyes. She gave Maggie a brief rundown of the day's activities. "But I can't promise anything," she finished. "Just because I took her around Portland doesn't mean she's sold on Out Coffee."

"You're so good," Maggie said. She ran her hands through

her short, graying hair. "What would I do without you?"

"You would be fine, Maggie," Tate said, trying not to notice the inexplicable pile of official-looking papers stuck in between two of the espresso machines.

"Hey, if you don't need me," Tate said, "I'm going back out to my garden for a while."

"Can I go?" Krystal asked, bounding off the counter.

Maggie looked around. The shop was quiet.

"For an hour," she said reluctantly. "Be back here to help me close."

As soon as Tate and Krystal arrived at the community garden, Krystal leapt off Tate's motorcycle and continued to bounce in circles around her.

"Did you have fun with the girl? With Hillary Clinton?" Krystal asked.

Tate shrugged.

"Did you kiss her? K-I-S-S-I-N-G," Krystal spelled out. She was practically singing.

"No."

"Are you going to?"

"No," Tate said, swallowing hard. "Why are you all wound up?"

"I told you!"

Tate was relieved that Krystal did not seem inclined to press her for more details from her afternoon with Laura. Then she remembered the letter from Krystal's father.

"Come on, let's weed something," Tate said.

She headed toward her garden plot with Krystal on her heels.

"Don't you want to know what he said?"

Tate gazed up at the network of straw paths, railroad ties, and orderly vegetable plots.

"Oh, Krystal," she said.

They reached the plot with the kiwi tree. Tate dug around in a plastic bin and retrieved two pairs of muddy gloves. She handed one to Krystal and pointed out the weeds in between rows of chard. Then she knelt down and began carefully extricating them.

"He said he wants to come stay with me for a little while when he gets out," Krystal continued, beaming. "He just needs me to help him pull together $2,000, and then he's going to get a place of his own in The Dalles."

Tate looked up at her and sat back on her heels.

"You don't have a place for him to stay," Tate said gently. "You live with Maggie."

"He is going to get his CDL. You know he can make sixty dollars an hour driving with a CDL, and I'm going to move to The Dalles with him," Krystal said, her voice growing shriller. She took a breath and turned away. "He wants me to move there with him."

Tate let out a deep sigh. Maggie was no good at these conversations about Frank Jackson. She invariably resorted to rhetoric about female solidarity and the "family we choose." But Tate didn't know what to offer instead.

"You know my mom kicked me out when I was a little younger than you," she said.

"Yeah. I know."

Tate patted the earth beside her, and Krystal sat down

heavily. Tate looked at her, her pink hair escaping its pony-tails, her Barbie-doll makeup at odds with the dirt furrows around her.

"Krystal, you know that people aren't always who we want them to be." Tate saw Laura leaning on the roof of her car in the parking garage, so elegant, so untouchable in her white as-cot. "You have to make a distinction between what you want and what's really going to happen."

Krystal flopped onto her back and stared up at the sky. "That one looks like a dog eating a cheeseburger," she said, pointing to a cloud above their heads. She said nothing for a long time.

Tate pulled a few weeds, glancing at Krystal as she did. She knew she could get this part right: silence. Maggie and Lill loved to talk. They were always talking to Krystal about the fu-ture and feminism and self-reliance. Tate lifted a clod of dirt to her nose and inhaled its rich, dark fragrance.

"Don't you think we have to believe in people?" Krystal asked eventually. "You know? Give them a second chance."

Of course Tate did. Her whole life was a second chance.

"Just be careful." Tate wanted to press the words into Krys-tal's forehead like a sacred seal. *Dream*, she wanted to say, *hope, play, but remember the minute he gets out of prison your real life starts.* "He could hurt you. I know you don't want to hear that. I know you don't think it will happen. But he could. He's hurt other girls. That's what he does."

"They say the woman was a drug dealer," Krystal said.

"That doesn't change what he did," Tate said, brushing the dirt off her gloves.

She expected Krystal to protest, but she just stared up at the sky.

"You're always careful," Krystal said finally.

Tate pulled off her gloves and ruffled Krystal's ponytails.

"Yep," she said and rose and walked into the shade of the kiwi tree. "And that's why I'm still alive." Just the rustle of leaves and the faint scent of fruit made her think of Laura and their kiss beneath the arbor. Her body filled with a longing that rested heavy in her heart.

"But Tate," Krystal called plaintively, "I love him."

# Chapter 11

When she entered her room, Laura went straight to her laptop and opened her e-mail. Work was her refuge. Her father had taught her that. There was no problem in life that could not be solved by work. In work, grief melted away. Disappointment became fuel for accomplishment. Questions crystallized into answers. But as she stared at the in-box, the names swam in front of her eyes. *Who are these people?* She closed the lid. The sunlight outside was fading from gold to blue and the first twinkle of city lights sparkled outside her hotel window.

She tried not to think of Tate. Tate dropping the diamond on the sidewalk. Tate striding away, her back upright, her head bowed. Tate in her tiny walk-in closet of an apartment. Somewhere Tate would be sharing a meal with her childhood best friend, sitting outside, watching the sky fade.

Laura felt restless. Her clothes were too tight. The air conditioner was too loud. She poured herself a glass of wine from the minibar, but the cheap merlot in a plastic glass just reminded her of everything she was missing. She flopped down on the bed and closed her eyes. *What am I doing?* It was the kind of question she had always thought welfare recipients should ask, or women with nine children, or old men who still worked at gas stations. Tate should be asking this question, but it was Laura, staring up at the textured plaster on the ceiling, who asked. *What am I doing?*

Without thinking, she slipped her hand under the hem of her skirt and pressed her clit through the fabric of her pantyhose, her body shaper, and her underwear. She relaxed into the pressure. Was that what she was doing with Tate? Just fulfilling a biological need? If that was the case she should be able to refuse, to put it out of her mind, but she couldn't.

She rarely masturbated. It embarrassed her. The weak orgasm she sometimes achieved and more often did not was not worth the vague feeling that she was doing something she should have given up at age four. But now she felt like someone deviled by an itch she could not reach. Her hands moved as if of their own accord, stripping layers of spandex and nylon until she could touch her bare flesh.

Her thoughts took her back to Tate's bed. To her surprise, it was not the memory of what Tate had done to her that aroused her the most—although she tried to touch herself as Tate had touched her, one finger inside her body, her other hand rubbing her clit—it was the thought of touching Tate. She remembered her own fingers exploring Tate's sex, how Tate's hips had thrust against her hand, how wet she had become. Tate's face had been so stern, so reserved, and her body so open. Her desire had made her seem vulnerable, and Laura had longed to protect her and pleasure her all at the same moment.

Now she imagined parting Tate's legs, pressing her lips into that delicate place. She imagined what it would be like to draw Tate's sex into her mouth. It was something she had never done with a woman, and in more lucid moments she worried that when she finally had the chance—allowed herself the chance—she would do it wrong and make a mess of the whole thing. But those fears were far from her mind. Now her own body swelled at the thought of kissing Tate.

Laura moved her fingers, imagining her tongue tracing the same pattern around Tate's clit. Each stroke made her shudder, each stroke made her body contract. The whole center of her body, from the tip of her clit to the deep mysterious recess of her womb, was on fire. But there was no relief. She rubbed harder, but the lubrication from her body made her slippery. The touch would not stay where she needed it. Her hand slipped too quickly away. And when she pressed down hard on her clit the promise of release seemed to slip back behind her flesh where she could not reach it.

She thought of Tate pulling her on top of her, holding her hips in her hands and rocking their bodies together. *Don't think about it. Just enjoy it.* But Tate was on the other side of the river. After what felt like hours, Laura stopped. Her body was as hot and tight as ever, only now she felt sore from the frantic rubbing, and the city lights made her feel exposed. She was thirteen stories up, but the sky outside was dark and she was practically onstage.

She was too frustrated to cry, but she let out a short sob as she thought of how easy it would be to call Tate. She knew instinctively that Tate would appear; she would not ask why. She would arrive at the hotel room door like a shy, noble suitor, her motorcycle helmet in hand, her face filled with concern. And Laura knew she could fall into Tate's arms and that Tate would hold her and kiss her. She could say anything to Tate. *I want you. I need you. I can't come. Please touch me.* Words she had never even imagined speaking. She knew she would be able to tell Tate everything.

Only she couldn't. She wiped her hand on the blanket. She couldn't tell Tate anything because there was no one—absolutely no one—in her life whom she could tell *about* Tate.

# Chapter 12

Vita and Tate sat on shredded lawn chairs in the vacant lot behind Tate's apartment, eating risotto. The moon was just as bright and watery as it had been a few days earlier when Laura walked into Out Coffee after closing. Then, it had filled Tate with restless potentiality. Tonight it had a melancholy, Bonnie Raitt kind of feeling.

"Where are the old Hungarians?" Vita asked. She had traded her leopard print for zebra stripes, and they glinted in the moonlight. "I'm surprised they're not out here badgering you. Their long-lost daughter. *Oh, Tate, we love. We love you.*" She imitated their lilting accent.

"They're just lonely," Tate shot back.

"I'm kidding."

"They don't have any family in Portland. They don't speak enough English. They don't have enough money to go out. It's sad. It shouldn't have to be like that. And it's Pawel and Rose, not the 'old Hungarians.'"

"Fine. I didn't mean anything," Vita said.

"Sorry."

They were silent for a while. Tate stared at her bowl, pushing the risotto from side to side without taking a bite.

"What's wrong?" Vita asked.

"Krystal got another letter from her father."

Vita snorted. "That girl's always got something. What's up, really?"

"Nothing." Tate stared into the garden.

The distant city noises formed their own kind of silence.

Vita waited a beat, then said, "You brood better than anyone I know. If I brooded like you did, I'd get all the girls."

"You do get all the girls," Tate noted. "Anyway, you said Cairo was the one."

"It's that profile," Vita said, ignoring Tate's comment. "The nose."

"Lay off."

"I love your nose. It's archetypal."

"Thanks, because that's what a woman wants to hear: She has an archetypal nose." Tate rolled her eyes.

"I'm just saying. We're going to talk about your nose until you tell me what's wrong with your heart."

"Nothing," Tate said again.

"If you don't tell me, I'll go find that woman you like and tell her every embarrassing thing you've ever done."

"You'll make half of it up." Tate threw her head back in mock despair. "I do like her."

Tate put her bowl down on the ground by her feet.

"I know you do, so why aren't you talking about her?" Vita asked.

"Because she's a Republican senator's daughter."

"I know. I looked her up online. I am so far ahead of you on this one." Vita scraped her spoon along her empty bowl and eyed Tate's half-finished dinner.

Tate picked the bowl up and handed it to her. "You're incorrigible."

"So what's her being a senator's daughter got to do with anything?"

"She's not interested. The only good thing is that she's still considering Out Coffee."

"No. She's not," Vita said. "I'm sorry, but this has nothing to do with the coffee shop. She just wants to get in your pants."

"You say things." Tate shook her head. "You open your mouth and things come out, but they have no bearing on reality. You can't know that."

"Yes I can. I'm sorry, Out Coffee is a losing business proposition," Vita said. "While you've been busy propping up Maggie, I've been managing one of the most successful bars in Portland, owned by one of the shrewdest lesbian entrepreneurs you're going to meet. Out is in a terrible location. It's a difficult business model. The retail space is too big for the business. The market is saturated. And Maggie has the business savvy of Mother Teresa. It's going under. I'm sorry to be blunt, but if you didn't already see that, then you're blind.

"And those sandwich boutiques this Laura Enfield woman wants to move in, they are hot. And they would be great for

Portland, especially that neighborhood. They have totally cap-italized on the organic, locally grown, free-range market. Everything that enters that store is compostable except for the customers." Vita paused. "Who are compostable too I guess, but you see what I mean."

Tate rested her chin on her knuckles.

"Yes."

"No. You don't," Vita protested. "That face says you don't."

"What do you want me to say?"

"I'm saying Laura Enfield is in this for *you*. That's what this little charade is all about whether she is ready to admit it or not, and you like her."

"I do."

"So...tell me about her. I'm your best friend. Why is this all such a secret suddenly? What's she like? What does she do? What does she do *to you*?"

Tate looked out over the moonlit lot with its weeds and its rusting shopping cart overturned beneath a wild cherry tree.

"That first night we played two out of three at 8-ball, she said if I won she'd tell me a secret or at least tell me something true," Tate said. "I lost. I scratched on the eight. But the thing is, when I'm with her, I feel like she's just on the verge of telling me that true thing. And I want to hear it. And I want to tell her...everything.

"Like tonight. She asked if I was happy. I told her all the crap, and then I told her we'd sit here and talk and it would make me happy. I knew that, but I knew it more when I said it to her."

For once Vita did not have a glib comeback. When she finally spoke she said, "I haven't seen you like this before."

"She was pretty clear the other night," Tate added. "Whether or not she wants something to happen she doesn't think it should. I don't want to get my heart broken again."

"Too late for that." Vita steepled her fingers under her chin. "But maybe right now, she's feeling like she messed up. She panicked. Maybe now she's wondering what she can possibly do to make up for it."

The following day, Tate woke early to ready Out Coffee. Then she rode back home to change in preparation for Laura's arrival at nine a.m. Her conversation with Vita had left her feeling at turns hopeful and guilty. If what Vita said was true, Laura had no intention of saving Out Coffee. But if what Vita said was true, then Laura had intentions for her. She alternated between these two poles a few more times while she washed her face. When she was finished, she ran a hand over her short hair and regarded the face that stared back at her in the bathroom mirror.

Happy. That was where her emotional pendulum finally came to rest. It had been so easy talking to Laura. Even though Tate had good friends who loved her, there was a corner of her heart that had been empty the day before and now was full of sunlight. *Today*, Tate thought as she shrugged into a white T-shirt, *I get to see her again*. She tried not to think about how short the day was or how likely it was that in a few days Laura would leave.

"*Push off, and sitting well in order smite the sounding furrows; for my purpose holds to sail beyond the sunset*," Tate quoted out loud. It was a poem she had memorized for her literature class nine years earlier. Then she thought, *Maybe there's still time.*

Everything seemed possible in Portland in the summer.

Unfortunately, Tate was not the only person who had been spurred to action by the beautiful day. When she got to Out Coffee, she saw a string of people standing outside. There was Maggie, a host of stern, craggy women in political T-shirts and leather vests, and several men with long, gray ponytails.

Tate pulled her Harley up short and removed her helmet.

"What's going on here?" she asked.

The women would have looked menacing, except that they looked so much like Maggie. Up close, Tate recognized them from Maggie's women's group. One waved to her. Another flashed a peace symbol. Two of them started singing "Kumbaya."

"We're all here!" Maggie called.

"Why are you all here?" Tate asked.

Maggie stood beside a woman in a CLINTON/GORE '96 T-shirt and a man with strings of handmade clay beads strung around his neck. And next to him stood…Abigail. Tate stopped short.

"Why is *she* here?" Tate demanded.

Abigail wore a green sundress. She really did have an exorbitant amount of freckles. They covered her from hairline to the plunging neckline of her dress. She was like a pale person perpetually walking in dappled shade or, perhaps, more like a white T-shirt on which someone had spilled a latte.

"Maggie said you needed me," Abigail called.

Her eyes were bright. She wore the same sweet, eager smile she had worn when they were first courting, before she decided that Tate could not understand her because Tate had never played the cello.

*Third cello,* Tate thought.

"Maggie said Out Coffee was getting bought out by some corporate bitch, and you were the only one who could save it," Abigail added.

"We're not going to let corporate America oppress us anymore," one of the leather-vested women yelled.

"No, we're not!" Maggie chimed in. She looked flushed and excited.

Someone yelled, "There she is!"

Tate turned to see Laura a few paces behind her, the Sebring parked on the other side of the street.

*Oh no,* she thought as Abigail led the crowd in a chorus of "Hell no, we won't go." She glanced from Maggie to Abigail, trying to decide whom to throttle first. Then everyone in the crowd lifted their arms in unison. The whole thing had suddenly gotten worse. They were—Tate now saw—handcuffed together. And at either end of the line, the last protestors, Abigail and a woman in a SAVE THE RAIN FORESTS T-shirt, were handcuffed to one of the drain spouts that ran from the roof of Out Coffee to the sidewalk.

"Freedom!" Maggie's voice rose over the rest of the crowd, clear and proud as though she was marching behind Martin Luther King Jr. and Cesar Chavez and Marx and Gloria Steinem and all the rest. "Freedom now!"

"But you're chained together," Tate pleaded. "You chain yourself to buildings when they are going to be bulldozed, when someone's going to cut down a heritage tree."

No one was listening.

"You can't demolish this building without demolishing us," Abigail yelled.

Tate glanced at Laura. She looked perplexed.

"No one is demolishing anything," Tate said. "Laura Enfield is here to see if her company wants to *rent* business space to Out Coffee. She wants to see if we are reputable business people."

"If they want to get in, they'll have to bulldoze our living bodies," the man with the beads said. "They will have to crush our entrails and crack every bone in our bodies and tear out our eyes."

It all seemed a little too visceral to Tate. The crowd cheered.

"Americans have become too complacent," Maggie added. "What happened to the union? When did we stop organizing?"

These were, in general, sentiments that Tate agreed with, inasmuch as one could agree with rhetorical questions shouted over a chorus of "Fuck the pigs! Fuck the pigs!"

But there was also the matter of Laura, standing at her elbow, saying, "Should I go?"

Tate was suddenly very aware of her proximity, the smell of her perfume, like the complicated smell of lemon blossoms.

"No. No. This is nothing," Tate said.

"Nothing?" Laura's eyebrow shot up.

"We do this all the time. It's like a Portland tradition," Tate said.

Krystal appeared at Laura's elbow.

"I could make you a cup of coffee," she offered, apparently forgetting that Laura would have to climb over or under the line of protestors chained in front of the door.

Near the end of the line, Maggie was swaying. Her eyes were closed. Tate imagined she was reliving her glory days as an activist in San Francisco. Perhaps she was getting doused by imaginary crowd-control hoses because she went down, pulling several protestors with her.

"It's so hot," she said, looking up at Tate from her newfound seat on the concrete. Her face went pale. "I can't feel my hands."

The handcuffs fit tightly, and her hands looked more swollen than usual. Tate was worried that Maggie had hurt herself. Old women fell, broke their hips, and went into nursing homes. She could not imagine Maggie stuck in some facility with "green" and "vale" in the name, far away in Gresham or Oregon City, without her friends and her causes.

"Are you okay?" Tate rushed to her side.

"No," Maggie said as though it was obvious.

"What's wrong?" Tate asked.

Maggie stared at her. "This isn't how it's supposed to happen. We're supposed to win." The man next to her tried to fan her, but one of his wrists was cuffed to Maggie and the other to another protestor.

"My dad could get out of these," Krystal said. "He knows how to open a pair of handcuffs like nothing."

Tate glanced down the block. A two-toned sedan was moving in their direction, slowing down, pulling to a stop on the opposite side of the street. It was not quite a police car, more like a prop from a 1980s B movie. The black portion of the car was covered with a matte paint that screamed *I did this in my garage and inhaled the fumes.* There was a white stripe painted up the front of the hood. There was also a logo on the door, something between the Marine Corp's globe and eagle and a barber pole. And there, in the front seat, filling the whole front window with her greasy pompadour, was Duke Bryce.

"Oh!" Abigail exclaimed.

"Laura, I think you'd better go," Tate said.

"I thought you did this all the time," Laura said with a slight smirk.

"Yeah…no."

Duke opened the car door and stepped out, one hand balled in a fist and a menacing look in her eyes.

Abigail yelled, "It's not what you think, Duke."

"You don't want to be a part of this," Tate said. "I'm sorry. You are a senator's daughter. I know these people look like they stepped out of the 1970s." She gestured to the line of protestors. "But every one of them has an iPhone and is waiting to right the world's wrongs on YouTube."

Laura glanced between Duke and Tate.

"I know her," Tate said. "She's my ex's current. This is all a mistake, just please go."

Laura looked behind her. On the other side of the street, the Oregon Adult Theater advertised its latest promotion on a bright yellow letter board: FEATURE-LENGTH FILMS! LIVE STRIPPERS! THE AMAZING CANDY COCKLES EVERY SATURDAY! Laura was clearly doing a little bit of cinematography in her head. She was standing in front of a pornographic the-ater, surrounded by hippies in handcuffs and lesbians shout-ing, "We're here! We're queer! We're drinking coffee!" There was no way for it to look like a photo op with the voters.

In the distance, Tate heard real police sirens.

"I think I'd better," Laura said.

She surveyed the crowd one more time, shook her head, and turned on her sharp, gold-tipped heels. Just like that. Tate wished Laura had hesitated for just a moment, at least idled in her car, but the Sebring pulled away, and Laura did not look back.

"I've had about enough of you," Duke bellowed.

Tate turned, looking helplessly at Duke and then Abigail.

"What are you talking about?"

"I see how she looks at you!" Duke added.

From the line of protesters, Abigail mounted her own protest.

"I don't. I never loved Tate."

"Down with the corporate overlords!" one of the men yelled.

"She dumped me for an oboist," Tate said. "Or hasn't she told you how she cheated on me and told me it was my fault because I didn't like Vivaldi?"

"Oh, I know about the oboist." Duke managed to make *oboist* sound like a racial slur. "I'll deal with her later."

So Abigail was up to her old games, Tate thought.

"But right now, I'm dealing with you," Duke said. "You ready to settle this?"

Tate threw up her hands.

"There's nothing to settle. I don't even know why you're here…why I'm here…why any of these people are here." She pointed at Maggie. "I'm just trying to get her out of those handcuffs before she passes out."

Maggie's narrow frame almost disappeared between the protestors. She was sitting on the ground, leaning against the wall of Out Coffee, but Tate had the impression it was the woman in the Clinton/Gore T-shirt and the man with the beads who held her upright. Her breath came in gasps.

"Yeah? Is that all?" Duke asked. "You really expect me to believe that? You think I don't know what you're doing to her?"

"No. Yes. I'm not doing any…"

Tate did not see the blow coming. One minute she was standing in front of Duke wondering how it was possible that, after ruining her life once, Abigail could actually come back and do it again. Then the next minute, she felt a force like a small quarterback hit her side and suddenly her face was pressed against the hood of Duke's car.

"She's not going to save you this time," Duke said into her ear.

Duke's shoulder pressed into her back. All Tate could see was the seam where the black and white paint met. She thought she remembered Pawel saying he used to hypnotize chickens by laying them on a line painted on the ground. Back in Hungary. Right before he chopped off their heads with a hatchet.

"Let go of me," Tate cried.

"Not until you leave Abigail alone."

"I don't even like her."

"I don't believe you."

Duke had her pinned to the car, but she could still move her legs. She took the opportunity to plant her boot just above Duke's knee.

"Get off me."

She pushed her foot hard into the soft muscle above Duke's knee. She had not almost-graduated with a BA in physics for nothing. Torque was on her side. Duke stumbled backward, releasing her hold on Tate's shoulder.

Tate straightened.

"What the fuck?" Tate brushed the dust off her cheek.

"You scared?" Duke thumped her fist against her own chest. "You gonna fight me? You gonna fight like a girl? You gonna pull my hair?"

"I can't believe you *actually* beat your chest at me," Tate said.

It was all so absurd. Suddenly Tate had had enough. Enough of Duke. Enough of Abigail. Enough of Maggie making all the wrong choices for the right reasons. Enough of Laura always walking away.

Tate had played rugby for a few seasons and now, like riding a bicycle, it all came back. She lunged at Duke, crossing the space between them in a single stride. Just as she reached Duke she dropped her shoulder and performed a nonregulation, below-the-belt tackle. Duke went sprawling with Tate on top of her.

Krystal cheered.

Maggie revived long enough to cry, "We're feminists. Solidarity. Fight the patriarchy, not each other."

And just about then Tate realized that, while rugby may have come back to her, she had not been in a fight since she was nineteen, and that had won her a black eye and a lump on her jaw that lasted for a month. She had a good three inches on Duke, but Duke had a hundred pounds on her. In seconds, Duke had flipped Tate onto her back and planted a knee in her chest. She felt her breath escape like the air in a punctured balloon.

Tate was waiting for Duke's fist to connect with some part of her face that she would rather use for other purposes—an archetypal nose was not improved by being smashed into the frontal lobe—when she heard the police sirens turn down their street.

"They're coming for you." She choked out the words.

Duke looked around.

"They *will* arrest you," Tate gasped. "They won't even know you're a woman. They'll think some big fucking Elvis impersonator is trying to beat the shit out of a girl."

"You're a dyke, and everyone knows it," Duke said.

"I will play the helpless girl." Tate coughed. "I swear to God, I'll be Scarlett fucking O'Hara when those cops show up."

Duke dropped the fist she had raised over Tate's head and stood up, giving Tate's boot a last kick for good measure.

"Fuck you!" she said.

A moment later, a police cruiser pulled up and two young men stepped out, hands hovering over their guns.

"What's going on here?" one of them asked.

The other officer knelt beside Tate.

"Are you all right?"

Tate touched the back of her head where Duke had slammed her against the pavement.

"I think so."

The officer looked from Tate to Duke to the protest.

"What happened?" he asked.

"It's a long story," Tate said.

"She started it," Duke grumbled, but she had seen the wisdom in Tate's threat and headed for her car. The other police officer stopped her and spoke to her in low tones that Tate could not hear.

"Can you get them apart?" Tate asked the man who knelt by her side. "Maggie over there, she's not doing so well."

An hour later, the protestors were separated with the help of a fire truck and a pair of bolt cutters. The police officers had taken a statement. Duke had driven away. Krystal, Maggie, and several of Maggie's friends were installed in the front window of Out Coffee, retelling the events with increasing bravado. And Tate was back at the front counter, tending to a long line of customers and fielding calls from their supplier, who had sent the morning's delivery with a new driver who was now hopelessly lost on the other side of the river.

She sighed as she hung up the phone and began frothing milk for yet another cappuccino. How many had she made in her life? A thousand? Ten thousand? A small part of her wished Duke had beaten her to a pulp or at least clocked her once. Maybe then things would have changed. The police would have taken her to the hospital. Maggie would have apologized for calling Abigail. Abigail would finally have seen that

Duke was a mistake. Maybe Krystal would have seen violence for the useless waste that it was and pushed her father out of her heart. Maybe Laura would have found out where she was and rushed to her side, crying, *I should never have left you.*

As it was, Tate was back at the counter, and Laura was probably in her hotel room making plans for her next corporate merger. Tate considered calling her, to tell her that everything had worked out, but the shop was busy. Maggie and Krystal were both useless. And Laura did not care.

# Chapter 13

With the morning suddenly free, Laura headed downtown to the shopping district she and Tate had skirted on their tour of Portland's stranger art galleries. She did not find any of her favorite shops—no Armani, no Burberry—but she did find a Nordstrom and a rather elegant, glass-fronted shopping mall with a J.Crew and an Ann Taylor. She was pleased to see that there were places in Portland where one could buy something other than hemp bracelets and skateboards. Some places. Not many.

However, after twenty minutes, Nordstrom had lost its usual appeal. The lights felt sharp. The constant fluttering of the staff was obsequious, not helpful. In an atrium beneath the second-floor escalators, a pianist was playing. Laura thought it was Chopin. But a moment later, she found "A Spoonful of Sugar" incessantly running through her mind, and she realized he was playing Disney tunes, arranged for piano with a kind of classical flair.

She was almost relieved when Brenda called.

"Where are you?" Brenda said. "I hear bad music."

Laura headed toward the only window on the second floor, secluded in an alcove beyond the juniors' section. The music faded.

"Escalator music," she offered by way of explanation.

Brenda did not care.

"I saw your credit card invoice," Brenda said. "You're still in Portland."

"Thank you, Sherlock Holmes."

"I thought you'd be headed down to Palm Springs by now."

In the background, Laura could hear Brenda's other phone lines ringing. She looked out the window. Below her, the city street was quiet. Even at eleven a.m., Portland was not fully awake. If New York City was the city that never slept, Portland was the city that got up late. Laura pondered this while Brenda talked, but then Brenda stopped, waiting for an answer.

"So?" Brenda asked.

There was a half second of silence on Brenda's end, and then her phone exploded again.

"What was that again? I don't get a lot of bars out here," Laura said.

"The Palm Springs project. Gregory Bonhoffer. Our biggest investor. He says his financial advisor told him to get out of real estate and out fast. Some ridiculousness about overlending and another mortgage crisis. I told him to forget the bank. If that's the issue, we'll go someplace else for the mortgage. But you have to get down there and remind him that real estate is the little black dress of investing. It never goes out of style. He only wants to hear it from you."

"I'm sure Gregory Bonhoffer wants to hear that he is buying a little black dress for $8.2 million."

"No one else can take over the Bonhoffer case," Brenda said. "He's touchy. Let Dayton and Craig take the City Ridge Commercial Plaza project. Just get down there before this explodes."

"No!" It came out too quickly.

The junior section sales clerk looked up from her register. Two teenage girls scuttled away from a nearby table where they had been sifting through tank tops.

"I'm doing some market research for the City Ridge Commercial Plaza," Laura said, trying to quash the earnestness that she heard in her own voice. That was not how she and Brenda talked. "There's a coffee shop in that building, a local tradition. That sort of thing. Close them down, and everyone hates us."

"Are they making money?"

"I haven't looked at their books yet," she lied.

"What's this place called?"

Laura hesitated.

"Out in Portland."

"How clever," Brenda said with bland irony.

"I want to know what this coffee shop needs to do to stay on their lease," Laura said. "That's all. Is it profit? Money in the bank? How can I be sure that they stay in the City Ridge Plaza and the hippies don't start calling us the Antichrist?"

"And remind me why we care?" That was a typical response

for Brenda, but then Brenda yelled to someone in her office,
"Can you turn off those goddamn phones?" And that was not
typical. Nothing delighted Brenda Phillips, and nothing ruffled her helmet of Brillo-permed hair. "Just tell me what I can
do to get you to Palm Springs," Brenda demanded.

She was angry. It occurred to Laura that she was not the
only one who had mixed feelings about her father's campaign.
Doug Vester might see the benefits of supporting Stan Enfield
by paying for his daughter's leave. But Brenda was just another
working-class girl from Charleston who had clawed her way
up the corporate ladder. Soon she would have all Laura's work
dumped on her desk and no way to complain about it because
Doug Vester, Stan Enfield, and by association Laura, were gods
in Brenda Phillips's world. Laura could almost hear Brenda remembering this, calculating, trying to figure out how hard she
could press on Laura without crossing the men who provided
her living.

"Just talk to the board, Brenda."

"About this coffee shop?"

"Yes."

There was another silence on Brenda's end.

"Out in Portland?" she asked finally.

"Yes." Laura kept her tone casual.

"If I talk to the board, will you be in Palm Springs by Wed-
nesday?"

Laura heard the frost in Brenda's voice. Laura was a problem. Her leave was a problem. Out in Portland was a problem.

"Yes," Laura said. "And thank you, Brenda."

Brenda hung up without saying "You're welcome."

* * *

Laura tried to enjoy the rest of her morning, but she couldn't. On every corner, she saw a quirky, no-name coffee shop, a dusty pharmacy, or a little deli with hand-painted signs and sausages hanging in the window. *Starbucks*, she thought as she walked. *Rite Aid. Subway. Starbucks. Subway. CVS. Starbucks.* She listed the conquerors all the way to her hotel. It would be so much cleaner, more predictable, and more efficient. One Walmart every twelve miles. One Walgreens every ten. One McDonald's every seven. And one Starbucks on every corner. Two weeks ago, she would not have minded. She liked the consistency. She *liked* Starbucks. But for once she was not thinking about investors, shares, or development opportunities.

When she got to her hotel, she cleared off the table and opened her laptop. There had to be some way to save Out Coffee. Not for profit. Not for Clark-Vester. Perhaps not even for Tate, but for herself, so that when she left she could remember Out Coffee as it had been that first night she walked in, the smell of coffee mixing with the smells of the evening street, the dim light lending the old fixtures a gentle patina. In her mind's eye, Tate would always be standing at the counter, watching the door, waiting for her.

By the time it got dark, Laura had to admit that she was not concentrating. She had five browser tabs and a dozen spreadsheets open on her laptop, and she could not remember what she was doing with a single one of them. She had heard police sirens approaching as she drove away from Out Coffee. Tate could be in jail. Tate could be locked in an undocumented cell, the victim of some deep-seated anti-protestor bias. These things happened. Most police were honorable, but that didn't mean there weren't a few homophobic assholes who would rough up a woman like Tate—or worse. And she had just left Tate in the middle of calamity, with her beloved Maggie about to pass out from heatstroke, the protestors rallying for revolution, and the police approaching.

Laura was in her car, keys in the ignition, before she'd stopped to think.

Out Coffee was nearly empty when she arrived. It was almost ten, almost closing time. She glanced through the door, hoping the reflection on the glass would hide her. Tate was nowhere in sight. She couldn't ask Maggie about Tate's whereabouts. Maggie hated her. The other woman, Lill, seemed only tangentially related to the coffee shop. She hesitated, hand on the door. It wasn't a feeling she was used to. She was used to marching in, placing the contract on the table, and walking out with exactly what she wanted. No, not what she wanted, what she asked for.

She was about to turn away when the girl with the pink hair spotted her through the glass and beckoned frantically. Slowly, Laura pushed the door open.

"Shhh," the girl said when Laura approached the counter. "Maggie is in the back. Can I get you a coffee?"

Laura shook her head. "I was just…checking on Tate."

"Tate went to do the bank drop. You have to have a coffee, and don't say decaf because that's lame."

The girl ran around the counter and grabbed Laura's hand, dragging her to a seat by the window. She must have been in her twenties, Laura guessed, but she moved like a child, unco-ordinated and guileless. It was both cute and annoying.

"Stay here!" the girl said.

A moment later, she returned with a cup.

"It's my signature drink," she explained. "It's called the Dragon-ator."

Laura took a sip. It was ferociously strong.

"I'm Krystal," the girl said, sliding into the seat across from Laura. "But I probably won't be here for much longer because my dad is getting out of prison and we're going to get a place together."

"What did your father do?" Laura asked a split second before it occurred to her that this was probably not an appropri-ate question for the girl-child in front of her.

Krystal hesitated.

"They say he killed this woman." She traced a knothole on the wooden tabletop. "She was dealing meth anyway, and she was a prostitute. Dad says they put the wrench in his truck. They didn't even do a DNA test on the blood. It could've been anyone's. I watch *CSI*. If they don't do a blood test, they don't know anything."

"I'm not sure that's true," Laura said.

"No, I saw it," Krystal said. "I saw it on TV." She glanced over Laura's shoulder and out the window. "They wouldn't put it on TV if it didn't happen...at least sometimes. He's getting out. He wants me to come live with him in The Dalles." She chipped at the table with one pink-lacquered nail.

"How long have you worked at the coffee shop?" Laura asked to change the subject.

Krystal sighed. "Since forever! Two years. Since I was eighteen."

*Two years*, Laura thought. How quickly two years disappeared. Or four. Or ten.

From the back storeroom, Maggie called out, "Everything okay up there?"

"Totally," Krystal called back. "Just waiting for Tate to come back." In a quiet voice she said, "You and Tate are totally cute."

Laura stiffened.

"I mean it's just like in the movies," Krystal added. "You can't be together, but you *have* to be together."

"There is nothing between Ms. Grafton and myself," Laura said quickly. She felt her face flush.

Krystal cocked her head.

"That's what Tate says too," Krystal said, and Laura had the uncanny sensation that Krystal was watching her face for a reaction, perhaps reading the truth.

# Chapter 14

Tate was not surprised to return to Out Coffee and find that Krystal had not locked the front door at ten on the dot. She *was* surprised to look around and find Krystal and Laura sitting together, Krystal talking quickly and Laura looking like she wanted to bolt.

"Tate?" Laura raised one hand tentatively.

Tate hurriedly wiped her hands on her jeans. She felt grimy from the day's work in the hot coffee shop. Laura looked as cool and pale as the moonlight.

"Hi." Tate stopped, wiped her hands again, ran a hand across her hair.

Laura stood up. "I'm sorry," she said. "Are you all right?"

"You didn't hear," Krystal said. "After you left, Tate got in a fight."

"Oh!" Laura's concern seemed genuine. For a second, Tate

thought she was going to reach out and touch her, but then Laura clasped her hands in front of her.

"You should have seen her," Krystal said. "Tate was awesome. Duke came after her and threw her on the car. Then Tate was, like, POW!" Krystal kicked her foot out. "Duke went flying, and then Tate went after her like a quarterback or a linebacker or whatever. She slammed into Duke." Krystal bumped Tate with her shoulder to illustrate. "Tate was, like, 'I'm gonna kill you, you motherfucker.' Duke was crying and begging her to get off. Then the police rolled up with their guns and everything."

"Oh, no," Laura said. "Did you get in trouble?"

Krystal snorted. "The police weren't gonna mess with Tate. No way!"

Tate put an arm around Krystal's shoulders.

"Krystal makes me look good." She squeezed Krystal and ruffled her pink hair. "The police saved my ass. I was about to get the shit beat out of me when the cops showed up."

"Are you okay?" Laura pressed. "I…I'm sorry I left."

Laura *had* left; Tate reminded herself. She had told Laura to go, but Laura *could* have stayed. She had practically run back to her Sebring. And yet, there was something in the way Laura stood now, tentatively leaning forward, while clasping her hands in front of her, staring at Tate intently. If it was not love in her eyes, at least it was awe.

"Are you sure you're okay?" Laura asked again.

Tate felt Laura's eyes slide down her neck, down the labrys tattoo, and lower.

"Of course she's okay," Krystal interjected. "She's probably gonna go find Duke tonight and fuck her up. I mean, people don't mess with Tate and get away with it."

"No!" Laura reached out. This time she touched Tate's hand.

Tate was about to say, *Good God, no! She'd kill me.* Then she reconsidered.

"Oh, I don't know. Maybe I'll go find her."

She gave a casual shrug that she hoped said, *I beat up 250-pound drag kings every day. It's just no big deal for a tough woman like me.*

"Please," Laura said, still touching her hand. "Don't."

Tate turned Laura's hand over and stroked the center of her palm.

"I have to go help Maggie with the inventory," Krystal said, as if on cue.

"I guess I could let Duke go if something else came up," Tate said when Krystal was gone. "What are you doing tonight?"

Laura drew in a sharp breath.

"Nothing."

# Chapter 15

Back at her hotel, Laura pulled on her body shaper, then jeans, a low-cut blouse, and a dark blazer. She turned in front of the bathroom mirror. The jacket was a perfect fit and the Spanx corset squeezed her curves into a more perfect version of themselves. But that was a problem. What about the awkward moment when Tate released the buttons of Laura's jeans only to find her body encased in an armature of spandex? It would take a good three minutes to wriggle out of the body shaper, and that was not an image one wanted to share with a new lover. It was like being swallowed by a python, only in reverse.

Laura stopped. Tate would not be unbuttoning anything. She had promised herself. She could not do that. Not to herself. Not to Tate. This late-night rendezvous was not a business meeting, but it was not a date either. It was…She paused as she searched for the right words…It was a chance to say good-bye and maybe spend a little bit of time together before the end. *Now*, she thought. That was all she could ask for. She glanced at her watch: eleven thirty. Tate would be there in a few minutes.

She slid a credit card into the pocket of her jeans and headed for the elevator. When she arrived in the lobby, she was so busy looking for Tate, she did not immediately hear the familiar voice call out to her.

"Hey boss, over here. Over here!"

It was Craig.

*Shit*, she swore under her breath.

Craig and Dayton had taken their usual place at the bar. By the empty beers in front of them, she guessed they had been there for a while.

"Come join us!" Craig said.

Laura glanced around. There was no way to pretend she had not heard him. Reluctantly, she walked over.

"A beer for our boss. No, make that a whiskey," Craig called to the bartender.

"Where are you off to?" Craig asked. "You look good." He was drunk.

She felt his eyes slide down her neck. She pulled her blazer tighter around her.

"I'm just going out for a walk."

"Lookin' like that. Dang!" Dayton said, although Laura was pretty sure he didn't mean it.

Craig chuckled as though Dayton's insubordination was a clever joke only he got.

The whiskey arrived.

"It's almost midnight," Craig said, pushing it toward her. "Lighten up."

Laura glanced around. Tate was not in the bar. She was not in the foyer either. Laura prayed she was late, that she had forgotten, that she had been hung up at work. She patted her pocket, looking for her cell phone, but she had left it in the room. She had wanted to be unburdened. Free. Now she saw the lobby doors swing open. She closed her eyes. *Please, no*, she thought. And Tate stepped into the lobby in full leather chaps, leather jacket, her black motorcycle helmet under one arm. She could not have looked gayer if she had worn a flak jacket with DYKE emblazoned across the front like part of a lesbian SWAT team.

"You meeting someone?" Craig pressed.

"No one," Laura said. "I'm just walking."

From where she stood in the lounge she could see Tate clearly, but she guessed Tate could not spot her through the maze of booths, mirrored columns, and keno machines in the bar.

"You okay?" Craig asked, his concern still tinged with lechery. He might as well have tacked on *hot little lady* to everything he said.

Laura glared at him. "Of course."

She took a sip of the whiskey. Thirty yards away, Tate leaned against the wall, watching the elevator. Five minutes passed and then ten. Craig and Dayton had turned their attention to a boxing match on the TV. *Just go*, Laura thought, her heart squeezing into a fist inside her chest. She had been wrong to visit Out Coffee that evening, wrong to accept Tate's invitation. It was too late, too intimate. And Craig and Dayton were right there, despising her, looking for any reason to discredit her with their superiors at Clark-Vester.

"What are you looking at?" Craig asked.

"Hey, isn't that that dyke from the City Ridge Commercial Plaza?" Dayton added.

Blessedly, Tate turned away from them at exactly that moment. Laura watched her back as she walked over to the front desk. Behind the counter, the pretty twentysomething who worked the swing shift beamed, tossed her blond curls from side to side, and then frowned with mock sincerity. Laura guessed that the girl was explaining the hotel privacy policy. Did Tate have a room number? No? She was very sorry. She could not give out room numbers.

Laura saw Tate glance up at the ceiling as if taking a guess at which of the three hundred rooms Laura occupied. Then she stepped away from the counter with an apologetic shake of her head. She was not the type to badger the hotel staff or push the issue after the clerk had said no.

*Good-bye, Tate*, Laura thought.

Then, as she watched, the girl called after Tate and Tate turned back around. The girl slid a piece of paper across the counter. Tate held up her hand in protest, but the girl cocked her head and said something else. Tate nodded, smiled, took the paper, and headed for the door. And Laura wondered why the girl had broken the hotel policy for her. Did she know? Could she feel Laura's longing from across the room? Was it just an intuition? A sign? An angel?

Laura took a sip of whiskey. Then her thoughts stopped

short. She knew that coquettish turn of the head. She recognized Tate's flattered refusal and then her polite acceptance. She saw Tate slide the paper into an inner pocket of her leather jacket. The acrid whiskey hit the back of her windpipe and she choked, waving away Craig's "Easy now, boss."

Back home in Alabama, a woman like Tate would have been unfathomably plain. In her full leather gear, with her head shaved, and her brow furrowed, she looked like a heroine from a sci-fi movie, some kind of post-apocalyptic ninja. Without thinking it all the way through, Laura had assumed that Tate's beauty was a secret only she knew. But suddenly it was clear. In this topsy-turvy city where people grew lawns on their roofs and vegetables in their lawns, Tate Grafton was gorgeous.

That girl—that insipid twenty-year-old—had not given her Laura's room number, she had given Tate her own number. And Tate had said no, but she had pocketed the number. And why not? That girl had not called her across town only to stand her up. That girl had not made love to her and then fled. That girl was not trying to buy the coffee shop where she made her living.

The jealousy that washed over Laura felt like a physical illness, as though her body temperature had risen and her blood pressure had dropped. She felt her cheeks flush and her mouth go dry.

"I've got to go." She pushed the whiskey away.

Tate was almost a block away when Laura emerged from the hotel.

"Tate," she called out.

Tate turned.

She ran toward Tate, coming up short a few inches away from her. Breathless. Too close.

"I'm sorry. I got hung up with work," she lied. "I got away as fast as I could." She reached out and touched the heavy leather of Tate's jacket, her fingertips over Tate's heart. "Am I too late?"

# Chapter 16

At Vita's urging, Tate had put on her chaps and her leather jacket. On the ride across town, Tate had wondered why she had taken fashion advice from a woman who wore only animal print. Still the outfit seemed to have the right effect on Laura, who hurried to greet her and then stood so close Tate could smell her citrus-blossom perfume.

Laura raised her eyes and met Tate's. She held a suit jacket draped over one arm, and she wore the kind of garment Vita had names for—bustier, camisole, slip—but which were as mysterious to Tate as the women who wore them. It revealed Laura's arms, her long neck, the swell of her breasts as she breathed. It showcased the sharp, nervous flutter of her pulse in her long neck. And then Tate realized she had looked for too long. Laura had asked her a question, and she had almost forgotten to answer.

"Where are we going?" Laura asked again.

"You almost missed it," Tate said, touching Laura's elbow and guiding her toward the crosswalk. "Down the block. There is something I want to show you."

This had also been Vita's idea, which made Tate nervous. Taking dating advice from Vita was like taking it from a spider that ate their lover post-coitus. But it was too late to change her mind. Now she could only hope.

"Just around the corner," she said.

Tate led Laura down Naito Parkway. To their right, Waterfront Park was dark. Beyond that, the river reflected Portland's skyline and the Hawthorne Bridge to the north, the Marquam Bridge to the south. A few homeless men stirred in the depths of the park, their cigarette tips glowing. Tate felt Laura edge closer to her.

A few blocks down, Tate had scoped out a park bench on the sidewalk.

"Let's sit here."

Across the street two police officers passed a cup of coffee back and forth. There was no traffic on the road.

Tate put her hand on Laura's knee and was surprised when Laura did not flinch.

"Listen," Tate said.

The night was warm and still and the sounds of the city carried. A truck beeped as it backed up. A door rattled. A dog barked. Someone yelled, "Hold that door." Then they heard a distant cheer, a kind of traveling hoot, a great collective cry of glee as though a hundred people had all opened their mailboxes simultaneously to find that they had won the sweepstakes.

Laura squinted down the wide road.

"Is it a parade?" she asked.

"Kind of."

"A road race?"

"A bike race."

"At midnight?"

"It's always at midnight."

"Why would you have a bike race at midnight?"

The hooting grew louder. Now they could hear the whoops of the bikers along with the cheers of passersby. The bikers drew closer, their feet whirling together, their backs arched.

"They're naked!" Laura covered her mouth.

The bikers had reached them now. The first was a gray-haired man so lean every striation of muscle showed on his legs. Then there were two young men in neon-green sneakers and glowing green bracelets and nothing else. Then it was all bodies: fat, round bodies and skinny bicycler bodies. Men with their parts flapping over their seats. Women with flowers in their loose hair and big pendulous breasts. Old, gray bodies. Lithe, young bodies. One man with cerebral palsy on a motor-assisted bike. There was even a man on a skateboard being pulled by a black Lab. And everyone was cheering and waving.

Laura's eyes were wide above the hand that she had clamped to her mouth. Then she dropped her hand and added her cheer to the rest, and Tate added hers. And as the race passed, and all they saw were a myriad of pale Oregonian rumps in the moonlight, they sat back and laughed.

"The cops are just standing there," Laura said when she caught her breath. "Aren't they going to arrest them?"

"No. It's Portland."

After the race, they sat for a while, talking easily. Tate filled Laura in on the drama at Out Coffee. Laura described an officious boss who kept track of her every move by credit card receipt. Finally, Laura said, "I suppose I should get back."

They stood and strolled toward the hotel. It seemed to Tate that Laura took a very long time walking the few blocks back. Still, the moment of parting was drawing near. Her bike was parked across from the hotel, and there was no reason to follow Laura across the street without an invitation.

"You know…" Tate paused in front of her Harley.

Laura stopped too.

"You really haven't seen Portland until you've been over the bridges on a bike."

"I've never been on a motorcycle."

"I have an extra helmet."

Laura hesitated. "I wouldn't know what I was doing."

"I've been riding these roads since I was eighteen. All you have to do is hold on."

Laura glanced in the direction of the bicycles as though summoning up some vicarious courage.

*Say yes*, Tate thought.

"Okay," Laura said.

Tate's heart soared.

She slipped her leather jacket on Laura's shoulders and a helmet over her head, stroking her hair into place between

Laura's face and the thick foam cushioning of the helmet. They were so close.

"It's this easy," Tate said. "All you have to do is climb on behind me. Put your feet here."

It was awkward riding the first blocks with Laura. She teetered on the back of the seat and held Tate's waist the way she would shake a stranger's hand. But every time Tate accelerated she clutched the hem of Tate's T-shirt. Every time they turned, Laura would lean away from the turn. Finally, Tate pulled over.

For a second, Laura thought Tate was going to ask her to get off.

"It's not working, is it?" she asked. "I know. I told you, I've never done this before."

Tate flipped up her visor and looked over her shoulder.

"Just relax."

Tate reached behind her and touched Laura's leg.

"Slide forward," she said. "You have to touch me. Put your arms here." She drew Laura's arms around her waist. "Can you feel my body?"

Laura nodded. She could feel Tate's back against her chest, Tate's hard, flat stomach beneath her hands.

"Now when I move, you move with me," Tate said. "Can you feel it?" Tate said so softly Laura was not sure she had heard.

All she knew was a second later, Tate squeezed some lever and the motorcycle roared to life. She could feel its vibrations through her whole body, and she became exquisitely aware of the spread of her legs, of Tate's ass between her thighs, of the slope of the seat drawing their bodies together. But as they set off over the Broadway Bridge, she forgot even that longing. She felt only the speed, the rush of lights, the roar of the engine, and the height of the bridges—each one higher than the next until the city sat so far below them, she felt like they were about to lift off into the sky.

# Chapter 17

When they reached the hotel again, Tate parked in the empty valet dock. There were staff inside the hotel, but the street was empty. Laura returned the leather jacket and pulled off the helmet. With her hair disheveled and mascara smudged by the wind or tears, she looked more beautiful than ever. Tate had to imagine Laura-the-politician's-daughter and transpose that woman's face over the one that looked up at her to remind herself how close she was to heartbreak.

"Tell me something," Tate said. She still felt the glow of Laura's embrace. Her lungs were still filled with the cool air that drifted down the forested hillside of Saint Johns.

"What would you do if I kissed you?"

Laura looked at her with more tender longing than Tate had ever seen before in any woman's eyes.

"I'd run," Laura said.

Tate bowed her head to hide her hurt.

Then Laura's hands were in her hair, Laura's tongue on hers. The kiss was so hard and sudden Tate stumbled back.

Then it was over and Laura was inside the lobby, stepping into an elevator, disappearing.

Instead of going up to her apartment, Tate sat in the vacant lot behind her house, listening to the distant freeway and the crickets. Even Pawel and Rose had turned off their late-night shows and gone to bed. It was the witching hour between late night and early morning, the loneliest hour. *Every time*, she thought.

She had been sitting for at least an hour when she was aware of a car pulling up in front of her apartment. For a moment, she wondered if it was Vita, borrowing Cairo's Jeep. But it wasn't a Jeep. It was the long, low curve of a cream-colored Sebring.

Tate watched as Laura got out of her car. She knew she was invisible where she sat on the rickety picnic bench in the overgrown lot. *Don't move*, Tate told herself. She thought of all the other girls she had known. Abigail with her cello. The physics professor she had loved so dearly, who would never return her love. The out-of-work accountant who stole the title to her truck. The tattoo artist who had dumped her when she refused to sit for a full back tattoo of a mermaid. And way back in high school, there was the brief affair with Vita, who made a great friend but a terrible girlfriend, even by terrible-high-school-girlfriend standards.

"Tate?" Laura called softly, looking up at the windows of the house, trying to judge which door to knock on.

Tate was no good with women. She always picked the wrong girl, and she always suffered for it. She knew that, and she knew that, and she knew that, and she called back, "Laura. I'm here."

Laura's kiss was as fierce and urgent as it had been outside the hotel, but this time it lasted. She pushed Tate back against the rough side of the house and leaned her whole body against Tate, her leg between Tate's thighs, her soft breasts pressed against Tate's chest, her hands in Tate's cropped hair, and her tongue in Tate's mouth. When Laura finally pulled back it was to whisper.

"Take me upstairs."

Tate felt weak. She knew she had only a minute before she lost all good sense.

"I want you," she said, surprised at how raw her own voice sounded. "But I want to know that you will be here tomorrow. Because if you're going to leave before I wake up, the answer is no."

"I'm supposed to be in Palm Springs," Laura said. "I'm from Alabama."

"You can't just disappear."

"I can't promise that I'll move to Portland, that I'll stay here forever. I have a whole life outside this city."

"I'm not asking for forever," Tate said, "just for tomorrow."

Laura's yes was a sigh.

Once in the apartment, Laura pulled Tate to her and kissed her hard on the lips, holding the back of Tate's head and drawing her into the kiss.

"I want you," she whispered.

She slipped her hands under Tate's shirt and pulled it over her head. Then she pulled off Tate's sports bra, scratching Tate's back in her haste and kissing Tate's naked shoulders once she had thrown the garment to the floor.

"God, you're beautiful," she said, in between kisses.

Her movements were frantic, as though she could not decide whether to kiss Tate or bite her or rub against her. Quickly, almost angrily, she discarded her own shirt and bra, as though their presence hurt her.

She was gorgeous in the moonlight that filtered through the window. Her breasts were larger than Tate's, heavier, and more feminine. Her nipples jutted out from small areola. Her belly was soft and marked by the slight indentation of her abs beneath a silky layer of skin the color of cream.

Tate cupped her breast and thumbed her nipple.

"Harder," Laura whispered.

Tate pinched her gently.

"Harder."

This time Tate pinched hard. A pink flush marked Laura's chest. Laura's nipples hardened. She closed her eyes and leaned her head back, drawing Tate's other hand to her other breast. Tate squeezed both her nipples, harder than she thought right, but Laura nodded. A shiver, like a bolt of electricity, seemed to go through her body, and she clutched Tate's hips to hers.

"In my hotel." Laura unbuckled Tate's belt and ran her hand inside Tate's jeans. "I masturbated. I wanted you. I touched myself, like you did. But I needed you. I need you." She kissed Tate, and then stepped back, shedding her skirt, her underwear, and her nylons in one swift movement. Her nylons ripped in her haste. When she was completely naked she lay down on the bed, reaching one hand up to Tate. "Come here. Lay on top of me. Fuck me."

Tate dropped her jeans and lay beside her, leaning over her, supporting her weight on one elbow.

"No," Laura said. "Hold me down." She clutched Tate to her.

Tate let her full weight settle on Laura's body. Laura wound her legs around Tate's, as though trying to touch as much of her skin as possible. Tate had never felt so utterly wanted in her whole life.

"You're so strong," Laura whispered.

Tate felt Laura's thigh press against her sex and she moaned.

"Yes," Laura echoed.

Tate thrust her hips against Laura as urgently as her body demanded, thinking about nothing but chasing the pleasure that raced through her clit. And even as she forgot herself in the pleasure of Laura's body, and even as Laura gripped her with a fierceness that had lost all manners, it felt like a wonderful collaboration, fun and raw and exciting. Her breath and Laura's breath, racing together. Her pulse beating against Laura's skin. Their bodies understood each other. Their blood spoke the same language.

Then Laura shifted beneath her, just a little bit, a slight angle of her hips upward. Tate felt a deeper heat as Laura's open labia touched hers. Tate's whole body flooded with desire, the pleasure of a second before multiplied by the tiny shift. The sensation was electric. Laura grabbed Tate's hips and held them and leaned up to meet Tate's kiss. All the while Tate felt Laura's desire like a tightly coiled spring. Every movement was full of its energy.

"I'm so close," Laura gasped. "It's so good."

Tate thrust against her, relieved by the pressure and tortured by it. Then some mixture of heat and motion, pleasure and anticipation, released Tate from her bondage and she came helplessly, panting as she felt her weight sink into Laura's body.

"I'm sorry," Tate gasped.

But Laura clearly did not hear her, for her head was thrown back and her mouth open in a silent cry. When the orgasm released her, she pressed her face into Tate's shoulder. Tate thought she heard Laura whisper, "I can't do this," but Laura's words were already stumbling into sleep. Her breath slowed. Her head fell back on the pillow. Gently, Tate rolled off Laura and nestled her in the covers. She wrapped an arm around Laura's waist and drew her close.

"Don't go," Tate whispered before she too drifted to sleep. "Just don't go."

# Chapter 18

In her dream, Laura was at a cotillion dance, a relic of her childhood transported into adult life. The dancers swung past her in a blur, both familiar and unfamiliar at the same time. Brenda was there, seeming to wear her mother's face, and, in the dream, Craig was her ex-husband. On one wall of the dance hall, a banner read ENFIELD FOR SENATE, but it was Laura running for senate, not her father. The partners changed, and the room faded into another scene, a bar perhaps, or a dance hall. Laura looked around but suddenly everything was strange and shadowy, and she didn't recognize anyone.

"Sweetheart," someone whispered. "Laura."

Laura woke to Tate leaning over her.

"Don't wake up," Tate said. "I have to go to work, just for an hour, to get things ready. Don't worry. I'll be back."

Laura's eye flew open.

"You're beautiful," Tate said, cupping Laura's face in one hand. "Go back to sleep." Just as Tate was closing the apartment door, she added, "Please stay."

Or Laura *thought* she heard "Please stay." Tate had spoken so softly her words got lost in the scrape of the door across the floor.

Laura waited until she heard the motorcycle roar away before she sat up. The apartment could not have been more than seven hundred square feet. The bed took up most of the floor space. There was also a table, two chairs, a stove with two burners, and a tiny refrigerator. Just enough for one person to survive. Minimally.

"Who lives like this?"

She did not answer aloud, although the answer came quickly: *Me.*

She rose, shielding her nakedness with a sheet. The window was screened with only a filmy blue curtain, like a scrim of sky.

Tate had left a vintage silk robe on a chair. Laura picked it up and pressed it to her face without thinking. It smelled of Tate's cologne, a mix of cedar and tea rose. She breathed deeply.

A note on the chair read: *Dear Laura, I had to go to work for an hour, but I took the rest of the day off. There is coffee in the pot, just turn it on. The password to my laptop is javadyke1976 if you need to do some work.*

Laura opened the laptop out of habit, certain there was something she should be doing but uncertain what it was.

*Leave Portland*, she told herself. *Never look back.* That's what she was supposed to do. Instead she sat at the small kitchen table and looked around.

On second glance, there was nothing of her spare hotel room in Tate's studio apartment. Only the square footage was the same. Every surface in the apartment bore a trace of Tate's life, from the hand-painted floor mat in the kitchen to the tray of seedlings on the windowsill. Shelves of books lined the walls, bearing authors Laura had been assigned in college but had skipped in favor of business texts: Melville, Hugo, Wolfe, Dickens. On the wall above the kitchen sink, a framed collage of photographs showed Tate and two friends clutching Frisbees in their teeth, Tate and Maggie accepting a plaque at a banquet, Tate and another woman grinning on a windy beach.

It occurred to Laura she did not have one friend she could call to ask the question she so desperately needed answered: Should she flee or should she do what her body told her and pull off the robe and lie naked in the sunlight waiting for Tate's return?

"I have to go," she said out loud. "Get dressed and go."

She stood, searching the floor for her bra, her slacks. Tears clouded her eyes but she blinked them back.

"Go."

She froze, her blouse in hand. She had always treated sex with her husband like business, something to be dispatched of quickly, with minimal contact with the adversary. She did not like him probing her with his fingers. Nor did she like manipulating him with hers. And when he lay on top of her, she felt pressed and breathless.

When Tate had lain on top of her it wasn't enough, and she had pulled Tate closer, clawing her back, biting her, trying to touch as much of her body as she could. She had been clumsy in the attempt. She had been awkward and rough. And she had cried things she could never imagine saying. The Hungarian couple downstairs had probably heard. They had probably turned on Lawrence Welk. It was all mortifying. And still she remembered how Tate's back had arched and her angular face had softened with a look of relief as though she had waited her whole life for Laura's embrace. And Laura knew she had waited her whole life for that look.

She sank down on the bed. No. It wasn't even a bed. It was a futon.

"No one sleeps on a futon," she said and put her head in her hands.

With her husband, and the two brief, awkward lovers she had had before him, there had always come a moment of clarity when, in the middle of their lovemaking, she thought, *Why is his tongue in my mouth?* Now, at thirty-seven, she finally realized what all the fuss was about. She finally realized what she should have learned in the back of some girl's pickup truck at age seventeen. And she began to cry.

She had cried unreservedly for about five minutes—long enough to ruin her face but not long enough to dispel the feeling that her life was over—when she heard a key turn in the door. *I can't do this*, she thought. The daylight made it all so real, like a spotlight highlighting the difference between this life and her life. She leapt to her feet, grabbing her suit jacket as though Ann Taylor could change everything. At the same time, she caught her face in the mirror—blotchy, red, and utterly pathetic—and thought, *She can't see me like this.*

She wiped at her eyes, doing nothing to fix the issue. Then the door opened, and suddenly she had real problems, because the woman who walked in, dropping her enormous purse on the floor, was not Tate Grafton. The woman looked like an '80s rock star, complete with leopard print bodysuit, red leather jacket, and hair teased to a height that could broadcast cell phone signals. The woman wore enough bracelets to kill a man. One swipe from her wrist and even the strong would fall.

*Tate's girlfriend.* It was the only thing Laura could think. She had been so wrapped up in her own story, it had never even occurred to her that sweet, earnest Tate might have secrets of her own. Perhaps she too was torn between the life she had and a life she could barely allow herself to want. Now the girlfriend had come home, from whatever hard-rock adventure she had been on, to find proof of her lover's infidelity, nearly but not entirely dressed. Ann Taylor could do nothing for her now.

*She's going to kill me.* The thought flashed across her mind like a snapshot from the ten o'clock news. They were called "crimes of passion," Laura knew. People who committed them got off.

"I'm sorry. I won't come back," Laura said.

She grabbed her shoes off the floor and made a run for it. She thought she could rush past the newcomer, but an arm blocked her path.

"I swear. It was a mistake. You'll never see me again."

Then another arm clamped around her shoulders, and she was engulfed. The woman squeezed her tightly. Laura sobbed in surprise.

* * *

"Hey there," the rock star said, pulling Laura even tighter. "You okay?" There was no venom in her voice. "I didn't scare you, did I?"

Laura stopped crying long enough to notice that the hold was more a hug than a death grip. She pulled back and looked at the woman again. She recognized her.

"You're Tate's friend," she said. "From the bar."

"Vita," the woman said, wrestling Laura back into a half-hug. "Tate is going to kill me when she finds out I walked in on you." Vita finally released her. "I just came by to get some CDs. I'm having a party tonight, and we're going old-school. I wanted vinyl, but no one's got anything good on vinyl anymore. You're Laura, right? Are you okay?"

"I'm fine," Laura whispered. "I should go."

"Tate must have really screwed up if you're crying already." Vita shook her head. "I'm sure, whatever she did, she didn't mean it. She is a total idiot with women, but she's got a good heart. We've been friends for years." Vita pointed to a picture of two little girls of about eight. "That's me on the left."

"She mentioned you," Laura said.

"Oh, did she? I'm flattered." Vita put her hand on Laura's shoulder and guided her toward the kitchen table. "Stay. Just for a minute. I have to meet Tate's mystery woman." She sniffed the air. "Coffee. I think I will." She turned on the percolator and sat down across from Laura. "Why so sad?"

Laura sat because she felt her eyes welling up again, and she knew that speaking would bring on the deluge, and because she did not know what else to do.

"Tate's hot isn't she?" Vita said enthusiastically.

*I can't have this conversation*, Laura thought. But apparently she didn't have to because the rock star was having both sides of it for her.

"She *is* hot. If she wasn't my best friend…damn! Those cheekbones. And you spent the night with her, I see." Vita noticed the note on the table and read it. "And you're not crying because she left you, because she is coming back in an hour…to kill me when she finds me here. Tate says I 'meddle.' I don't meddle. I just want what's best for her. And she's got good stuff that she doesn't mind me borrowing…as long as she doesn't notice it's gone."

The coffee pot hissed. Vita stood and brought two cups to the table.

"Cream? Sugar? Is Tate your first girl?"

"Splenda," Laura whispered.

"That stuff gives you cancer. You'd better just have sugar. Better be fat than have cancer, right?"

Vita put a mason jar of cream and a bowl of brown lumps in front of Laura.

"It's better. It's raw," Vita said, gesturing to the sugar bowl.

Laura took a sip of her black coffee and scalded her tongue.

"So?" Vita prodded. "Tate's your first girl, isn't she?"

"It's none of your business." Laura clutched her blazer to her chest.

"She was! It's like you were deflowered, and I am here to witness it. And you're so *old*."

"Excuse me?" The rudeness shook Laura out of shock. "I don't know you. I am not talking to you about this. I have to go."

"No. No. No. Stay. I didn't mean it like that. It's awesome. Everyone's coming out at sixteen now. My friend's daughter is five, and she's already told her mom she wants to be a lesbian when she grows up. No. It's wonderful that you're what...? Thirty?"

Laura softened a little bit at this underestimate.

"This is an important moment in your life, and you're old enough to appreciate it. It's good that you're this old."

Laura felt Vita's gaze travel up and down her body and wished, desperately, that she was more thoroughly dressed.

"And you're sure this is your first?" Vita asked, gulping her hot coffee as though it were water. "You didn't go to prom with a gay boy and then go make out with your girlfriend while he made out with his boyfriend in the back of, say, a 1984 Chevy Cavalier station wagon?"

"No!"

"You didn't kiss on girls at prep school? Didn't get on the four-year plan at college?"

"I don't even know what that is."

"You know...you hook up with your freshman-year roommate and have a couple girlfriends in college. Then you graduate and marry an aspiring politician from Yale."

Laura dumped cream and a few brown lumps in her coffee and stirred vigorously. She sipped her coffee. It was surprisingly good.

"Come on," Vita said. "Tate has been talking about you nonstop, and she's never going to introduce us. She's afraid I'll embarrass her."

That was easy to imagine.

"This might be the only chance I get to talk to you...for months if Tate has it her way."

*Months*, Laura thought. There would be no months. The thought made her sad.

"I skipped right to the politician," she said.

"So you're a late bloomer." Vita shrugged. "That's cool. You don't have to cry about that. I wish I could go back and relive my first. Did you know you can reduce your chances of getting cervical cancer by almost 100 percent if you sleep exclusively with women? Did you know that? You only have to get Pap smears every three years."

Laura did not know that, and she pressed her fingertips to her forehead trying to understand how her life had gotten to this point and how it had gotten there so *quickly*. First there was no Splenda; then she was getting a lecture on how many Pap smears she would need if she became a lesbian.

"I'm supposed to be in Palm Springs," she said.

"There are a lot of gays there too. And did you know you're less likely to get murdered by your spouse? Which means you probably won't get murdered at all," Vita went on, clearly undeterred by the existential crisis taking place on the opposite side of the kitchen table. "Women always get murdered by their husbands. Everyone knows that."

"Why are you telling me this?" Laura asked.

"I'm trying to make you feel better."

Despite everything, Laura felt a smile pull at her cheeks.

"This is supposed to make me feel better?"

"That is why you're crying, right? Because you're gay, and this is new. I'm just telling you some of the unsung advantages." Vita counted on her bejeweled fingers. "No cervical cancer. Not getting murdered. Not getting pregnant. But if you want kids—not my thing, personally—but if you like the sticky little buggers you know there are almost zero reported incidents of childhood sexual abuse in lesbian households. *And* you always have someone to give you a tampon if you run out. But you know what the best part is?"

Laura opened her mouth, closed it, and shook her head.

"The best part is that you picked Tate. Or she picked you. If we hadn't already tried it in high school and realized we were completely incompatible, I would fight you for her to the death!"

"What about not getting murdered?"

Vita laughed a big, hyena laugh.

"I like you. Don't worry. Tate is my best friend, nothing else. And she's a good person. She's solid. What you see is what you get, and you can depend on her. Plus she's got that jaw line. What I would do for that bone structure!" She paused, suddenly serious. "So why are you running off?"

"I have to leave Portland tomorrow. For good. Forever."

"So? That's tomorrow."

Laura glanced out of the window at the vacant lot below, with its overturned shopping cart, its broken-down picnic bench, and the snowfall of cottonwood tufts drifting in the sunlight. It seemed like the whole city sang that song. From the hookah smokers to the lazy traffic jams in which no one honked, it seemed like the whole city shrugged and said, *So? That's tomorrow.*

# Chapter 19

Tate had braced herself for the possibility that Laura would not be in the apartment when she got back. She was ready for disappointment. She was ready for the sudden amplification of sound—a lawnmower, an engine revving—that filled a room once a lover had left. She was not ready for the sight of Laura, wearing half a business suit, sitting across from Vita, in some fantastic morning-after outfit that seemed to include a hairpiece made out of a dead Afghan hound.

"You're talking about Enron," Vita was saying, waving a bejeweled hand in the air. "You are talking beast of the apocalypse, resident evil."

"I'm talking about business," Laura replied with equal vigor. "This is the language of American business, and if you don't speak it, you can't compete." She popped a raw sugar cube in her mouth.

"So if everyone jumps off a cliff with Satan, we should too?"

"Well...yes!"

They were so engrossed in their talk they did not notice Tate's arrival for a good ten seconds, which was still not enough time for Tate to process the sight.

"Vita!" she said when she found her voice.

They both looked up.

"I came to borrow some CDs," Vita said, "and I met Laura."

"I see that."

Tate was going to say something practical about keys and privacy and boundaries. But Vita and Laura looked so oddly happy together, the sunlight streaming through the window, their coffee steaming, and neither of them wearing enough clothes to be seen in public. They looked...like friends.

"I see you found the coffee," Tate mumbled.

"There's more in the pot." Vita nodded briskly, as though Tate had just arrived late to a scheduled meeting. "Laura has been outlining her plan to sell your soul to the devil, and while I don't generally approve, I think she may be right. This is your only option."

"What?"

Tate was trying not to stare at Laura's breasts as they swelled beneath the filmy camisole.

"Your plan?" Tate pulled up a chair.

"To save Out Coffee," Vita added.

"I thought we were a lost cause."

"It's going to be a tough sell," Laura began. "The board is all about the bottom line, and we don't have a lot of time to get that up."

The explanation that followed reminded Tate of an economics class she had dozed through in college. Apparently Vita and Laura had already been over the lesson during the two hours Tate was at Out Coffee. Vita had not dozed off. She kept clarifying, but the clarifications only distracted Tate from the difficult task of appearing deeply interested while not actually looking at Laura. She couldn't look because Laura was so beautiful in her camisole, with her disheveled hair, so sexy with her talk about "corporate underpinnings" and "fiduciary duties."

Tate tried to listen. She gathered, at least, that Laura's plan was a blend of fund-raising and accounting fraud. Out Coffee would report its projected earnings as real earnings. They would base the projected earnings not on past history, but on a supreme optimist's version of what a coffee shop *might* make in Portland if God loved them more than He loved Jesus and starving children. Then they would raise prices, switch to nonorganic, non–fair trade products, and buy from a corporate wholesaler. This would ensure the shop looked profitable to Laura's business partners. At the same time, they would raise the four months' rent required to continue their lease, provided it was approved by some group of tycoons Laura referred to only as "the board."

"That's $8,000," Tate said, when Laura finished. "Maggie can't raise that kind of money."

"It's sixteen, actually. The Clark-Vester Group will double the rent."

"We don't have $16,000."

"You've got two kidneys," Vita said helpfully.

"Maggie's already mortgaged her whole life."

"It's not that much money." Laura reached out as though she was going to touch Tate's hand, then glanced at Vita and withdrew. "I know it sounds like a lot, but it's not really. You'll find a way. There is a window open. I got the board to reconsider your eviction, but you have to revise your books, and you have to have the cash in hand."

Tate's mind was still reeling as she sat down at the table in the back room at Out Coffee. Laura sat beside her. Maggie and Lill sat on the other side. And Krystal, who was supposed to be working the counter, leaned in the doorway. Tate wished she was still in bed with Laura. Barring that, she wished she had an hour in her garden to think about everything that had happened in the last few days—from Laura's arrival at her house the night before, to Laura's insistence that they had only a week to secure Out Coffee's future, and that they had to talk about it immediately because Laura was leaving Portland the next day.

As it was, Tate found herself saying, "You remember Laura Enfield," as if everyone's attention was not fixed on Laura.

"Of course I do," Maggie said.

She looked angry, her mouth set in a down-turned fissure. The words KEEP YOUR LAWS OFF MY BODY draped across her T-shirt.

"Laura has a plan that could get us a lease in the new building," Tate said.

"It's not a new building," Maggie grumbled. "It's the same building. We're just getting kicked out."

"The Clark-Vester Group plans to do extensive remodeling.

It's going to be a beautiful space," Laura said. "State-of-the-art, LEED certified. I'd like to see you in that building."

"Will you be doing gray-water reclamation from the roof?" Lill asked, stirring a piece of lemongrass in her green tea.

"Laura wants to help us," Tate said. "She thinks we can stay, but it's going to take a lot of work."

"Why?" Maggie asked. "Why help us? A week ago you wanted to close us down."

Tate offered a vague explanation about Clark-Vester supporting emerging businesses; she had no idea if it was true. Lill said Maggie had to be open to the "possibilities of the universe." Laura said that small-business leases could offer Clark-Vester a significant tax break, especially given Portland's small-business incentive packages. Maggie crossed her arms and replied with a stubborn string of "but whys." The conversation circled around and around like the fan above their heads.

Finally, Krystal sighed from her post in the doorway.

"Duh!" she said.

Tate shot her a look.

Krystal bugged her eyes out at Tate.

"I'm sorry," she said. "You guys are so dense. She has a crush on Tate."

"Krystal!" Tate hissed.

"I doubt that very much," Maggie said.

"Sexuality can be very fluid," Lill said, tasting her lemongrass.

"You guys are so out of it." Krystal leaned her head against the doorframe. A customer rang the bell at the front counter, and she sighed again. "I don't get why it's such a big deal. I'll just go make more coffee while you sit around and talk about everything except the stuff that matters."

"Tate and Ms. Enfield have nothing in common," Maggie said to Krystal's retreating back. "That is a ridiculous fantasy."

Tate opened her mouth to protest—although what exactly she planned on saying she did not know. Then she glanced at Laura, whose posture had gone even more upright than usual. Her face was pale, her hands tightly laced together. *She's scared,* Tate thought.

"Just listen," Tate said.

Laura outlined her plan: the creative bookkeeping, the cheap supplies, the $16,000.

"It all sounds like a bunch of lies to me," Maggie said, when Laura finished. "We lie to ourselves. We lie to our customers. We lie to the bookkeeper."

"No, technically, your bookkeeper lies for you," Laura said.

Maggie snorted. "We lie, and we lie, and we lie. Then we buy cheap junk from Walmart, and we lie to the customers who trust us and what we stand for. And who's to say you don't come around a month later and tell the IRS to check our books? Wouldn't that be convenient? You get your $16,000 and then, oops, we're all in jail for tax fraud."

"This has nothing to do with taxes. You'll report earnings and expenditures to the IRS just like you always do. This is just a different way of interpreting the numbers you share with the board."

Exasperation entered Laura's voice, concealed behind the smooth flow of words, and Tate glimpsed the woman Laura was in the rest of her life. Formidable. Unyielding. It made her gentleness, her fear, more poignant. Tate felt her breath go shallow and her heart sink in her chest. Laura was leaving tomorrow.

"If we need to lie to corporate America to keep Out Coffee open, why not?" Tate said.

"You're not doing anything illegal," Laura added.

Lill placed her palms together as if in prayer. She took a deep breath.

"I feel…at peace with this."

"Good?" Laura looked at Tate.

"I mean, I know an accountant who can rework our books," Lill added. "I did Reiki on her."

Laura shrugged. "Get me her number, and we'll talk about what you need to do. Two years' worth of records should be enough. This isn't a big line item for the board."

Maggie slapped both hands on the table. "We're not doing this. I don't trust her. If we're going to save Out Coffee, we're going to do it the right way. We'll have a rally. We'll do a zine. We'll get people involved. This is *their* coffee shop, *their* community, *our* community. We'll sign a petition. I don't think Clark-Vester is going to look at two thousand signatures and tell us we're not viable."

"You're not being practical," Lill said.

"If you think you can run this shop, then come back and run it," Maggie said.

"As I recall, I'm the only one who ever did run it," Lill snapped back. "At least until you indentured Tatum."

"Then why did you leave?" Maggie demanded.

"Because you closed me out."

"Because you left me!" Maggie folded her arms more tightly across her chest.

"I embraced my heterosexuality," Lill said. "You, of all people, should understand that. I was given a gift of insight into my sexual orientation. I was a kid when we got together. I didn't know. I thought I was a woman-oriented woman, and I am, spiritually, but not physically. And now you're supposed to be my best friend, and you still hate me because I'm straight."

"You left me when I needed you. That has nothing to do with sexual orientation. And you." She pointed at Laura. "You need to think about the women who worked and sacrificed to break the glass ceiling and get you where you are today." Maggie glanced back and forth between them as though they were two sides of the same unfortunate coin.

Laura said nothing.

Lill pleaded, "I didn't leave you because I didn't love you. I left because it's not who I am. It's not *you*, it's *me*. It's my life. That's what you always taught me. It's my body, and it's my life."

Maggie slumped in her chair and rested her chin in her rugged hands.

"I lost you, Lill, and now I'm losing Out in Portland," she said.

Laura turned to Tate. "I should go."

"No," Tate said quietly. To Lill and Maggie, she added, "Please stop. Please listen."

They both looked up.

"I trust Laura. Now, trust me. We can save Out Coffee. Laura's not asking us to break any laws, just to bend them a little. You chained yourself to the building. You know: We can't start a revolution if we follow all the fine print. Think about Stonewall. What if those drag queens had said, 'No, we're going to play by the rules'?"

"We're not revolting," Maggie said sorrowfully. "We're just trying to run a coffee shop."

"Out Coffee is more than a coffee shop, and you know it." Tate leaned forward. "This is our revolution. It's an economic revolution. It's not about race or gender or orientation. It's about money—who has it and how they keep it and what that does to the people who can't get into the system. Big business closes doors for people. They say what we can buy, when we can opt out, who gets health insurance, what chemicals go in our food. They tell us what we have to say to every customer who walks in the door and how many seconds we have to say it. We have to create an alternative."

Tate glanced at Laura expecting to see her rolling her eyes or at least wearing the strained expression of someone who was trying not to roll her eyes. But her face was solemn.

"I live my whole life in a hotel," Laura said. "And every room, in every city, is exactly the same. Out Coffee is different. Those hotel rooms aren't ever home. But there is a little bit of home here. For everyone."

Tate held her breath, waiting for Laura to continue, but she said nothing more. Her words hung in the air, and everyone looked at Maggie.

Finally Maggie sighed. "Go back to your hotel," she said quietly. "You can't be part of them and help us. You can't live in a hotel and build a community."

"But…" Laura said.

"Just go." The anger had drained out of Maggie's voice. "You won't ever understand."


Tate walked Laura out. On the sidewalk outside Out Coffee, they stood awkwardly like teenagers after a first kiss.

"I'm sorry," Laura said.

"It's her decision. You tried."

"What are you going to do now?"

Tate stared down the street to the distant point where the Portland skyline appeared between buildings. She didn't know.

"Maybe go down to the port and load trucks. The long-shoremen are striking. I could probably pick up a couple weeks as a scab. I hate it, but the strike is over some territory squabble between the longshoremen and the electricians' union. It's not a real labor issue. Then…" She stuck her hands in her pockets and exhaled into the clear, blue sky. "Who knows? I've been at Out Coffee my whole life."

"Oh, Tate."

"I'm sorry about what Krystal said," Tate said quickly, because something in Laura's "Oh, Tate" made her want to cry. "She's twenty, but I swear, sometimes, she acts like she's ten. She doesn't have a filter."

"Whatever she thinks is true," Laura said.

When Tate turned back to Laura, Laura wore a sad, thoughtful smile.

"Are you really leaving tomorrow?" Tate asked.

"Yes," Laura said. "Of course."

It was so unfair, Tate thought, to meet Laura in such a strange, magical way and then to lose her so quickly.

"I'll miss you," Laura added quietly. "I'll miss all of this. But I have to be in Palm Springs tomorrow."

Tate looked away and pulled a flower off the honeysuckle that curled up the power pole outside Out Coffee and crushed it between her fingers, releasing the sweet scent.

"Tomorrow," Tate repeated.

It was still summer. The nights were getting shorter, but they were still suffused with the same watery-blue brightness that had lured Tate from reason the night Laura had first walked into Out Coffee. In that light, a woman newly and foolishly in love could still shave a few minutes off eternity. That was the beauty of a Portland summer. You lived longer on those blue days when the sun lit the sky until ten at night, and the ground never lost its warmth.

"Vita is having a party tonight. You haven't really seen Portland until you've been to one of Vita's parties," Tate said.

"I don't know." Laura turned to go. "I've got a lot to do." But then, in a gesture so fleeting it barely existed, she brushed a soft kiss across Tate's lips. "What time?"

# Chapter 20

Back at the Marriott, Laura plugged in her cell, which had been lying dead at the bottom of her purse. It buzzed immediately, announcing a message. Four messages, actually. All of them from Brenda.

"Craig said he saw you leaving the hotel with one of the women from the City Ridge Commercial Plaza project. Laura, what's going on? You're supposed to be in Palm Springs. Craig and Dayton can handle everything in Portland. We don't need you there."

The remaining voice mails carried the same message but in curter tones. Laura felt her heart race. *He saw you leaving the hotel with one of the women from the City Ridge Commercial Plaza project.* She wondered if Craig had guessed the truth. Had he intimated that there was more going on than just business? She had met Tate around midnight. She was dressed up.

They had stayed out late. What part of that suggested a real estate transaction?

She called the front desk.

"I'd like to change the credit card on my reservation. Yes, I'd like to put the room on my personal card."

She would have to send Craig and Dayton to Seattle—anywhere but here, and that was the nearest project. They weren't needed there, but they weren't needed in Portland either. Although she could arguably use them in Palm Springs, the project was definitely something she could handle alone.

Once she hung up with the front desk, she called Craig to tell him the plan.

"Thank God," he said. "Finally. And where are you off to?"

"Palm Springs."

"Ah. The little black dress of investing."

"Exactly."

*That was easy*, Laura thought. But nothing was easy—not Portland, not Tate, not Brenda, not the work she had to do for her father. She sat in front of her open laptop for several minutes before she placed the last call.

"Fidel's Pizza, Palm Springs. Pickup or delivery?" the voice on the other end asked.

She almost hung up.

"Pickup," she said finally.

She used her Clark-Vester credit card.

*There you go, Brenda*, she thought bitterly. *I'm in Palm Springs.*

# Chapter 21

A little before ten that evening, Laura appeared in Tate's doorway, in a sky-blue dress, her hair loose around her shoulders, and a great confetti of peony blooms in her arms. Together they strolled through the quiet streets to Vita's apartment, known by locals as the Church, since it was, in fact, the sanctuary, Sunday school rooms, and pastoral office of a converted Methodist church. It was also, despite an ever-changing cast of tenants, the best party spot in Portland. Vita and her roommates—a dancer from the Portland ballet and an acupuncture student—preferred theme parties. That night's theme was Gold Lamé Yacht. In honor of the Gold Lamé Yacht, Vita's roommates had spray-painted dozens of toy ships gold. These hung from the rafters of the sanctuary from invisible fishing line. The Beach Boys played softly on a stereo. A buffet table was laden with wine and slabs of blue cheese.

Tate could see Laura's eyes widen as they stepped into the

Alice in Wonderland splendor of the church sanctuary converted into a living room converted into the deck of a golden sailboat. Tate considered a quip about Laura's anchor-patterned ascot, but resisted, feeling Laura's hand clasp hers.

Vita greeted Tate and Laura with a hug each.

"Come in. Join the usual suspects," she sang out, then slipped back into the mix of people.

In the center of the room, Cairo was dancing languidly, scarves whirling around her like a kaleidoscope. Tate recognized several regulars from Out Coffee and many more from the Mirage, including Abigail, whom Tate made a special point to ignore. Even Krystal had been invited. She sat at the kitchen table looking awkward but pleased to be part of the grown-ups' party. Tate did not even stop to worry what Krystal would tell Maggie about her and Laura, their arms around each other, Laura's cheek on her shoulder. There was only tonight.

The music turned up. The guests kept arriving. Tate installed herself deep in a papasan chair. Laura sat down beside her, the slope of the papasan sliding their bodies together. They watched as the room filled. Vita's roommate, the acupuncturist, pulled out a set of stilts and tiptoed around the sanctuary. Someone brought in an enormous pumpkin filled with soup. A man in a gold tutu tried to show two women how to tango.

"He's a real dancer," Krystal said, plopping down on the floor by Tate's feet. "He's in the ballet."

"I know," Tate said. "You're not drinking, right?"

"My dad would get me a drink."

*With a roofie and a shot of bad heroin*, Tate thought. But she just ruffled Krystal's hair with one hand and said, "Think of me as your evil stepmom."

"You're more like my big sister," Krystal said, pensively. "Because we're so alike."

Tate shot Laura a look, rolling her eyes.

Krystal swiveled her head around so she could see Laura.

"And I read Tate's horoscope," Krystal added. "It said, 'This month a fit of emotional eating will send you crawling back to the stale candy hearts you have left over from last Valentine's Day. Pay attention. They will spell out a different message this time.'"

Laura raised her head from Tate's shoulder.

"That was in the horoscope?"

"In *Willamette Week*. Yes. Probably," Tate said.

"It means you and Tate would be perfect for each other," Krystal said, staring across the dance floor at the darkened stained glass window on the other side of the room. "I knew the minute you walked into the coffee shop."

Tate leaned over Krystal's shoulder.

"Don't talk to Maggie about it, okay?"

"Naw," Krystal said. "I got your back. *Mom* won't find out."

Tate blushed, but it was only happiness making its way from her heart to her cheeks.

Then the man in the gold tutu called for a new dance partner, and Krystal stood up, saying, "Me. Me."

"She is precocious," Laura said once Krystal was clomping across the floor, her face set in an expression that was probably meant to be a seductive frown but looked something like a blowfish. "Is she really just like you?"

"She's smarter than I was, but she's more troubled," Tate said.

"I like her," Laura said, smiling her wry smile. "She's got that stupid kind of hope that gets people killed."

"Great," Tate said.

Laura's smile faded. "I never had that kind of hope."

Tate leaned her cheek on the top of Laura's head, trying to make sense of a world in which Frank Jackson could kill a girl with a wrench and his daughter could dance the tango in a room that looked like the inside of a golden candy wrapper. A world in which Laura could lean against her, stroking her ribs, her fingers just grazing the side of her breast. And a world in which Laura could leave. The next day. Forever.

Two more couples had joined Krystal and the man in the tutu, and they glided, stomped, and slid back and forth across the sanctuary, each pair making a dramatic turn a second before they crashed into the wall. Vita made a theatrical bow and asked Cairo to dance, and then there were eight bodies parting the crowd of guests.

"Vita is a character," Laura said.

"She has a new girlfriend every week," Tate said. "Every week it's 'the one.'"

"That's the one for tonight?" Laura nodded toward Cairo.

"Yeah, although she's been the one for a month. Maybe we can all change."

"And what about the woman over there? What's her story?" Laura pointed to a tiny woman with a puff of dark, gray hair.

"Barb. She shows dogs. She has a dozen Irish setters at home."

"And over there…the man in the green dress?"

"Mica. He and his partner got together when they tied for the queen of the Rose Court. That's the drag queen beauty pageant."

Tate pointed out a few more local characters. Laura snuggled closer to her.

"And what do they say about you?" Laura asked, gesturing toward the crowd.

"Besides the fact that I grow the best heirloom tomatoes in east Portland?" Tate asked.

Laura laughed. "Besides that."

"They probably say I've spent way too long working at Maggie's coffee shop."

"I didn't mean what I said the other night," Laura said.

Tate pulled her closer.

"They say I always fall hard for the wrong woman." She pressed her lips to Laura's temple to soften her words. Then, speaking into the sweet, citrus-blossom scent of Laura's hair, she added, "They say, 'This time she is much prettier.' They say, 'This time, she's leaving even faster than the rest.' They say, 'Some people just have that kind of luck.'"

Tate closed her eyes. Laura said nothing. Tate heard the sound of music and boots clomping across the floor and girls laughing.

"Now turn," the diva in the gold tutu called out.

"I'm going to get a drink," Laura said.

Tate opened her eyes.

"I'm sorry," Tate said.

Laura smiled. "And then we're going to learn to tango."

* * *

More guests arrived and eventually the room got too crowded for dancing. Laura went in search of another drink, and Tate reclaimed her seat in the papasan chair. She was watching Laura from across the room when Abigail sidled up behind her chair and popped around its circumference like an orange sprite.

"Tate," she said as though she had not expected to find Tate there.

Tate looked at her.

"Is she your girlfriend?" Abigail asked.

"That's Laura."

"I heard she was from Kentucky."

"Alabama."

On the other side of the room, Laura poured herself a sip of red wine in the bottom of a large wineglass. A moment later, Vita threw her arm around Laura.

"You call that a drink?" Vita grabbed a bottle of wine off the counter and dumped half the bottle into Laura's glass. "Now, that's a drink."

Laura laughed, and the two of them toasted with overfull glasses. Tate thought how much fun it would be to have both of them in her life: her best friend and this strange, beautiful woman who was like a Pegasus that had alighted in Tate's earthbound existence.

Abigail was still talking. Clearly it was important, at least to her, because she kept stepping in front of Tate and blocking her view. Finally, Tate had to tune in.

"You know they all said I was the backbone of the string

section," Abigail was saying. "It's not so much about tone. It's about strength of tonal unity. That's what they missed, and I miss it too, but not in the same way."

"What?"

"I quit the orchestra."

"You got tired of Vivaldi?"

"I let it come between *us*. I can see that now. That's why I broke up with Duke."

"Duke." Tate tried to piece together what Abigail had just said. She did not want to admit she had not been listening and risk the possibility of Abigail delivering the whole speech again. "Shouldn't you have broken up with Duke because she's crazy and she beats people up?"

"It doesn't matter." Abigail knelt down. "What matters is that I'm here for you, if you want me."

"I'm with someone."

"She won't stay." Abigail put a hand on Tate's knee. "I'm not saying that to be mean. It's just a fact. But I'm here."

Across the room, Laura tossed her head and laughed. Her hair swam around her face like a golden storm. Behind her, someone opened a back door. Her dress rippled in the breeze. The breeze carried in the smell of charcoal fire, honeysuckle, a whiff of cigarette, and behind that the distant smell of the river. Tate thought, *She'll never stay.* Then Laura was standing in front of her. Tate rose. She took the drink out of Laura's hand and set it on a table. Then she cupped Laura's slender neck in her hand and kissed her, because tomorrow's sadness belonged to a woman who had not yet been born.

\* \* \*

After the party, they returned to Tate's apartment. Since she met Laura, Tate had spent many hours lying awake, imagining how skillfully she would make love to Laura, how she would wait—practically a stone butch—tending to Laura's every need before her own. But it was Laura who took the lead, pushing Tate down on the futon and straddling her. Then slowly she worked her way down Tate's body, kissing and licking and massaging Tate's shoulders, her breasts, her nipples. When Tate tried to reciprocate, Laura chided her gently.

"I want to do this for you. I've been waiting too long already."

"I know," Tate said, thinking about the long, dry months at the end of her relationship with Abigail and afterward.

"No." Laura's kiss came to rest on Tate's stomach, just below her belly button. "You don't know," she whispered. "When was the last time you had sex with a woman?" Laura asked. "Besides me."

"Nine months. Maybe a year. The last time I had good sex, besides you, was a lot longer than that."

"You know you're the only woman I've been with," Laura said, laying her cheek on Tate's belly and looking up at her.

"You said you came out in your twenties," Tate said gently.

"I guessed when I was in my teens. I knew for sure I was gay by the time I was twenty, after I met my husband but before we got married." Laura stroked one finger through Tate's pubic hair, sending a shiver of pleasure down Tate's legs and up her spine.

"And you married him anyway?" Tate tried to follow the conversation as Laura continued stroking her.

SomEthing True 203

"I didn't think he would cure me or anything," Laura said. "I didn't even think it was bad being gay, but it was my father's first run at senate. The media was obsessed with my marriage. It was in the news more than his campaign. 'A modern fairy tale,' they called it. 'The new Kennedys.'"

"And your father won."

"Yes."

"And you got divorced."

"Yes. But it was my ex who asked for the divorce. I thought he was just in it for the press, like me, but he actually wanted a life together. He loved me." Laura paused. "I didn't understand that."

"But you didn't meet a girl you liked after that?"

"Not until now." Laura slid her hand between Tate's legs. Tate drew a quick breath. "Honestly, at first I didn't care. I was busy. I had a career, and I was so good at it."

Laura moved her finger in and out of Tate's sex, gently, absentmindedly, as though she had forgotten what she was doing. Although Tate had not.

"I thought I could just turn off my sexuality. Priests do. Nuns do. That's what I told myself. But the more I tried, the more I thought about sex. I wanted it. I thought about it all the time."

Laura circled Tate's clit with a slick finger.

"I don't think that's very strange." Tate's voice strained.

"Before I left my last project in Chicago, I decided I'd have a one-night stand in a city I knew I'd never come back to. I'd never had a one-night stand before in my life. I didn't know how. But my boss called and said I was going to Portland. We don't do business in Portland. Portland's barely on the map. I thought, *This is my chance.*"

Tate rested her hand on Laura's to stop the delicious circling of her fingers at least long enough for Tate to concentrate on Laura's confession.

"I thought if I could do that once—if I could do *this* once, maybe twice a year—it would be enough. And I knew it was a mistake to pick you of all the women in Portland, but that ex of yours is so awful and you're so beautiful." Laura sighed. "And I didn't expect you would come to the meeting. I thought if I could just…"

"Just…"

"I thought after I slept with you, I wouldn't want it anymore."

Tate relaxed back on her pillow and released the gentle hold she had on Laura's hand.

"I don't think that it works that way."

"I know," Laura said. "When I left that morning, I wanted you so much. I want to make you feel as good as you make me feel." Her lips rested in the soft hair above Tate's sex. "May I?"

Some vague inhibition in the back of Tate's mind told her she should say no. She wanted it too much. Her body was too eager. She was supposed to be in control. But any rules or inhibitions she could remember slipped away as Laura kissed the inside of her thigh.

"Here," Laura said. She kissed closer to Tate's sex. "Or here?"

"Yes," Tate breathed.

Laura's first kiss was so light Tate could barely feel it, but it was at exactly the right spot, directly on her clit.

"Is that right?" Laura asked.

Tate's hips rose to meet Laura's lips.

"Or like this?"

Laura flicked the opening of Tate's sex with the tip of her tongue.

"Or this?"

Tate felt Laura's tongue moving around her clit in a slow, hot circle.

At that moment, there was nothing Laura could have done that would not have turned Tate on, but the blend of Laura's ardor with her shy questioning—"Is this all right?" "Is that too hard?"—was excruciating. Tate had never been a vocal lover, but finally she begged Laura, "Right there," she gasped. "Harder."

Laura kissed her again, then plunged her tongue inside Tate's body and then up along the side of her clit and over and around it. It was better than any sex Tate had ever had before, as though her body had suddenly opened itself to pleasure. She wanted to tell Laura how good it felt. Every muscle in her body was singing. And even as her hips lifted and her whole body strained against Laura's kiss, she was not thinking about orgasm. She was just feeling the wild, incredible pleasure and, even better than Laura's lips sucking her clit, pulling her toward orgasm, even better than that, she felt loved. When she did come the orgasm shook her whole body.

Laura cupped Tate's sex with one hand, pressed her hand there as Tate rode out the last tremors of the orgasm. Then she held Tate.

"Are you okay?" Laura asked.

Since Tate could not put into words how she felt, she showed Laura with her lips and her tongue, and when Laura came Tate thought she heard in Laura's cry the same pleasure she had felt. Then they slept through the night and late into the morning, deep in the sunshine of each other's arms.

Tate woke to the realization that Laura was leaving Portland and the further realization that, if she were a truly good person, she would wake Laura. Laura seemed like the type to take early-morning flights, and it was already ten a.m. As it was, Tate lay motionless, barely breathing. Perhaps Laura would sleep through her flight. Perhaps there would not be another flight that day. Perhaps the next day, aliens would arrive on earth and destroy all flying vessels. Maybe Laura would be grounded forever, and they would grow their own food in the community garden, and weave baskets, and knit sweaters, and live in harmony with nature. *And then die of strep throat*, Tate thought. No. There was no fantasy world in which Laura stayed happily in Portland.

Tate glanced over at her sleeping lover. Laura looked like an angel, her hair fanned out across the pillow in a golden halo.

*Don't go*, Tate thought helplessly, even as Laura's cell phone chimed from the bedside table. Laura opened her eyes and consulted her phone, apparently able to go from dead sleep to smartphone calendar in one ring of her alarm.

"My flight is in two hours and twenty minutes."

She stood in a quick, fluid motion, the sheets spilling off her. Tate admired the curve of her waist, the dimples above her tailbone. She was heavier than her tailored suits belied, plump even. Tate liked what she saw even more than she had admired the slim line of Laura's clothes. But there was no way to tell her that. Not now. And if not now, not ever.

Laura dressed like someone in a locker room, turning away from Tate and curving in on herself as she donned her bra, her dress, and some contraption that looked like underwear but squeezed Laura to half her real size. Tate did not even remember removing that much clothing the night before. It was like Laura had carried a secret morning-after outfit. In a moment, she was fully clothed, complete with a perfectly crisp, white blazer she produced from some mysterious recess of her purse. The businesswoman reasserted, reaffirmed, and ready to go. From the same purse, she pulled out a comb and began smoothing the tangles from her hair.

"You aren't coming back to Portland, are you?" Tate said. It wasn't really a question.

Laura paused in her brushing and looked down at Tate, who had risen on one elbow, the sheets spilling off her body.

"On the 18th, a rep from my company will come out to close the sale. It will probably be my boss, Brenda. She'll call another meeting with Out Coffee. If you have the financials and the money, you'll give it to her then. She'll probably say yes if you have cash in hand, but if she hesitates show her the books, like I said. Show her you're profitable."

Tate felt suddenly self-conscious and pulled the sheet around her shoulder.

"If she says yes," Laura continued, "you'll sign the new lease. I'd like to be there for that, but I don't know."

"I don't know if we're going to be able to raise the money. I don't know if Maggie will go along with any of it."

Laura coiled her hair into a French twist and pinned it at the back of her head.

"I hope you can," she said quietly.

*Three nights*, Tate thought. *Is that all?* There wasn't even room in their brief relationship for Tate to cry, *How could you do this to me?*

"I don't owe you anything," Laura said. Not an accusation, just a statement of fact.

*I am a fool*, Tate thought.

"I have work," Laura said.

"I know."

Tate wanted to drop down on her knees and say, *Please stay. Please stay.* But what did she have to offer? A tiny apartment and barely enough money to keep her lights on? A few friends? A good party? And in that moment, everything that she had not done came reeling back to her: the degree she never finished, the scholarship she turned down, the life she could have had. She could have been a professor or an engineer living in a Victorian in the northwest hills, with her own garden, a nice car, and a purebred dog. Maybe then, Laura would have stayed. At least then Tate could have asked.

"I don't have any other option." Laura pressed the heels of her hands to her eyes. "I have to go."

"I know."

"I'm going to be late. I don't even know where the airport is from here, and the TSA in Portland takes forever. No one reads the instructions. How hard is it to take your shoes off before you get to the scanner?"

There was nothing to do now, Tate realized. Laura was gone already.

"I can take you to the airport," she said. "It's fifteen minutes from here. You've got all the time in the world."

It was only fifteen minutes, but Tate had imagined a last ride together, Laura on the bike behind her, the wind blowing their words away. She imagined stopping at the terminal, giving Laura a kiss in front of all the travelers, then roaring off into her own grief. But, of course, Laura had the rental car, and luggage that she had packed in the trunk the night before. Tate ended up riding beside her in silence. When they got to the rent-a-car kiosk, Laura asked, "How are you going to get home?" in a way that suggested she did not understand why Tate had come with her in the first place.

Tate knew she could not kiss her. Vita's party had been a magical exception. In the world of Hertz rent-a-car agents and business travelers, Laura kept an arm's length between them.

"The TriMet stops at the airport. I'll take that back," Tate said.

"Hop in," the rental car agent said, gesturing to a large, gray van idling in the fire lane. "I'll drive you up to the terminal."

Tate sat first, and Laura sat on the opposite side of the van, staring ahead, motionless. When the van dropped them off at the terminal, Tate followed Laura as far as she could and still, ostensibly, be walking toward the train.

"What airline are you taking?" she asked.

"United."

They were almost there. The line was short. Tate knew she

had about forty seconds in which to preserve her dignity. Hug Laura, or at least touch her arm. Say, *Thank you.* Say, *Call me if you're going to be in town again.* Then stride off. Vita would have a plan, something about leaving them wanting more. Something about getting the last word in. But Tate's window of cool detachment closed with her on the wrong side. At Laura's side. Tagging along like a spaniel.

At the front of the United line, Laura punched her flight number into the computer kiosk, then moved to the next open attendant without looking at Tate.

"Palm Springs. One way," the man behind the counter confirmed. "One bag."

He asked the usual questions about strangers with packages, flammable liquids, hazardous weapons.

"Who says yes?" Laura asked, curtly. "Who says, 'Yes, I picked up a bomb from this guy in the parking garage'?"

"Ma'am, you're not supposed to joke about it," the clerk said. "Has your luggage been in your full control since you left home? Yes or no."

"Yes."

"And has anyone asked you to carry…"

"Of course not."

"Have a nice flight then."

Tate expected Laura to say something sharp, but Laura paused, then asked, "Are there still seats on that plane?"

"Two left, yes," the clerk said.

Laura turned to Tate for the first time since they had entered the terminal.

"Come with me."

# Chapter 22

Tate saw Laura's house long before they reached it. From the flats of Palm Springs, it had looked like a circular, gray pagoda perched on a cliff above town. She had noted it, half expecting Laura to look up, and say, *And there is the house of John Travolta.* Or George Bush's cousin or Martha Stewart's aunt. But Laura had said nothing, and Tate dismissed its distant wealth, until, after a steep, winding road, they pulled into a driveway, and Tate realized they were there.

The sun was even brighter on the hilltop. Tate stepped instinctively into the shadow of the house, shielding her eyes as she tried to look up at the eaves.

"This is your house?"

"It's my family's house," Laura said, pressing a sequence of numbers into a lockbox disguised behind a sconce.

"It's the one we saw from the road."

Tate had never been in a house that one could see from

a distance. Tate's dwellings were visible from across the street...if you were paying attention.

"I guess so," Laura said.

Tate paused in the doorway, awestruck. If she had tried to imagine a house so wealthy it could afford its own promontory, she would have pictured something garish or at least something bland: a faux French chateau or a ranch house on steroids. But the room Tate stepped into was as beautiful as the desert rock it rose from. Beyond the foyer spread a step-down living room four times the size of her apartment, its panoramic window revealing 180 degrees of valley glowing in the sunlight. The floor was stone tile. The furniture was upholstered in a palette of beige, and in one corner of the room rested a pile of what appeared to be boulders but were, in fact, pillows fashioned to look like giant river rocks. On one wall an enormous abstract swirled rose and gold, perfectly echoing the colors in the landscape below.

"It's beautiful," Tate said.

"Thank you." Laura smiled. "I decorated it. Take a look around."

When Tate came back from her exploration, Laura had changed into a new suit. She stood in the kitchen, a marble and brushed-steel extension of the living room, typing on her laptop with one hand and checking off items on a spreadsheet with the other. She looked up.

"Did you like it?"

"When do you have time to decorate?"

Laura held her place on the spreadsheet with a manicured finger.

"Years ago. My family used to come here for vacation." The smile she gave Tate seemed to be half pride, half embarrassment. "No one ever comes here anymore, but I'm glad you could see it."

For a moment, they stood looking at each other. Tate took in Laura's suit. The skirt was shorter, the cut more feminine. She had changed into higher heels, curled the locks of hair that framed her face, and put on an opal necklace on a heavy, gold rope. She was lovely, but as Tate regarded her, she thought, *It's drag.*

*I see you*, she thought.

Laura looked away.

"I have to go to work," she said.

That night Laura returned late, laden with bags from which she drew boxes of steaming food.

"I didn't know what you'd want, so I got something from each of my favorite restaurants." She unloaded her sacks. "I've already eaten. I had to. Our buyer owns the least interesting steak house in town."

She pulled off her heels and tossed them under the kitchen table with a disregard that Tate had not managed for anything in the house. It had taken Tate half an hour to work up the courage to sit on the sofa and another hour before she took one of the books off the shelf in the library.

"How was your day?" Laura asked.

Tate pulled her into an embrace.

"I missed you," she said, surprised by her own candor.

"I missed you too." Laura relaxed into her arms.

"And after about an hour, I worked up the courage to sit on your furniture."

Laura drew back to give her a quizzical look.

"It's not that stuffy, is it?"

"It's not stuffy at all. It's just beautiful. You own your own cliff. I've never been anywhere like this."

"I don't own it. My family owns it, or some conglomerate. Someone who needs a tax credit owns it. I don't know anymore. Someone knows," she said, leaning her head on Tate's shoulder.

"How can you not know who owns your house?"

"My family is very rich." She pronounced each word carefully, as if reciting an embarrassing truth. "When you are that rich, you have people to keep track of things like that."

"Things like mansions?"

"And endowments. Companies."

Tate closed her eyes and kissed Laura's forehead. *This will never work*, she thought.

"I don't own anything," she said. "By now Vita's probably stolen my bike. What's left after that isn't even worth a renter's insurance policy."

Laura was silent for a minute, and Tate wondered if she had broken some unspoken code of the wealthy, a promise not to admit there was anyone living beneath the mansion. But when Laura spoke, she said, "You have things that are worth more than this house." She leaned up and kissed Tate again. "After dinner, I want to show you something."

Tate was almost too happy to eat, and the few bites she placed in her mouth were so satisfying she wondered how she had ever needed more than a morsel to sustain her. When she was done, Laura led her into one of the bedrooms, where she tossed Tate a cashmere sweater from the closet, as though cashmere sweaters were something one kept in supply for guests, like Dixie cups and washcloths.

"It gets cold," she said.

Laura herself changed into a pair of jeans, a tweed blazer, and riding boots.

Then they headed out into the night.

"Where are we going?" Tate asked.

"My favorite place. You know I love this house, but I love it because it's *here*, in the desert. I want you to see the desert for yourself." Laura reached for Tate's hand and led her away from the circular driveway into the desert. Tate kept looking back. The house seemed to grow larger, not smaller, as they moved away, perhaps because it took a hundred meters before Tate could see the building in its entirety. The first story seemed to rise, organically, from the rock beneath it. Then there was a sloping roof and a smaller story with a lower ceiling, and then, on top of that, a kind of observatory that was all windows.

"That's a bedroom," Laura said. "We'll sleep there tonight. It's gorgeous in the morning." She squeezed Tate's hand. "Watch your step."

They walked for another ten minutes, Laura maneuvering easily through the rocks and sage, Tate watching the ground beneath her boots. Finally, Laura stopped.

"Here," she said.

Beneath their feet was a large, flat stone, worn clear of dirt, as though they stood on the bones of the earth.

"Sit," Laura said, lowering herself onto the rock.

Tate sat down beside her, draping her arm around Laura's shoulders.

"I used to come here with my brother. I haven't been back in almost ten years," Laura mused. She touched the rock with the flat of her hand.

Tate copied her gesture. The air was cool, but the rock held the heat of the day. Below them, Tate could see the lights of Palm Springs, casting an orange glow, but not enough to hide the stars overhead. Laura leaned against her.

"We used to have fun," Laura said, "even during the first couple of campaigns. We were still shocked that it was us. It felt like this adventure that we knew would end. I remember my brother and I used to sit here and drink my father's whiskey and talk about how crazy it was that people actually trusted *our* dad to run the country." Laura gave a sharp laugh that sounded like crystal breaking.

Even sitting on a rock in the desert, Laura's posture was upright.

"My mother was the first one to seriously think my father might be in politics for the rest of his life. She raised my little sister, Natalie, to think of us as a political family. Then one day it was the family business, and we were all politicians. The perfect Enfield family."

Tate massaged Laura's neck.

"I told my brother how I felt about girls once," Laura said. "We were drinking, but I remember. I was still in high school. He was home on a vacation from college. I felt so close to him, so I told him. He hugged me, and he told me he thought it must be hard. Then he told me to be careful. He knew what was coming. He saw it. He said, 'When you get a little older, you'll see there are some things you can't do and still win.' Now he won't even admit that we came up here to drink underage."

"How scandalous," Tate said gently.

"That's what public office does to you. It makes your whole life into one snapshot. If there is anything that doesn't fit, it has to be erased. It doesn't even matter if it happened when you were a kid or a hundred years ago or if it happened to your cousin's ex-boyfriend. Life becomes this big ledger, and everything counts against you."

Laura looked up quickly, and she didn't say it. But Tate read the words in Laura's eyes: *You count against me.*

In the distance a night bird let out a single, mournful call. Beyond that, somewhere in the canyon, a coyote warbled to its mates, and they answered in unison. Laura did not move.

"Of course, they're all *tremendously* happy, and they have nothing to hide," she said. "That's the party line. The only thing that will make them happier is having me back in Alabama so the whole family can campaign together."

"But you're not going, are you?"

"Of course I am."

"Why?"

"What political family doesn't have a skeleton in the closet?" Laura's smile was flirtatious and sad at the same time.

"That's not a reason."

"I love them," Laura said, staring into the distance as if reading a distant teleprompter. "You chose your family. You picked the people you care about. Not everyone gets to do that."

Tate wanted to say *Yes, pick me*, but she hesitated. It was true, she had picked Vita. Maggie had picked her. Lill had picked Maggie. Krystal had shown up like a baby floating down the river in a bulrush basket, but they had fished her in, tethered her to the shore, made her their own. They were all bound together by love and choice and commitments they had made both consciously and unconsciously. It was better than the family Laura described. It was certainly better than Debby-Lynn and Jared and Tommy Spaeth. Still, like so many wholesome things—vegan food, rebuilt laptops, organic lettuce—the reality paled compared to the ideal.

"What are you thinking?" Laura asked.

"I don't know what to do about Maggie." It was a relief to finally say it. "She's old. She can't work at a coffee shop forever. She doesn't have a lot of other skills. She doesn't have any savings or a partner. She has a hundred people who love her and would put her up for a month, but that's not the same thing. And I don't make enough money to support her even if I did take over the shop."

Tate lay back on the warm stone. Laura lay beside her and took her hand.

"Has it ever occurred to you that she's not your responsibility?" Laura asked.

Tate stared up at the stars.

"How can she not be?"

"Soon she'll get Social Security and Medicare, and there are rental subsidies available for elders. She could sell her house."

"It would kill her to sell, plus she wouldn't get anything. I don't even understand her mortgages. She's paid on that house for twenty years, but she says she doesn't have any equity."

"She probably got a third or fourth mortgage."

"Shit." Tate closed her eyes. There was so much she needed to do, so many things she had to figure out, and she did not want to be anywhere but there on the warm rock, beside Laura.

"I can help you," Laura said. "We could look at her paper-work together and figure out the best plan of action. It sounds like she's not always been that responsible." She spoke tenta-tively. "That's not your fault."

Tate said nothing, waiting for her thoughts to pass on to other topics, but they didn't, and finally she said, "She took me in when no one else would." Tate sat up. "And because of that her partner left her, and because of that her business went south, and because of that she probably can't raise the money to win over your board and convince them to let her stay. And all of that has something to do with the fact that I was sixteen, and no one in the world loved me—except for Vita—and Maggie didn't even know me, and she just took me in."

Tate's voice cracked, but she wasn't sure if the tears were for Maggie's generosity or for the enormity of her own debt. She wiped her eyes with the heel of her hand, hoping Laura had not noticed, but Laura had already sat up and wrapped her arms around her.

"How is it not my fault?" Tate asked, pressing her face against Laura's neck. "If I go follow some crazy dream that doesn't involve her, I'm selling out everything."

"You're not," Laura whispered.

"But she is my responsibility."

"No, Tate. She isn't. She just isn't."

When they returned, Laura led Tate up to the room on the very top of the house. Standing inside it was like standing on the top of the world. They were surrounded on all sides by windows and skylights; their privacy was the vast expanse of cliff and sky that separated them from the next living person.

Laura slipped her hands under Tate's shirt and lifted it over her head.

"I want to see you naked. I want to taste you."

The eager hush in her voice aroused Tate almost as much as her touch. She let Laura strip her of her clothing, watched as Laura cast her own clothes aside. At first Laura's movements were clumsy with haste. Her kiss was rough, her breathing labored. But after Laura had come once, riding her sex against Tate's thigh, she grew languid and her movements slowed.

Gently, she pushed Tate's legs apart, kissing her way down Tate's thigh and then nuzzling the soft, dark hair above Tate's sex. She opened Tate with her fingers and exhaled a breath against Tate's open sex. Tate shivered.

"Can you feel that?" Laura asked.

"Yes." Tate's voice was rough.

Laura directed her breath against Tate's clit.

"And that?"

Tate nodded. Her body stretched with anticipation. She had not come yet, and she was on fire with yearning, but unlike the nights she had spent with Abigail, there was no anxiety in the straining of her hips.

"Look at the stars," Laura said.

Directly above her, a skylight revealed a sweep of the Milky Way, visible above the glow of the distant city.

"You're beautiful," Laura whispered.

Then she lapped the whole surface of Tate's sex with the flat of her tongue, starting with the tip of her tongue inside, and enveloping the folds of her labia and her swollen clit.

Tate cried out at the sudden pleasure and pressed herself against Laura's tongue.

"Oh, yes! God!"

Then her words were lost in delight. She felt like every star had landed on her skin, shimmering and electric. When she came, she laughed because the happiness in her heart and the pleasure in her body had blended into one feeling, one expression, as though the whole galaxy laughed with her. Laura laughed too as she mounted Tate again and rode out another orgasm.

As Tate drifted off to sleep she could not remember if she was indoors or outside, and she dreamed that she was in the desert.

She was walking along a rocky path. In front of her, her mother and Maggie were old women trudging along with canes in their hands. But when she called to them to see if they needed help, they both laughed.

"The fair is just starting," Debby-Lynn said. In the dream, she had a long, silver braid, not the blond permanent she had worn from Tate's infancy to the last day Tate saw her through the window of Jared Spaeth's front room. "We can always be late, but why would we want to?"

The dream-Maggie pointed, and the desert bushes parted, and Tate saw an open-air market. Red and indigo scarves adorned stalls full of handmade goods. Krystal and her friends, some in colorful clothing and others naked, danced around open fires. Plates of bananas and other fruits Tate did not recognize glistened in the shadows beyond the fire. Suddenly Maggie and her mother were absorbed into the crowd.

"I can't see you," Tate called after them. "Come back."

Then, in her dreams, Laura was standing before her naked.

"See me," she said.

Sunlight filled the upstairs sunroom like liquid gold. Tate stretched. Beside her Laura stirred, then opened her eyes and smiled.

"You like the view?" Laura asked.

The room provided a view of the entire valley, but Tate was not looking at that landscape.

"Yes," she said, running her hand across Laura's belly. "Very much."

"Don't be silly," Laura said, but the warmth in her eyes said *Be silly.*

Laura rolled off the bed and stood at the window. She spread her arms open to Palm Springs, baring her naked body to the city. Tate got up and stood beside her. There was no one for miles. The city was barely more than a grid. Still it was exhilarating.

Laura turned and wrapped her arms around Tate, pressing their bodies together, and Tate thought, *Maybe, just maybe, this will all work out.* Then she felt Laura stiffen.

"What is it?" Tate asked.

"I heard something."

"What?"

"There is someone in the house."

*Of course*, Tate thought. She was happy, so now she would have to be killed, probably by an escaped convict with a history of eating his victims' ears. Everyone would say it was a freak occurrence. QUIET NEIGHBORHOOD SHOCKED BY BRUTAL KILLING, the headline would read. Back home her friends would say, *It figures. She just met a nice girl.*

"Quick." Tate tossed Laura's robe across the bed. "Put this on and your shoes too."

Tate pulled on her jeans and the sweater she had borrowed from one of the well-stocked closets. She glanced around. There was no place to hide in the rooftop sunroom and no way to lock the door since the "door" was a spiral staircase that rose from the floor below.

"The room beneath us, does the door lock?" she asked.

"I can't remember."

Tate dropped to her knees, listening at the top of the stairs. She heard it too now: voices, a door slam. But they were still far away, somewhere deep inside the house. She tiptoed down the staircase. The room below was eerily still. She checked the door. It locked, although the push button would not keep an intruder out for long. She pressed it anyway, then beckoned to Laura to come down.

Laura took her hand, and, for a second, they stood frozen, staring at the door.

"I'm calling the police," Tate said. She had left her phone somewhere in the house, but there was a landline on the table. "You sure there's no one in here, like a maid or a chef or something?"

She had the vague impression that wealthy people had staff. Perhaps there was a housekeeper, a faucet sanitizer, a painting restorer. Or perhaps one of California's many disenfranchised had come with a shotgun. She lifted the phone.

"What's the address?"

Laura said nothing. She stood transfixed, listening.

"The address?" Tate asked again.

When Laura still said nothing, Tate dialed 9…1…Even if she did not know the address, the police would be able to trace the call. For that matter, she could just say "the huge house on top of the cliff," and they would know. She was about to press the third number, when Laura leapt across the room and slammed the lever on the base of the phone.

"Stop!" Laura said.

Tate heard the dial tone.

"It's my family."

"We have to get you out of here."

Laura had dressed completely in the time it took Tate to readjust the phone in its cradle and say, "What's the big deal then?" Laura now wore a charcoal-gray dress, nautical scarf, and pantyhose. Tate did not even know how it happened.

"Where did they come from?" she asked, perplexed by the

transformation. Did Laura keep an arsenal of professional clothes in some hiding place? Did pantyhose spontaneously grow on women like Laura in emergencies?

"I don't know," Laura said. "They probably flew in from Alabama."

"What?"

Laura smoothed an invisible wrinkle out of her dress.

"My family. They probably heard that I was here and flew in from Alabama. I'm sorry. You have to go. They can't see you."

Tate was so startled it took her a moment to form the words: "Go where?"

Laura looked around the room.

"In the closet."

"No!"

"Then sneak out to the rock where we were last night. I'll get them out of here, and I'll come find you."

The voices in the house were drawing closer. Tate thought she could distinguish an older woman, a young woman, and a man. Maybe the father. Maybe the brother.

"They didn't catch us having sex, if that's what you're worried about. Just tell them that I'm your friend."

Friends—what a sad cliché. If Abigail had asked her to pretend to be a "friend" she would have refused on principle. But she was willing to bend her principles to ease the worry on Laura's face. Anyway, Laura *was* her friend, in a way. A kind of gorgeous friend, who would certainly break her heart into a million pieces but probably leave her thinking it was all worth it in the end. That kind of friend.

"Tell them I live in Palm Springs. Tell them I drank too

much last night, and you let me crash here. Tell them I'm your friend from college."

Laura ran a hand over her perfect hair.

"I don't have friends." Laura gave a shrug and a thin smile.

"Everyone has friends."

"I don't have friends like you." It was just a fact. "Don't be mad." She strode to the window and looked out, her breath fogging the glass. "You didn't tell Maggie."

"That's different."

Laura turned from the window.

"Hide in the closet," Laura instructed. "Then go down the back stairs. If they catch you say you're the new gardener."

Tate looked down at her own outfit: motorcycle boots, jeans, and a sweater belonging to some previous occupant of the mansion, a large insignia emblazoned on the left breast. Snakes and a shield and an anchor. Of course, an anchor.

"What about the schoolboy I mugged to get this sweater?"

"It was my brother's. He'll never remember."

"I look as much like a gardener as you do."

"And we don't have a garden." Laura took Tate's hands. "If they see you, they'll guess. At least my brother will. The important thing is that they know you'll lie. They just want the fiction. They tell everyone I'm engaged to a lawyer in Atlanta."

"What?" Tate pulled her hands from Laura's.

"I hardly know him. He's probably gay too," she said, as though the thought had just occurred to her. "It looks good in the literature. You can't have a single daughter over thirty. And if I'm honest with them, they'll start worrying who else I might be honest with."

"You mean, like yourself?" Tate shot back.

The footsteps in the hallway were drawing closer. Tate could make out the flurry of questions tossed back and forth between them.

"You have no idea what the political landscape of the country looks like." Laura lowered her voice. "If I come out, I'm risking everything my father has worked for, and he is a good man. You don't know what the competition is like. They're clan members. They want to criminalize birth control. My father is a moderate."

"Where I come from we don't lie about who we are. We make mistakes. We do dumb things. We're not perfect, but we don't lie about who we are."

"Where you're from is a fantasy. Even the conservatives are liberal in Portland. You can't go out there and be honest." Laura spoke as if Tate had just proposed walking on water.

"I am not going to stand in front of your family and tell them I'm a gardener for a house with no garden who stole your brother's sweater," Tate said.

Suddenly, there was a knock on the door.

"Laura?" a man's voice called out. "Are you decent?"

*No*, Tate mouthed.

"One sec," Laura called out, her cheerful voice at odds with the look on her face.

She grabbed Tate's elbow. It was not a lover's touch. It was the grip mall cops used to drag shoplifters to the office to await their fate. Tate wrenched her arm free.

"Get in." Laura pointed to the closet. "Now."

From outside the door, an older woman sang out, "Yoo-hoo! Laura-bear, I'm coming in."

"My mother," Laura whispered.

"I came out when I was ten." Tate took a step toward the door, the waiting mother, the man's voice, the whole Enfield clan.

"That's the whole problem." Laura gave Tate one last, appraising glance. "You look it." Then she grabbed Tate's arm again and pushed her into the large walk-in closet.

The closet wasn't really that bad. A sliver of light came in from beneath the door illuminating a space slightly smaller than Tate's apartment. The whole space smelled pleasantly of cologne and expensive textiles. Tate wondered if Laura expected her to insinuate herself behind a rack of slacks. Would her family check the closet?

Tate heard a door open.

"What are you doing here?" That was Laura.

Several footsteps entered the room. It sounded like someone landed on the bed with a bounce.

"Natalie. Mom."

So it was Laura's sister, mother and, Tate guessed by the man's voice, her brother.

"Laura," her brother said. "I didn't know you still used this house."

"Apparently you did," Laura said, "because you're here. Or are you here on vacation?"

"Your mother and sister were visiting friends in LA, and they heard from Dora that you had ordered a room made up."

"You're stalking me."

At least Laura was not enthusiastic about seeing her family. That was something, Tate thought.

"And we saw you were here with someone." Natalie affected a childish, singsong voice that made Tate want to burst out of the closet and hit her over the head with a shoe. She really did sound a lot like Abigail.

"Are there spy cameras in here? What the hell?" Laura said.

The man's voice interrupted. "We just checked the alarm records. You know it records movement in the house. Utilities usage. You don't flush the toilet when you're not home."

"Did you finally meet someone?" Laura's mother asked.

Laura stumbled over her words. "I had to pull a few overnighters with the accountant from the Bonhoffer account. It was just easier to work here."

"Was he cute?" That was Natalie again.

"Yes. Gorgeous. And he fucked me senseless every night. I'm probably pregnant with his love child."

"Laura!" her mother exclaimed.

"Come on now, Nat was just asking," her brother said.

"Is that why you're here?"

Tate took a quiet step toward the door of the closet, trying to picture the scene outside. She knew what Vita would say. *Carpe fucking diem.* Vita would tell her to take her shirt off, jump out, and scream, *She's a dyke!* Instead she listened.

"They heard that you were here, and they just couldn't contain themselves," Laura's brother continued. "They wanted to tell you the good news."

"Tell her," Natalie urged.

"Your father..." her mother said dramatically.

"Our father..." her brother added.

"...is going to be president of the United States of America!" Natalie crowed.

"He's being considered for a presidential nomination," the brother said. "Nat is getting ahead of herself, but it's true. Some very influential people have been mentioning his name. They like our campaign. They say we're 'untarnished.'"

"We?" Laura asked.

*Say it*, Tate urged. *Just tell them. It's that simple.*

"The Enfield campaign. All of us together," her mother said with treacly sweetness.

The brother was clearly trying to play it cool, but Tate could hear the excitement in his voice. "So we thought we'd fly up, pay you a visit, and talk to you about working on the campaign. There's going to be a press conference tomorrow."

"You've been out of the loop," her mother added. "Your father would like to strategize with you before the conference."

"I'll have to think about it," Laura said.

"What could possibly be more exciting than campaigning for the president of the United States of America?" her mother asked.

*Lesbian sex*, Tate thought. *Love. Everything!* But she had already sunk to the floor, her knees tucked under her chin, her arms wrapped around her legs like a child. She knew the answer.

"Of course," Laura said, her voice flat. "It's wonderful. Let's go downstairs, and you can brief me. Who's going to be at the press conference?"

# Chapter 23

Laura had been sitting in the living room listening to political strategy for over an hour, all the while trying to devise her own strategy to get her family out of the house and Tate out of the bedroom closet. So far she had not been able to budge her family. She had not even gotten a word in edgewise. It was all polling stats, issue treatments, and the aesthetics of campaign materials. It was still early in the morning—too early for a drink, which was too bad because the desire to strangle someone was growing with each thinly veiled reference to Laura's fictional accountant.

Natalie dropped another one, and John said, "You know Natalie is right. You've got to establish some sort of stable, monogamous relationship."

"I don't see why you can't get married," her mother added. "You're a lovely young lady."

Laura rose and walked toward the window.

"No one here is young," she said, more to the landscape than to her family.

"Speak for yourself," Natalie said.

"Natalie, you were born old." Laura scanned the desert below. Miles of unadulterated rock, scrub brush, and rattlesnakes surrounded the house. And something else. A figure moving in the distance. A woman making her way from rock to rock, the early sun casting a long shadow at her feet.

Tate.

Overhead, a hawk circled on the hot air currents. Beyond her, Palm Springs spread itself out like a distant mirage. As Laura watched, Tate paused, looked up at the sky, and then set off again, heading downhill, toward the highway, toward the city. It occurred to Laura, she had never seen anything more elegant, more resolute. In that silhouette was everything John Wayne was meant to be all wrapped up in the body of a lean, muscular woman. She almost stopped her brother in midsentence to show him. That's what he wanted for his campaign flyers. That integrity. That grace.

"I have to go," Laura said.

"Where?" her mother asked.

"Out."

"What's going on?" John called after her.

"We were talking to you," Natalie said.

Laura ignored them. She slipped on the most practical pair of shoes she could find in the front hall closet. Then she ran into the desert, calling for Tate.

She did not get far. She had drawn a map of Tate's trajectory in her mind, but when she reached the desert she wasn't sure.

Every time she headed in one direction she thought maybe Tate had gone another way. She listened. Every sound could have been Tate's distant footsteps. Every sound could have been the breeze blowing against the spruce trees. Laura scrambled down to a lookout point where she knew she could see the valley, but there was no sign of anyone.

"Tate!" Her voice echoed off the rocks. No one answered.

Finally, sweaty and past tears, she trudged back to the family tribunal that awaited her. Someone had poured a round of mint juleps.

"What was that about?" her mother asked as she entered the living room.

She was aware of her disheveled hair, her red face, and her family's cool reserve. She turned. They all sipped their drinks in unison. It was cultish.

"How do you do that?" Laura asked.

"What?" her mother and Natalie said together.

Except for her long, red hair and freckles her sister was a carbon copy of their mother.

Laura wandered into the kitchen, surveyed the mint julep fixings, and poured a shot of rum in a glass. She took a swig, feeling the liquor burn her throat.

"It was a woman," Laura blurted out. "I was here with a woman."

Laura thought she could hear the houndstooth rustle as her mother and sister stiffened simultaneously.

"The accountant?" John asked. "It's a small thing. Just be more careful. We don't want any impression of impropriety.

You know once Dad is nominated, we're going to be in the tabloids. There's just no way around it, and they don't care if it's true."

"It is true!" Laura slammed her glass down on the counter.

"I know you were just here with a female accountant, but the tabloids can make anything into a scandal," John said, as if explaining a simple lesson to a dim student.

She knew what he meant, and she knew why he was explaining it again. She understood his deliberate tone. *Don't. Tell. Anyone.* That's what he was saying. He remembered their conversation on the rock, so many years ago. He knew why she traveled, why she had no real home, why there was no warmth in her life or her face or her heart. He knew, and he had no pity.

"I was here with my *lover*!" Laura said.

For a moment, the sunlight coming through the window froze to amber and everyone sat motionless. Laura had the uncanny feeling that if she stood up and walked out, the family would remain petrified, like an installation at a wax museum. *First Family on the Eve of Ruin*, the artist would title it.

Unfortunately, they had not been reduced to figurines. Natalie broke the silence.

"You can't do this to us." It wasn't a plea. It was a statement.

Then everyone was talking at once, everyone except Laura. She sat rigid on the couch, her hands clutching her empty glass. It was ten minutes before they quieted down. Then John stood, the alpha male presiding over his women.

"I'm going to sit here." He motioned to Laura's sofa.

"Fine."

He sat and waited a beat.

"Do you love America?" John asked finally.

A month ago, she would have given a knee-jerk yes. Of course, she loved America. Now, she thought of Maggie standing behind the counter of Out Coffee. She thought of Krystal with her pink ponytails, sheltered by the only people who would take her in, dreaming of a father in prison. She thought of Tate, with her stern face and endless loyalty. She thought of this network of work and love and sacrifice, where the small pleasures had to be enough because often that was all there was. America. She did love it, and it had nothing to do with the Stan Enfield campaign.

"You value AMERICA," John continued, pronouncing *America* in all caps. "You have a responsibility to bring your gifts to the service of AMERICA."

"Don't talk to me," Laura said. She knew the buzzwords: *value, future, accountability.* "I don't give a shit about your America."

Out of the corner of her eye, Laura saw her mother open her mouth to protest, but John stopped her with a glance. He was planning a new approach. He leaned back, throwing an arm across the sofa behind her.

"Ah, Laura!" he said cheerfully. "We should come out here more often, spend more time together. We used to do that. Remember?"

"We miss you," Natalie said with so much venom, Laura was certain rattlesnakes dropped dead in the rocks around the house just at the sound of it.

"Everyone makes mistakes," John added. "We're all human.

And we can be that here, with family, but outside of this house we have a duty, a responsibility just as much as any soldier. We have an obligation to be role models to AMERICA."

"And I can't be a role model if I sleep with women?" Laura asked bitterly.

"It's confusing." John shrugged. "People don't know what to think."

"And Dad needs the conservative Baptist vote, which means no gays." Laura knew the statistics.

"You were happy when you were married."

John squeezed her shoulders, and Laura flinched.

"I've never been happy." She did not know how true it was until she heard the razor edge in her own voice. "Not until I met her."

"Maybe you could help us find a way to reach the moderate liberal," John continued. "Maybe you could campaign around some social issues. Maybe there will even be a time when you could 'come out' if that is something you really decide you want to do. But not now. We are standing on the edge of a cliff, and we can either soar with the eagles or fall."

Laura thought of Tate, standing beneath the hawk and the sky. Laura had never seen anyone be so cool in her entire life, and there was nothing she could say to her family that would make them understand the pathos of a gay Portland barista walking through the desert. Going home.

"We are going back to Alabama tomorrow," John added.

In her family's mind it was already settled. Laura would fly back to Alabama on a private jet. She would hardly need to call Brenda to give her notice. The Clark-Vester Group and the Enfields had a long-standing relationship, which was, Laura knew when she was being honest, the only reason she had ever been hired.

"No," Laura said and hurried out of the room before her family could see her cry. "I'm going back to Portland."

# Chapter 24

Tate watched Palm Springs shrink beneath the wing of her plane and felt nothing. She knew on some level that her heart was breaking. She could barely remember the steep descent from the bluff to the highway below. It was just a blur of heat and dust and shifting gravel. She patted the pocket of her jacket. At least she had her keys, her wallet, and her own jacket, even if the rest of her clothes belonged to brother Enfield.

"Hard day?" the man in the seat beside her asked, looking askance at her dusty clothes.

"Yep."

The pilot announced cruising altitude and Tate fell into a deep, suffocating sleep. When she woke, they had landed. On the TriMet home she watched her own reflection in the window. She could see why the man on the plane had looked at her uncomfortably. It wasn't the dirt on her jeans. It was the look in her eyes. *I'm too old for this*, Tate thought.

* * *

Tate returned home and threw herself on the futon. She considered calling Laura. Then she replayed the conversation she had heard through the door of Laura's closet. A presidential nomination. An accountant. Laura's voice taking on the same tone it had had at their meeting in Beaverton. *Let's go downstairs and you can brief me. Who's at the press conference?* Anyway, she had left her cell phone in Palm Springs. It was probably for the best.

She did not want to stare at the four walls of her studio apartment and think about Laura. She went downstairs. After several failed attempts, she got the engine of her ancient Harley to turn over and headed to Vita's.

At least she could tell Vita the story. Perhaps in the retelling, some part of it would become comic or at least remarkable. Perhaps, true to form, Vita would retell the story to each of her roommates, and by the end of the night Tate would have been locked in a basement, rescued by FBI agents, then chased through the desert amid a rain of bullets.

True to its original calling the door to the Church was never locked, and Tate let herself in when she arrived.

"Hello?" she called as she climbed the stairs.

The living room/sanctuary was dark, the air was heavy with incense. Melissa Etheridge blared from a crackling speaker. For a moment, she thought she had stumbled on a performance-art installation by one of the roommates.

"I'm sorry," she called out. "Is Vita here?"

It was only then that she noticed the figure slumped across

the kitchen counter, her head near the speaker, a bottle in one hand.

"Vita?"

On the speaker, Melissa Etheridge wailed.

Vita straightened, slightly, and took a swig off the bottle. Southern Comfort, Tate noted. Vita's mascara had run. Her hair had deflated while still maintaining a certain rat's nest quality.

"What does it all mean? Life!" Vita pounded the bottle on the counter. "Nothing. That's what it means."

It actually would have made a fairly good performance piece if it had been staged. It was a modern rendition of *No Exit.*

"What's wrong?" Tate asked, hovering in the doorway because a quick exit felt like the most attractive course of action at that moment.

"She left me." Vita's words slurred, and she swayed on her stool. "Cairo left me."

There was no exit this time. Melissa soared to a crescendo. Vita turned up the volume until the music was so loud Tate thought it would recalibrate her heartbeat. The song ended and began again. Tate crossed the room and turned off the music. Melissa Etheridge playing on repeat was never a good sign.

"I'm sorry, Vita."

Vita turned, bottle in hand.

"Where the fuck have you been? I called you and you didn't call me back." She was drunk. "How could you, Tate. You're supposed to be my best friend." Vita took another gulp of Southern Comfort and looked at the bottle. "You're my only real friend."

"How can you drink that stuff?" Tate said wearily.

"I don't see why you care, since you never call me." Vita rested her head on her arms, staring across the countertop at a bowl of shriveled oranges. "Where were you?"

Tate had half a mind to pull up a stool, take a swig of the Southern Comfort, turn Melissa Etheridge back on, and tell Vita exactly where she had been and why she was back. But that wouldn't help either of them.

"I lost my phone."

She pulled the bottle from Vita's rubbery grasp and poured the rest of the brown liquor into the sink, filling the air with its cough syrup smell.

"That's mine," Vita whined.

"You've had enough."

"You don't get to lose your phone," Vita said, draping even more of her body across the counter. Tate put her hand on Vita's back.

"What happened?"

"Life is shit. That's what happened. She said she wasn't ready to make a commitment. She said she didn't want to *limit* herself to the experiences she could have with one person."

Tate looked down at Vita. Only the look of abject misery on Vita's face kept Tate from reminding Vita that she had used the same line on every woman she had ever dated. How many brokenhearted girls had cornered Tate outside the Mirage, begging her to intervene on their behalf? She did a quick tally: at least seven.

"Say something," Vita said, looking up.

And there was the rugby player. She made eight. The white

girl with dreadlocks, the drag king, the stripper, the woman from Austria.

"What do I do?" Vita said.

Tate stopped counting.

"I don't understand. How she could just leave? What do I do? You've been dumped a hundred times. You must know."

"Thanks."

"But you *have to* know! Why am I so unhappy? What do I *do*?"

*Why are we so unhappy?* Tate thought. She patted the Aqua-Net disaster that was Vita's hair.

"*You* never do anything." Vita answered her own question. "You just go quiet and sit around looking stoic with those god-damn cheekbones. Why did we break up, Tate? You and me, why?"

"Because we were sixteen, and you set my porch on fire."

"I did it for you." Vita reached for Tate's face. "You're so pretty. You know I love you."

Tate took a step back.

"I love you too, Vita. And you're drunk."

"How do I get her back?"

"You don't. You cry. You watch *L Word* reruns. You say you're going to go vegan and stop drinking, but you don't actually do it. That's what you do when you get dumped. Because people don't come back."

In the back of her mind, Tate thought she must still be in shock. It was the only way she could deliver the words without weeping.

"Of course they do," Vita said.

"In movies." Tate sighed. She didn't know what else to say or how much. There had to be some sort of inverse relationship between alcohol and talk therapy. The more one drank, the less point there was in processing details. "Do you remember the rugby player you dated?"

"Yeah."

"And the biology major from PSU, and the woman with multiple personalities? Did you ever think about going back to them?"

"No." Vita's eyes were wide.

Tate heard her own voice as if from a great distance, a gentle friend delivering the news directly because delay would only cause more pain.

"Did you know that they all asked me what they could do to win you back? Do you know what I told them?"

Vita waited.

"I told them there was nothing they could do."

*There is nothing I can do.*

"But I love her."

*But I love her.*

"I know you do," Tate said quietly. *But it doesn't matter.*

# Chapter 25

There had been a moment when Laura thought she could make the afternoon flight from Palm Springs to Portland. She had swept her clothing off a chair, tossed her laptop—still on—into her luggage, and rushed past her family to her rental car waiting outside. She had sped to the airport, nearly running several red lights, but the flight had already left.

"Can you tell me if there was a passenger named Tate Grafton on the airplane?" she had asked the clerk, knowing the airline would not reveal the identity of passengers, even if she had paid for Tate's expensive, last-minute, flexible-departure ticket.

The next flight to Portland was at eight the following morning. Laura booked her seat and retreated from the counter, her haste turning into lethargy. She booked a room in a nearby hotel. Then she sat in the air-conditioned chill, staring out the window. Her view offered only the backside of another hotel and a slice of the pool. She tried to call Tate a dozen times, but Tate did not answer.

Time passed like a geological age. Nothing moved, not the stiff laminate curtains, not the palm trees by the pool. Laura moved from chair to bed to chair and felt like she sat in each position for hours, but when she checked the clock only minutes had gone by.

Around five she called the hotel's front desk and asked if they offered room service.

"I'm sorry, no," the friendly woman's voice said. "But various restaurants deliver."

Laura offered a hundred-dollar tip if the receptionist would send someone to fetch a bottle of gin and a bucket of ice.

She had drunk a considerable amount when her phone rang with an unlisted number. She leapt to answer it, then dropped the phone on the bed when she heard her brother's voice.

"Hello? Laura?" she heard him call from the tiny smartphone. "Laura, don't be childish. Talk to me."

She poured another ounce of gin into her glass, picked up the phone and her room key, and walked barefoot into the hall, not caring who saw her.

"What?" she asked.

"Have you been drinking?" her brother asked.

"Yes."

She moved toward the end of the hall and the door that led onto the pool. Apparently this was not a popular hotel with parents and children. She would have expected to find the pool full of kids, but it was empty, the water as smooth as a mirror. Beyond the pool, she could see a mini-mart, a dusty highway, and the arid desert Palm Springs pretended not to be.

"Laura." John's voice was urgent. "I'm glad I caught you. Look, I'm sorry about everything. Okay. Can we just skip that part for now?"

"What part?"

She wasn't in the mood for cajoling. No threats of expulsion from the family circle, no doomsday forecast for the world without Stan Enfield, no promise could drag her back to Alabama. She felt very calm. The air outside was still, the noises muffled, and yet her vision felt clearer. She could see the horizon in one direction and the mountains in another. The day was hot, but the sun was dimming. A few house lights in the distant mountains were just flickering on in the early twilight. Standing at the edge of the fence that surrounded the pool, she could be anywhere, any desert.

*I'm drunk*, she thought, but she didn't care. Let the family sit around sipping their mint juleps and judging her. A gust of wind blew into the pool area, carrying a wave of dust that blew around her bare feet.

"I know you don't want to come home," John said.

"I'm not coming home."

"It's just that…"

"*Home* is hardly the right word for it, John."

"It's Dad." John drew in a deep breath. "I told him what you said… what you are… and that you plan on living that life in public, no matter what it does to our family."

Laura moved the phone away from her ear and put John on speaker.

"I'm not doing anything *to* our family," she said. "I am living my life. You never asked about me? Have you ever thought about what life on the Stan Enfield campaign trail has done to me? You like this. You're perfect for it, but I don't want my whole life to be a lie because *you* think I'm inconvenient."

She was drawing a breath, ready to keep going, when John interrupted.

"Dad's had a heart attack, Laura."

Laura froze, the phone in one hand, her drink in the other. "What?"

"I told him about you, and he had a heart attack. Mom and Natalie have already flown out on a charter flight to be with him."

"But he's in great shape." Laura saw her father's broad shoulders, his campaign smile, his wide wave to the crowd.

"Laura, listen to me. They don't think he's going to make it."

# Chapter 26

There was only one option for a woman heartbroken at the height of summer in a city of bridges with a Harley as old and familiar as a twin brother. Tate stood on the sidewalk outside the Church, breathing in the smells of the city. Then she mounted the bike and pulled on the helmet, comforted by its familiar warmth. It had been too long since she rode alone just for the sake of the ride.

It was hard to feel sad as she urged the bike past seventy, up onto the Broadway Bridge, so wide and high it felt like someone had paved the sky. She thought of the time she had taken Laura on this ride. Over the years, Tate had taken a dozen different friends and a handful of lovers on her bike. Usually it was no more intimate than riding in a crowded TriMet bus. The movement of the vehicle jostled them together, but it wasn't sensual. With Laura it had been. The ride had been awkward at first. Then Laura had wrapped her arms around

Tate's waist and pressed her chest to Tate's back, and they were one body. Tate remembered that as she crested the Broadway Bridge and soared back down into northwest Portland. She remembered how Laura had leaned into her as they rode, using every turn as a chance to draw nearer. She remembered leaning into a curve, feeling Laura's arms tighten around her, Laura's hands caressing her sides. At that moment, she had been suddenly and completely certain that Laura was as hungry to touch her as she was to touch Laura.

Now she leaned into a turn, the bike almost horizontal, speed holding her a few feet off the ground.

She thought, *I can get her back.* She had lost her cell phone and with it Laura's number, but there had to be a number for Laura's development company. Only this time, Tate would be like Vita—at least, pre-Cairo Vita. She'd be bold but aloof.

*How did you get this number?* Laura's voice would catch in her throat when she realized who was on the other end of the phone.

*The president's daughter isn't hard to track down.*

Tate played the conversation out in her mind as she rumbled over the bridge.

*I can't see you again.*

*I don't want to see you. I want to feel you.*

*Oh Tate, I need you!*

And even if she did not call Laura at Clark-Vester, Tate trusted what she had felt in Laura's touch. She had told Vita it wouldn't work. No one came back. But she had to be wrong. Laura wanted her. Laura would come back. She had to.

In the meantime, Tate thought, she really would go vegan

and stop drinking. She would install the pull-up bar that had been stashed under her futon for two years. She would join a gym. Perhaps she would get another tattoo. The labrys had been an eighteen-year-old's impulse purchase. She could get something more dramatic, a full sleeve of mermaids fornicating, or a phoenix, or dragons eating a phoenix on top of mermaids fornicating.

Then one day, Laura would walk through the front door of Out Coffee, see Tate surrounded by a flock of admiring baby dykes, be consumed with jealousy, and fall into Tate's muscular and well-inked arms. She could almost smell Laura's perfume.

That was the problem with breakups. People made resolutions, but they never followed through. Only this time, she would. She would be a different woman when Laura walked back into her life.

She took the Steel Bridge at seventy-five, not even scanning her rearview mirror for police. It didn't matter. She could outrun them. The bike was old, but she knew it like her own breath. She could take 99W at 90 mph, be in Oregon City in ten minutes, Washington State in twenty.

She circled back to catch the Hawthorne Bridge and return to downtown. She would ride each bridge—eleven of them—all the way down to the two-lane Sellwood Bridge that arched so high it did not need to draw open for the ships. Then she would return to her apartment, do two hundred push-ups and start planning her rebirth from the ashes.

Except that the Hawthorne Bridge was open when she got there. A line of cars waited for the tall freight liner to pass through the open mouth of the drawbridge. She idled. The boat was moving very slowly.

A few specks of rain hit her visor as though Portland was reminding her of the long winter to come. The car in front of her rolled up its windows. She zipped up her leather, but her T-shirt was already damp. In fact, she was cold throughout. And tired. And the bike was making a coughing sound that warned her of another expensive repair.

Before she realized she was crying, a sob escaped her lips.

Laura did not care if she got a tattoo of mermaids fornicating. Laura had not pushed her into a closet and denounced their love because Tate's biceps were not sufficiently inked or because her triceps were inadequately defined. She would not love Tate more if Tate started chewing on lemongrass sticks and drinking pulverized wheatgrass or whatever concoction Lill was pushing these days.

A thunderclap—a rarity in Portland—exploded. The rain hit her like a dam breaking. The whole awful day came back to her in a wave.

She remembered the sudden fear she had felt when she thought someone had broken into Laura's house. Once again, she felt the bitterness of Laura's closet. It wasn't just that Laura wasn't willing to come out or even be seen with her. The pain was simpler than that. Even after her conscious mind knew they were not going to be killed by an intruder, her body had been afraid. She had been scared, and Laura had pushed her into the dark to be alone. Another sob wracked her body.

Before her, the ship passed. The drawbridge began to lower slowly. The traffic light turned green. The brake lights in front of her winked off. This part of the bridge was made of a metal grate, the river clearly visible below. The trick to riding the grate was to loosen up. Let the emptiness between the rails pull at the tires. Let the bike wobble a little as the metal pulled it back and forth. But Tate could not relax. She jerked the bike into position, even as she cried into the soft foam of her helmet.

All she could think was that after everything Laura had done and not done, the only thing that would ease the pain in her chest was the feel of Laura's arms around her, to hear Laura's voice in her ear whispering some endearment. *Sweetheart. Baby.* The very person who broke her heart was the only person who could comfort her.

She revved the bike, ignored its cough, and started off in the direction of the city. She felt the wind on her hands, the rumble of the bike beneath her. She saw the headlights of an oncoming van. The visor hid her tears, but she knew the other drivers could see her shaking with sobs. She didn't care. No one could comfort her. What could Vita say? For all Tate knew, Vita had found another bottle of Southern Comfort and was halfway through. And Maggie would hit the liquor if she learned the truth about Tate and Laura. She had no one to go to. And she wept too because she knew that Laura proba-bly *would* come back to Portland—at least once—and that she could probably sleep with her again if she wanted. And that she must not because every moment they spent together only delayed the inevitable end. The longer she postponed it, the more it would hurt. For the first time in her life, Tate thought she might not have the strength to survive another heartbreak.

The bike weaved. Angrily she revved the engine and muscled it back into the center of the lane. At least this she could control. At least here she had power. Then she felt it: the first fraction of a second in which the traction of the front tire slipped on the wet metal and the power in the back tire pushed, and the laws of physics that had held her upright on the Broadway Bridge betrayed her.

The next thing she felt was her helmet hitting the metal bridge. Then the sound of brakes screeching. A car horn. Then she was moving very fast, but on her back, staring up at the infrastructure of the drawbridge, her leather jacket dragging against the metal grate, the hot bulk of her bike skidding along the bridge on its side with a metallic roar. A second later everything went silent.

# Chapter 27

Laura entered the hospital through the ER entrance and asked a woman at the intake desk for directions to her father's room. The woman pointed to an elevator. Laura waited for a long time, breathing in the smell of disinfectant hiding urine. She pulled the Saint Laurent scarf out of the breast pocket of her suit and pressed it to her nose. The place smelled contagious.

"Coming through," a voice said behind her.

Two EMTs headed toward the elevator, rolling an old woman on a hospital bed. One of the young men pushed a series of buttons on the elevator panel, and it opened immediately.

"You can ride with us," he said, holding the door for Laura.

She did not want to be close to the woman in the gurney. The woman was clearly at the end of her life, about 120 years old by the look of her. An IV trailed off one of her papery arms, and the veins in her face stood out blue beneath her skin.

"I think I'm going to be sick," the woman murmured.

One of the men slid a blue-gloved hand under her back and lifted her up. The other handed her a bag, and she spit in it.

Her father was not like that, Laura thought. He was not frail with blue-gray skin. He was a tall, barrel-chested man with a broad smile and a firm handshake. She rode the elevator up to the cardiac ward.

What if this was the end? What if it was all her fault?

When Laura arrived at the cardiac ward, she found her sister, Natalie, installed at a small table in the hall, glaring at her laptop.

"Welcome home," Natalie said when she caught sight of Laura.

"How is he?" Laura asked.

Natalie shrugged. "He's in the hospital." Her face said, *Because of you.* She pointed to one of the rooms. "In there."

Cautiously, Laura pushed open the door to her father's private room. Inside the room was quiet. The TV played silently above her father's bed. And in the bed, Stan Enfield looked like a man feigning sleep. His body still exuded vigor. His cheeks were ruddy. His chest rose and fell in big, manly breaths.

"Dad?"

Still his eyes remained closed.

Laura pulled up a chair, careful to lift it and move it rather than scrape it along the linoleum floor. She did not know if she should wake him or not.

"Dad?"

She touched his hand. It was warm. On another screen, a heart monitor noted a steady, even beat. Except for that, there was no equipment. No IV. No ventilator. No tubes running beneath the blankets.

Her father's eyelids flickered.

"Dad." Laura squeezed his hand.

"How are you, Laura?"

"I'm fine. How are you, Dad? Are you going to be all right? No one will talk to me. I didn't mean for this to happen..." Laura trailed off.

Stan continued to hold her hand, but with a feathery grip, not the strong grip of a professional hand shaker.

"When a man and a woman," he wheezed, "come together to bear a child, they put everything in God's hands. They can't say 'I want one like this and one like that.' They can't say, 'Make my child just like me, and let her support me in everything I do.'"

"But I do support you."

Stan closed his eyes as if holding them open took too much energy.

"But when a child grows up, when a person becomes an adult," he continued, "it *is* possible to ask them to do what they know is right for their country."

Laura squeezed her father's hand, then pulled away. There was another world in which he said, *You know I'll always love you.* There was another world in which he said, *As long as you are happy.* That was what she wanted to hear. But happiness had nothing to do with the Enfield family.

"John said this happened because of me," Laura whispered. "I was shocked."

"Because I was with a woman? Do you really think it's that wrong?"

"Off the record?"

"Yes."

Her father's eyes flickered open.

He coughed. "I don't care about the gays. I care about America."

Laura knew she should drop it. She should ask him about his prognosis, about the nurses, about the hospital food. She should find a copy of one of the magazines he liked and read him interesting headlines while he dozed.

Instead she said, "But you've campaigned on an anti-gay platform."

"Anti–gay marriage. And I've won, every time. We won. Don't you see? It's today's issue. We get votes, and then we go on to do great things. And what do the gays lose? The right to be just as miserable as normal people, and we get to build the country up. I want to build America, Laura, but I thought I had more time." He coughed again. "I don't know if I'll make it much longer."

"Don't say that, Dad."

A nurse in blue scrubs entered the room.

"We need to take your father down the hall for some tests," the man said quietly.

Laura rose slowly.

"You're going to be okay," she said.

Her father sighed. "I want to make America a better country, Laura. To do that I need votes, and this is how you get votes." He spoke slowly. "You could run for office too. You know that, right?"

"What if I was in love?" she asked.

"If you pursue this thing with a woman, if you come out...you'll never get the conservative vote, Laura. Never. You'll win more, you'll do more if you stay on our side."

The nurse cleared his throat. "We'd better get on with this," he said more matter-of-factly than Laura thought appropriate.

"I don't want to be president," Laura said.

"But what if *I* were? What if this heart attack doesn't kill me?" Her father pressed a hand to his chest. "They said I might not make it, but what if I do? I could win this. If you can just put your private life on hold for a few years."

Laura felt like she was sinking into quicksand.

"What if you get reelected?"

"Then it won't matter. Hell, it'll probably be a nonissue in six years."

"Really," the nurse said, turning to Laura, "you should go."

She wondered if he was gay. Perhaps he had heard the whole conversation. Perhaps he resented tending to a conservative senator. But he did it. Everyone did what they had to do.

Her father held out his hand. Reluctantly, Laura took it.

"Can I count on your support?" he said.

# Chapter 28

Tate blinked as several men in formal tuxedos surrounded her. One knelt down by her side.

"Can you hear me?" He had a very high voice despite his massive girth and heavy beard.

Her body felt numb. She tried to breathe. It felt like her lungs had been crushed.

"I can't breathe," she gasped.

"What happened?" someone else called.

Tate felt a sharp pain radiating from her foot up through her leg and into her groin.

"Get that bike off her," the man said, his falsetto at odds with his authoritative demeanor. "I'm a nurse. You're going to be okay."

A moment later the pain in her leg subsided.

The nurse squeezed her hand.

"Can you feel this?"

"What happened?" Tate whispered. "Where am I?"

"Can you feel this?" the man repeated.

He squeezed harder.

"Yes."

Somewhere through the rain and the crowd of legs, Tate thought she saw the puff of a tutu in the crowd of black-and-white suits.

"Am I dreaming?" she asked.

The man reached over and pulled one of her eyelids open.

"Someone get me a phone light!" he barked.

A moment later, the bright light of a cell phone's flashbulb seared her retina.

"Stop." Tate struggled in his grip.

"Don't move," the man said. Then, as if by habit more than to communicate with anyone, he announced, "Normal pupil dilation." He squeezed her other hand. "Can you feel this?"

"Yes." Tate pulled her hand away. The bridge was coming back into focus.

The man was not deterred. He touched her leg at the thigh, the knee, and the foot. Tate yelped when he touched the foot that had been trapped beneath the bike. Then he asked her to push against his palm, pull his hand toward her, and resist as he pushed his hand against hers.

"Okay. I'm going to take your helmet off. Let me know if you feel any pain."

Carefully, the man removed her helmet.

"Follow my finger with your eyes."

"I'm fine," Tate said, although her leg throbbed with a hot

pain. She watched the man's finger move back and forth across her field of vision. "I really am okay."

"Now stick out your tongue and move it side to side."

"Really!" she protested.

She struggled to a sitting position. Behind the nurse, she saw several of the other tuxedoed men directing traffic. One was indeed wearing a tutu over his tux. It was surreal.

"Where are you all going?" she asked.

"Just stick out your tongue."

"I told you, I'm fine," Tate said over her extended tongue.

"No sign of brain injury," the nurse said, "but we'll want to check you for concussion."

A couple of cyclists had also stopped nearby, as well as an old woman in a pickup. She got out of her truck and stood over Tate, her wiry gray hair emerging from beneath a John Deere baseball cap.

"What happened?" she asked.

"She must have spun out in the rain," the nurse said.

"This bridge is hell." The woman took a cigarette pack from her shirt pocket and lit one, shielding it from the rain in her cupped hand. She offered the pack to Tate, who shook her head.

"How's the bike?" she growled.

"Oh, God, I don't know," the nurse said. "Those things terrify me." He straightened his bow tie.

"Why y'all dressed up?" the woman asked.

"Portland Gay Men's Choir." The nurse gestured toward his van. "We're on the way to a concert."

The woman sniffed.

The nurse turned back to Tate.

"We should get you to a hospital," he said. "We don't mind. My boys and I'll take you."

Tate shook her head. She felt battered. The pain in her foot made her eyes water. But she was lucky. She hadn't been going fast. She flexed her arms gingerly.

"I'm okay."

"That was a nasty spill. I saw it. One minute you were up, and then bam!" the nurse said.

Now that the immediate emergency was over, he had the delivery of a cooking-show host. *I just throw the garlic in and bam!*

Tate rose, holding on to the guardrail to steady herself. Once on her feet, her vision blurred for a moment, then returned to normal. Her foot hurt, but she could put weight on it. She looked over the edge of the bridge. The smell of the river rose to meet her, cool and dark. On either side of the bridge, the lights of the city glittered.

"I'll be okay."

"You should really be checked out by a doctor," the nurse insisted.

She put her hand on the nurse's shoulder.

"You're sweet. Thank you. But right now a doctor's bill would hurt a lot more than this."

"Oh, no honey," the man said, putting a massive arm around Tate's waist to steady her as she swayed in the breeze that came up through the metal grate of the bridge. "You're looking awfully pale."

"I was only going ten miles per hour, if that," she said.

Behind the nurse, the choir had formed a worried circle. The woman in the John Deere cap urged them off the road.

"I'm losing my job," Tate said. She met the man's eyes. He had a big, black shovel of a beard and bright, little eyes. He was probably a bear, Tate thought. "The coffee shop where I work is being shut down. I've got about two weeks. Even if I get a new job tomorrow, I won't get paid before rent is due. The last thing I need is a thousand dollars in ER bills to say that, yes, I kissed the Hawthorne Bridge going six miles per hour. Look. I'm not bleeding. I'm standing up. I promise you. I'm fine."

"Do you have someone you can stay with?"

*Not really.*

"Absolutely."

"Hmm." The nurse snorted. "I would too if I had your cheekbones."

Then, with much negotiating, arm waving, and general discussion, it was decided that the woman in the John Deere cap would try to ride Tate's bike back to Tate's apartment. A baritone named Jeff would follow in her pickup, in case she didn't make it. The nurse, whose name was apparently Crown Princess Margarita, helped Tate into the van, where she was serenaded with an a capella version of Cyndi Lauper's "I Drove All Night."

She looked out the window of the van at the grizzled woman trying to start her motorcycle. *I'll never see it again*, she thought, but when the choir delivered her to her apartment, she saw the bike parked in front, the keys tucked under the front tire as promised.

Reluctantly, she knocked on Pawel and Rose's door. She

had planned on simply ignoring the nurse's advice and falling into bed, but Crown Princess Margarita insisted on talking to Pawel and Rose before he released his patient.

"We check on you every hour," Rose said after Tate explained the situation.

Pawel turned up Lawrence Welk as though a good, loud dose of Welk was all she needed.

*I'll never leave*, Tate thought as she drifted off to sleep. In her dreams she was flying high over the city, over the river and the ships and the leisurely traffic and the hookah bar and Out Coffee and the Church and the Mirage and the roses in Ladd's Addition. "I love you," she called again and again. And this time it was not for Laura. It was for the city.

# Chapter 29

When Tate limped into Out Coffee the following morning, the line was nearly out the door. For an optimistic moment, she thought Maggie had found some brilliant way to increase revenue. Then she noticed the customers' impatient stance.

Behind the counter, Maggie had lined up several cups with orders written on them, but she looked perplexed.

"I'm working as fast as I can," she mumbled. "I'm trying."

"If you can't appreciate quality," Krystal added, "go to 7-Eleven."

She had twisted her pink pigtails into little horns.

Very slowly Maggie tapped coffee grounds into a metal basket.

"Maybe you could all take a seat," Maggie said as though the customers were a class of bad children.

A man broke rank and left.

"Don't bother," he said to Tate as he passed. "You'll never get your coffee."

"I've got this," Tate said, pushing her way through the crowd and quickly washing her hands. "Maggie, go make sure the cream station is filled. Krystal, I'll get these orders out." To the line of customers, she announced, "Give me two minutes. We'll get you all taken care of."

An hour later, the morning rush had slowed down. Tate leaned against the counter and wiped her face, once again aware of the pain in her foot and the throbbing in her temple.

"What the hell happened to you?" Krystal squinted at her.

"Nothing."

When she looked up, Krystal's face had fallen into a look of concern.

"What?" Tate asked.

"Did that girl dump you?"

"Have you ever considered not prying into my life?"

Krystal opened her mouth in a shocked little O, as though someone had just struck her.

"I didn't mean it," Tate said. "I just…can't talk about it right now."

Krystal threw her arms around Tate, and Tate was enveloped in the smell of her bubble-gum perfume.

"I love you, Tate." Krystal squeezed harder, as though she could squeeze sadness out of Tate's rib cage. She certainly squeezed more pain into Tate's leg. "If she left you, she's a fucking idiot, and I'm going to call her, and tell her, and tell the whole world that's she's an idiot."

"And I'm sure that will make everything better," Tate said, trying to extricate herself from Krystal's affection.

"No, I'm serious," Krystal said, still holding on. "I'll get one of those planes. I'll get one of those planes, and I'll write 'Laura Enfield is a fuckup' all across the sky."

Tate pulled away. "And I'm going to make the bank drop," she said. "And you're not going to talk to Maggie about this or skywrite to Maggie about this, and we're both going to pretend none of this ever happened."

*But it did.* Tate tried to push the thought from her mind as she headed for the back room, where Maggie was folding a pile of clean dishcloths and looking shell-shocked.

"Where were you?" Maggie looked worried. "You were supposed to work yesterday. I called you. I thought you'd been killed on that motorcycle of yours. Or abducted. Or beaten. You know there are a lot more gay-bashings than the police want to admit. Human trafficking is on the rise, especially in Portland." She sounded distracted, as though she were reciting a half-remembered list. She did not seem to notice Tate's limp or the fading bruise on her face.

"I don't really want to talk about it," Tate said.

Back at the coffee shop after going to the bank, Tate didn't realize for several moments that Krystal was not waiting on the man who stood at the counter; she was fighting with him. It was not always easy to tell the difference with Krystal, but Maggie's defensive stance alerted Tate to the problem. That and the man's protests.

"Will you tell this teenager to get out of my face?" His voice rose several decibels louder than the space required.

Behind him, two other men stood sentinel, their white T-shirts and khakis contrasting with the man's dark business suit. They looked like security guards flanking a politician. For a brief moment, Tate wondered if it was Laura's father come to exact revenge for the deflowering of his daughter.

"How 'bout you go stick it!" Krystal countered. She held up a sheet of paper and slowly tore it in half. Then she tore the halves.

"What's going on?" Tate asked.

Krystal held up the paper, now torn in four squares. She ripped the stack in half again. The man grabbed Krystal's wrist and wrestled the paper from her.

"Ow!" Krystal yelled.

"Stop," Maggie said.

Tate marched up to the counter and clamped a hand on the man's shoulder.

"Let her go!" she said.

Slowly, the man withdrew his hand and crossed his arms.

"What's going on?" Tate asked again.

"We are serving a twenty-four-hour eviction notice," the man said, slapping the shredded paper down on the counter.

"You can't do that." Maggie stepped in between Krystal and the counter. "Don't use your patriarchal privilege to try to intimidate us. You're not going to kick us out of our own business."

Tate cleared her throat. "Our lease specifies one month notice, minimum, for termination."

"With an exception for reckless and wanton behavior," the man said.

"When?" Tate demanded.

The men in T-shirts seemed to get larger.

"Well, we could start with that little production you staged the other day: your protest," one said. "Let's see, you had people handcuffed to the building in the heat. You called the police. There was a fight. You endangered your customers. You utilized commercial property for political activities."

"That was a peaceful protest," Maggie said. "Those were citizens exercising their freedom of speech."

"Why didn't the landlord tell us?" Tate asked.

"The building has been sold," the man said. "The Clark-Vester Group owns this building. You have twenty-four hours to vacate the premises. Mr. Loeb and Mr. Duneo are going to stay here to oversee your departure. Be very careful how you leave and what you take. All assets belonging to the former title holder are now property of the Clark-Vester Group. Anything damaged or removed from the premises not belonging to individual employees or to Out in Portland LLC by proof-of-purchase receipt will be considered theft and prosecuted as such. Anyone left on the premises after..."—he checked his watch—"three thirty tomorrow will be arrested for trespassing."

"We have a right to a lawyer and a right to talk to your supervisor," Tate said.

"You have the right to shut up." He poked a finger at Tate's breastbone.

"We haven't done anything wrong!" Tate protested.

The man took a step back.

"Can you afford the lawyer who's going to tell the court that?"

With that, the men strutted over to the airpots, helped

themselves to coffee, and took up residence at a table by the window.

Tate looked around.

"Should we leave?" a woman seated near the counter asked.

The other customers were packing up their books and laptops and heading for the door.

"Yes. I think so," Tate mumbled.

A few minutes later, the customers were gone. Tate switched off the machines and took her books from underneath the counter. Krystal gathered up the assortment of lipsticks and hair ties she had left in the employee bathroom. Maggie bundled the Mariah Lesbioma dioramas into the back of her station wagon.

It was strange to close at three in the afternoon. It was strange how much of their lives had been lived in the shop and yet how little there was to take.

Tate caught one last glimpse of the shop. Except for the two men sitting by the window it could have been any sleepy Sunday, one of the many days Tate had worked there alone, not really thinking of the future or the past, but idly dreaming about the beautiful woman who might walk through the door at any moment.

*Look where that got me*, she thought as she flipped over the CLOSED sign.

Outside on the street, Krystal consulted her phone and said, "Maybe I should go to class tonight," but after that she stood expectantly staring at Tate.

"They can't just do that," Maggie said. She held a diorama to her chest. "I'm going to call Basic Rights Oregon. We'll do a phone campaign. We'll go door-to-door. We'll paper this city. Every bar. Every coffee shop. If they can do this to us, they can do it to anyone." She looked down at a diorama that involved a rubber tarantula sitting inside the papier-mâché folds of a green vagina. "Mariah will be devastated," she said, her voice suddenly maudlin. "This was her first exhibition. But she hasn't sold one piece, and now it's all over."

"I don't think she was ever going to sell anything," Tate said carefully.

Tate glanced down at the curb, then up at the telephone pole covered in band flyers. The Screaming Helicopters. The Fascist Lanterns. The Deep Oak Grove Mystery Band. Around the base of the telephone pole, the honeysuckle was withering.

"I have to call Lill," Maggie said, almost dropping the diorama in her haste. "She has to know. Tate, what am I going to do? I'll lose my house. Where's my phone? I think I left it in there. Tate? Tatum?"

But Tate was wrestling with something far greater than a missing phone. She was surveying the coffee shop door, the plastic CLOSED sign on its dirty string, the stillness of the shop where she had come for refuge as a teenager, where Maggie had fed her when no one else would, where she knew every piece of equipment as well as she knew her own hands. And she thought, *I'll never work here again.* And despite the pain in her foot and her concern for Maggie and the dawning realization that it was Laura who had shut down Out Coffee to hide her own involvement with Tate, Tate felt a moment of giddy exhilaration. *I don't work here anymore.*

An hour later, they were installed in a booth at a tiny Thai restaurant with a blue-and-yellow equality symbol on the door. As Tate expected, Krystal had not gone to class. Maggie had gone farther down the path of her imagined ruin. Lill had arrived with a stack of business cards from attorneys she met at Namaste Yoga. Vita had joined them too, although the state of Vita's eye makeup told Tate she might not be the one to cheer the group up.

"We've got to think this through." Tate sorted through the business cards Lill had handed her. "Do you actually know any of these people?"

Maggie tore her paper napkin into little shreds, declaring that hiring a lawyer was just giving in to the prison-industrial complex. Vita said she had slept with a couple of lawyers, but she couldn't remember their names.

Then Vita caught Tate's eye.

"You know who you should call," Vita said.

Tate shook her head in a way that she hoped was sufficiently subtle to allow Vita's comment to go unnoticed, but Vita had silenced the table.

"Who?" Maggie asked.

"Go on. Tell her," Vita urged.

"No."

"What?" Lill asked.

"Laura Enfield," Krystal sighed. "Duh."

Vita reached out and patted Tate's hand. "She's the only one who can help you."

"She wanted to help us before." Lill nodded her assent.

"No," Tate said.

"Why not?" Vita asked.

"Because it's over," Tate said, staring into her jasmine tea.

"I called it from day one. Why don't any of you listen to me?" Krystal said.

"What are we talking about?" Maggie asked.

"Tate's shagging Laura Enfield," Vita exclaimed, as though they had been playing a game of twenty questions that had gone on long beyond reason.

"But she's a developer!" Lill protested. "She's probably a conservative. She's probably right-wing!"

"Did you?" Maggie asked. "That Laura woman...she is a pawn of the patriarchy. She's trying to destroy everything we've worked for."

It hurt Tate to see the tears trembling at the corners of Maggie's dark eyes.

"Why would you share your body with someone who doesn't share your values?" Maggie asked. "Why would you do something like that?"

"Because she's hot!" Vita jumped in.

"Because I like her," Tate said. "...Liked her."

"You don't even know her." Maggie glanced out the window. "Is she even gay? Is she a bisexual?"

"There is nothing wrong with being bisexual," Krystal interjected.

"Maybe this is all part of her plan." Maggie turned back to

Tate, slapping her hand on the table. "Maybe you're part of her plan. That's what the patriarchy teaches women: to wear high heels they can't walk in, so they need a man to protect them, and then, when they need to take a little bit of agency over their own lives, what do they do? They use sex. The very thing they fear, the very thing that makes them vulnerable."

"Um." Krystal twisted a hank of hair around one finger and tilted her head. "I don't think Tate was trying to rape Laura 'cause she wore high heels."

"Krystal!" Maggie said. Maggie did not joke about rape.

"That woman is using everything she has to ruin us," Maggie said.

Tate spun her teacup around between her fingertips until the tea splashed on the table. "Laura didn't wake up in Alabama, throw a dart at a map, and say, 'I'm going to ruin Maggie Davidson's life.'"

"But that's what she did, didn't she?" Maggie countered.

*If she planned on ruining anyone's life it was probably mine*, Tate thought bitterly.

"Look, Maggie." Vita wiped a smear of black mascara from beneath both eyes. "Put your personal feelings aside for a minute. Tate has a *significant in* with this woman."

Vita managed to make the whole sentence sound dirty. Tate was glad to see that Cairo had not broken her spirit completely. But she didn't have an "in" with Laura.

"Not anymore," she said. "Okay?"

"Whatever." Vita spread out the words like a banquet. "Tate, you call Laura, cry, offer her sexual favors, and this all goes away."

"A woman like Laura Enfield is never going to be with Tate," Maggie said with a certainty that hurt all the more because Tate knew it was true. "Look at her. And look at you, Tate. You're a beautiful, strong, independent woman, but someone like that Laura woman isn't going to marry you. She's not going to take you home to her family. And one day, she's going to meet a man…"—Maggie shot a glare in Lill's direction—"…and decide what she really wants is a 'normal' life."

"Lill and Stephen aren't exactly normal," Vita said with a shrug.

"And what is normal, Vita?" Lill asked.

"She's probably repressed," Krystal added.

"Stop it." Tate stood up, knocking the table and making the teacups jump. "All of you. Laura broke it off. She dumped me. Go ahead and say 'You should have seen that coming.'"

Maggie opened her mouth and then closed it. Lill pressed her hands together and breathed deeply. Tate sat back down.

Vita said, "You could still call her."

"No. I can't." Tate lowered her voice. "I can't bear it. I can't see her again. It just…has to be over. I'm going home."

"Wait," Vita said. "Is she mad at you?"

"I don't know." Tate stared down at the glass tabletop.

"So she's just totally closeted and can't deal with being with a woman?" Vita asked.

"Basically," Tate said.

"I called it from the beginning! You have to see this," Krystal said, pulling out her phone and flipping through the screens, looking for something.

Tate did not care what.

Vita's eyes were brighter than Tate thought was appropriate.

"Call her," Vita said. "Make her feel guilty. Tell her there's one last thing she can do to make it all up to you."

"No," Tate said.

Vita pulled out her own phone. She tapped something onto the screen.

"I'll call her. There's got to be a number listed for the Clark-Vester Group."

"No!" Tate felt like a teenager in a cable special about peer pressure. This was the part where Vita pulled out a joint and told her that the first hit was free.

Still poking at her phone, Vita said, "Ah... Tate?"

And then, in much the same tone she used when watching videos of skateboard wipeouts or bear attacks, Vita said, "Oh. Oooh!"

"What?" Tate asked.

Vita looked up.

"Maybe you don't want to call her."

"What is it?" Tate asked again.

"Did you post these?" Vita turned the phone to Tate slowly.

At first, it was hard to make out the images tumbling across the screen, then Tate recognized the party at the Church. Then she recognized the tango lesson. She and Laura had danced for almost an hour under the tutelage of the ballet dancer. The camera focused on them, lingering on Tate's hand as she caressed Laura's back. The video ended with their kiss. Laura was still so beautiful. Tate felt as though the phone screen dimmed all the lights in the restaurant. Tate also felt her mouth go dry and her hands go cold.

"I didn't post that," Krystal said.

Everyone turned to her.

Vita passed the phone around.

When it returned to Vita, Vita said, "It was posted yesterday, about six p.m., by Orchid1975." She scrolled through a few more screens, then read. "'Senator and Republican presidential hopeful Stan Enfield denies any knowledge of the recently posted YouTube videos showing his daughter, Laura Enfield, engaged in sexual activity with another woman.'"

"We were dancing." Tate's voice came out in a whisper.

"You know what they say about sex," Vita said, cheerfully. "It can lead to dancing." She read on. "'Previously known as a moderate on the gay-marriage issue, Senator Enfield now says he will strongly oppose any gay-marriage or civil-union bills that come before him. He says he knows his daughter is heterosexual and has proof that she is involved with a male attorney from the prominent Beautrix firm.'" Vita stared at her phone for another minute. "You know, the strange thing is that whoever tagged these videos only tagged her."

The reality of the situation became clear to Tate like a wave crashing in slow motion.

"She thinks I did it," Tate said. "She thinks I posted these to out her."

The party's attention focused again on Krystal.

"I didn't do it!" Krystal protested.

"No one else at that party knew her," Vita said.

"Someone might have recognized her," Tate said. "She's the daughter of a politician."

"Yeah, but which one of *my* friends is going to recognize Stan Enfield, let alone his daughter?" Vita asked.

She had a point. Suddenly Vita snatched Krystal's phone away from her and tapped the screen furiously.

"Where is it?" she asked.

"I don't know what you're talking about..." Krystal's tone suggested that she knew exactly what Vita was looking for.

"You've always had a crush on Tate," Vita said.

"Have not."

"You're happy Laura broke up with her."

"I am not."

"Leave her alone," Maggie interrupted. "She hasn't done anything."

"Really?" Vita turned Krystal's phone around so Maggie could see the screen. "What's that?"

Tate did not need to look to know it was the video of Vita's party.

"I swear to God I didn't post it," Krystal said.

"You know it is possible for the phone company to pull anything off your phone," Lill said. "Nothing you do on that phone is private."

"Yeah!" Krystal folded her arms across her chest. "Nothing on my phone is private."

"This was private," Tate said quietly. She had gone past angry, like someone might walk past a bus stop. Past angry, past vengeful, past snide. She was just tired. Laura was gone, and wherever she was, she believed Tate had betrayed her. Out Coffee was gone, and it was Tate's fault. And it was Laura's fault. And it was Krystal's fault. And in some tangential way it was Vita's fault, and, even if Laura hadn't shut them down, the store probably would have gone under anyway, and that was Maggie's fault and maybe Lill's fault too.

"I'm going home," Tate said.

She didn't go back to her apartment. She did not have the energy for Pawel and Rose, who would be full of concern and eager to push her into an armchair in front of *The Price Is Right*. Even if she had not been in an accident, they would be waiting with a handful of junk mail for her to translate, a ploy for her company. *Come in. Have a cookie.* They were so lonely, and she just did not have the strength to add their loneliness to hers.

Instead she parked the Harley at the base of the community garden and limped up to her plot. The sunlight was turning orange as the sun slipped down between the buildings, casting long shadows among the tomatoes. Tate pulled a few blueberries off a vine, but they were sour. Inside the kiwi hut, the tree had started to smell of rusting fruit, a familiar sweet-rotten smell. She stretched out on the bench and listened to the sounds of the city until she fell asleep with her head on the hard wooden slats and her legs dangling over the edge.

Tate woke to the uncomfortable feeling of being watched. She opened her eyes to see a woman's figure silhouetted in the opening of the kiwi tree hut. She blinked. For a second, she thought it was Laura. She sat up shielding her eyes against the brightness outside.

"What are you doing?" the woman asked.

It was Abigail.

Tate dropped the hand from her eyes.

"What are *you* doing?"

"Maggie said I'd find you up here."

*Damn Maggie*, Tate thought. Maggie had never liked Abigail while they were dating, but in light of Laura Enfield, Tate gathered Abigail was looking better and better to the matriarch of gay Portland.

"What do you want?" Tate asked.

"Can I sit?"

Tate wished there was an alternate reality in which she could say, *Get the fuck out of my kiwi tree* and not sound like an idiot. As it was, she scooted to the edge of the bench so that Abigail could sit without touching her. Abigail plopped down right next to her, their thighs touching.

"Oh, Tate," Abigail said.

Nothing good began with "Oh, Tate." Tate scowled.

"What?"

"I heard about your girlfriend and Out Coffee. Maggie told me everything."

"And you've come to gloat."

"I've come to talk. I loved Out Coffee too. Everyone did. That's why I helped Maggie with the protest."

*Helped* was a funny word for it.

Abigail was wearing a green tunic that set off her fiery orange hair and dark eyes. It was the kind of contrast Tate had once found glamorous. Now Abigail reminded her of a J. R. R. Tolkien creature run through the wrong Instagram filter.

"Tate, I still love you. I was wrong about Duke. I was wrong about everything. The only thing I've ever been right about was you."

Tate stood before Abigail could do something embarrassing like grab her hand.

"If you know everything, then you know I'm not looking for anyone right now," she said.

"You knew it would never last with that woman." Abigail was using her "understanding voice." It made Tate want to kick her in the shin. "She was just playing with you. But I'm here, Tate. I'm real."

"We don't have anything in common." Tate sighed. She did not want to have this conversation.

"Be honest with yourself. Did you really have anything in common with *her*?"

Tate thought about the night in Palm Springs when she and Laura had watched the city lights and talked about their families. She said nothing to Abigail.

"Well? Did you?" Abigail pressed. "Did it ever occur to you that you were out of your league with her?"

*Every day.*

Tate spat back, "That's great coming from a third cello."

"What's that supposed to mean?" Abigail's eyes got darker.

Tate wasn't really sure. It had never meant anything to her.

"If you think that Armani-wearing pinup girl is your type, you better look in the mirror." Abigail stood, her face hardening into a more officious version of itself. "You don't even own your own car. You couldn't finish your bachelor's degree. You think you can compete with her? Did you think she was going to move into your studio apartment? Were you going to upgrade and get a one bedroom? Did you think she'd be a barback at the Mirage and ride around on your Harley? That thing is a piece of shit. I'm surprised you haven't gotten killed on it already."

"You know what?" Tate said. "You're right. She's never going to choose me. I already know that. I don't need you tromping up here to tell me. And you know what else? Compared to me and Laura, you and I are like, fucking, Siamese twins we've got so much in common. And you know what else? I'd trade our whole relationship for one week with Laura."

*Which is all I got anyway.*

Abigail folded her arms and glared at Tate.

"Get out." Tate did not care if she sounded like one of the crazy protestors who crawled up into old growth trees and let their beards grow. "This is my tree. This is my plot. My life has gone to shit, but this is still my goddamn kiwi! Go!"

"I'm leaving," Abigail said, as though it had been her idea in the first place. "I'm sorry you can't see what's right in front of you. You're obsessed with a straight girl. Most of us got over that when we were sixteen." She turned and exited the kiwi tree, slapping the branches away with unnecessary force. When she was outside, she turned. "Oh, and you'd better call Maggie. She sent me up here to find you. I wasn't just walking up here for my health. I guess that foster kid ran away, headed out to Eddyville. Maggie said you accused her of outing your girlfriend."

# Chapter 30

Tate had to borrow a phone from a man she found weeding spinach seedlings a few plots over.

"What's going on, Maggie?" she asked when she got Maggie on the phone. "Abigail just came out to the garden to tell me I'm a loser, she still loves me, and Krystal ran away."

"She wrote a letter. She's left."

It was the calm in Maggie's voice that frightened Tate. If Maggie had scolded or lectured or rattled off a list of human-trafficking statistics, she would have dismissed the whole thing. Krystal was always coming home late or going out without telling Maggie, and Maggie held Krystal on a tighter leash than she had ever used on Tate when Tate was young.

"Her father was released. She's gone to find him."

"Why?" But there was no why. He was her father. She loved him. *If he gets out, I'm going to be with him.* "Shit!"

"I know," Maggie said.

"He hurts women."

"I know."

"I'm coming over."

Tate found Maggie sitting at the kitchen table of her squat white house on Southeast 94th. In her hand, she held a piece of notebook paper, on which Tate saw Krystal's childish handwriting.

The letter read like a suicide note:

*Dear Maggie,*

*I know you don't understand why I have to do this, because you always say, "Friends are the family you make yourself." But blood is thicker than water. I never knew my real mother, but I have a real father, and he needs me right now. We'll be staying at my aunt's place in Eddyville. I would say, come and visit, but I know you can only see him through one lens, and he needs people who can see him as a whole person and not judge him.*

Tate raised her eyes to Maggie. "She's serious, isn't she?"

Maggie shrugged. Tate read on.

*Tell Tate and Vita, I didn't post those videos. I don't have a crush on Tate, and I'm tired of everyone thinking I'm this stupid kid who doesn't know anything. My father doesn't think that, and I know he accepts me for who I really am. Goodbye for now. Krystal.*

When she was done, she looked up at Maggie.

"What a load of crap."

"I did judge her, and I shouldn't have," Maggie said. "It was Laura's fault. Laura shut Out Coffee down. Laura was the one who couldn't be honest about who she was. It wasn't Krystal."

Tate stood and walked over to the kitchen sink. A dusty dream catcher hung over the sink alongside a philodendron that Tate remembered from her own childhood. She gazed out the window at the low chain-link fence that surrounded the yard and had once held in Maggie's teacup poodle, Ditto. The grass was brown. A single rose clung to a spindly rose bush by the fence.

"What are we going to do?" Maggie asked. "We can't just let her throw her life away. He'll hurt her."

Tate turned to face her slowly.

"We'll go get her."

As soon as Tate spoke, she felt the exhaustion of the past week settle on her. All she wanted to do was to lie down and to sleep for days, for weeks, until she could wake up as another person in another life. But there was no sleep like that except death, which, Tate thought glumly, was the likely outcome of charging into a murderous predator's lair to rescue Krystal from herself.

"'Blood is thicker than water,'" Tate said, tipping her head all the way back until all she could see was the textured ceiling. "As soon as she comes back, I'm going to throttle her."

Tate was still thinking the same thing a few hours later. Maggie, Tate, Lill, and Vita were all bundled into Lill's minivan, headed west. Lill had printed out pertinent court cases involving Frank Jackson and was reading them out loud to no one in particular.

"Aggravated assault of a minor. Female. 1995. Attempted rape, 2001. Rape, 2002. Soliciting a minor while in prison." Lill put the paper down for a second. "How do you even do that?" She went on. "Oh, here's the one we're looking for. In 2007 he pled guilty to the murder of Tabitha Kenelton. It says he raped her vaginally and anally with…"

"Stop," Tate said. "We know."

No one said anything else until they had exited the interstate and followed an ever-narrowing road into the coastal foothills.

Tate had been keeping enough attention on the road to avoid the log trucks that took the hairpin turns at 65 mph, but no more than that. She was deep in thought when Lill said, "Is this it?"

Tate reassessed the road ahead. Majestic fir trees lined both sides of the road.

"Where?" Tate asked.

"There." Lill pointed to a DOT sign: POPULATION 962.

At 55 mph Eddyville looked like two run-down double-wide trailers and a bridge. As they backtracked, it was clear there was a bit more to the town. Behind the double-wides were a few mossy ranch homes and at least one two-story house with sparkling white siding.

Signs pointed to Elk Creek Park and the post office. When Tate turned off the highway and onto a street that purported to be Main Street, they saw a minimart with a sign advertising cold beer, home cooking, and ammo.

The words had been hand-painted on the cinder-block wall of the store. They were well painted, Tate noticed, but done many years earlier, so the sign looked like one of those occasionally revealed when a Portland building was torn down and the brick side of the neighboring building was exposed. It was the kind of old relic that tourists liked to photograph, only here, she thought, it was just business as usual. Business as usual, except that there were no living human beings visible anywhere.

Tate pulled into the gravel parking lot. Outside the van, the air was unnaturally still. Tate remembered a headline she had read in the Oregonian: MAN JUMPS FROM MULTNOMAH FALLS, TO RESCUE DROWNING SQUIRE. Noble. Stupid. She could see her own headline forming: PORTLAND HIPSTER CONFRONTS MURDERER ARMED WITH... Tate glanced at her companions, who were stepping tentatively out of the van. ARMED WITH OTHER PORTLAND HIPSTER, AGING BARISTA, AND MONTESSORI MOTHER. *"I really thought we had what it takes,"* said Vita Galliano. *"We will always remember Tate Grafton."* It was all a really bad idea.

Before she could say anything, the door to the market opened. A woman appeared in the doorway, looking, for all the world, like a boulder with pink lipstick and a thinning perm.

"Y'all here for lunch?" she called.

This, Tate thought, was the part where the drug lord walked out and told them to leave while shooting the wheels of the van with his shotgun. When they turned the whole story into a B movie, she would get listed as Female Victim #1.

Maggie called back, "No. We're looking for Frank Jackson."

"Maggie!" Tate hissed. "Shh."

The woman's granite face grew harder.

"I don't know nothing 'bout Frank Jackson."

"We are here for lunch." Tate shot a meaningful look at her friends. "We're not really looking for Frank. We're looking for his daughter."

"Okay." The woman eyed them from under veils of electric-blue eye shadow and creased lids. "Special of the day's chicken-fried chicken."

Inside, the market was divided into three rooms. The room they entered looked like any minimart, minus most of the brand-name items plus twenty-five years' worth of dust. A door by the cash register led down a hot, narrow hallway and into a little diner. The smell of grease wafted from behind the counter. A buzzing radio played the Doors. At the back of this room, a door read LOUNGE. NO MINORS PERMITTED. A fading plastic sign showed a pregnant woman with a Do Not Enter sign pasted over her belly. ALCOHOL AND PREGNANCY DO NOT MIX.

"Have a seat wherever you like," the boulder said.

They sat. Lill opened the menu.

"Do you think they have vegan?"

"Don't ask," Tate said.

"What is chicken-fried chicken, anyway?" Vita whispered.

Tate rolled her eyes.

When the woman came back a few minutes later, they ordered coffee.

"So, you lookin' for someone?" the waitress asked.

"Maybe," Lill said, pulling a packet of stevia out of her fanny pack and adding it to her coffee.

"Outside you said you was looking for Frank Jackson or maybe not Frank Jackson," the waitress said. "You looking or no? 'Cause you're not gonna find him here."

There was a silence. Tate mustered her thoughts.

"None of my business," the waitress said, moving away from the table. "You girls have a good day."

"Wait," Tate said. There was something in the woman's antipathy that she trusted. The boulder did not like Frank Jackson any more than they did. "We are looking, and we don't know exactly how we're going to find our friend." She explained the situation.

"What's the girl's name?" the waitress asked.

"Krystal Jackson. Maggie, show her the letter," Tate said.

The waitress scowled as she read it.

"I don't got no pity for Frank Jackson. Don't know why this girl does. 'Blood is thicker than water.' Ha. So is the borax paste we use on the rats, but that don't mean I'm gonna drink it. You think Frank got this girl?"

"We think she went to him."

"Well she's not gonna wanna stay, and if I know anything 'bout the men in that family, he's not gonna let her leave. You'd better talk to my sister, Janice. That way. Through the bar. Coffee's on me. Anyone who's going up against Frank Jackson is a friend of ours. You're some brave women."

The encouragement did not make Tate feel any better. She wondered how it was possible that, a few days earlier, she had been lying naked in the arms of a beautiful real estate tycoon, while now she was destined to be killed by Frank Jackson.

She pushed open the door with the pregnant woman sign. It took a few moments for her eyes to adjust to the darkness. It was so dark, for a moment she thought the bar was closed.

"Well, y'already came this far," a voice called out.

Tate stepped into the darkness. The bar was not closed, and it was not empty. It was just the darkest pit she had ever walked into.

Tate could hear the clink of glasses, the knock of a pool ball dropping into a pocket, and then the murmur of voices starting up again as their arrival was noticed, noted, and dismissed.

As her eyes adjusted to the light, Tate made out a small square room with plastic booths, wood tables, a wall of mirrors embossed with beer logos, and a small television playing the keno games. Really, it was not that much different from the Mirage—except for the men and the elk's head mounted above the bar.

Tate ordered four Budweisers, stopping her companions with a look before Lill could say she was on a "cleanse" or before Vita could ask for a cosmo. But Maggie managed to get out, "A beer in the afternoon? No, I couldn't."

Tate despaired, but the bartender asked, "Well how's about a nice iced tea?"

He was a massive granite slab just like the waitress, but with a crew cut and a T-shirt, pulled tight over his belly, that read

NO GUTS, NO GLORY. He must have had a lot of glory, Tate thought, because he certainly had a lot of gut.

"Just drink the beer," Tate hissed.

"No, no," the bartender said. "This here's a lady, and she's delicate. An iced tea with a lemon, comin' up."

"Thank you." Maggie wiped her forehead. "It's hot out there."

"I bet you just wilt like a pretty flower."

Nothing about Maggie said "pretty flower"—lone pine, maybe; weathered sage, perhaps—but Maggie flashed the bartender an uncharacteristically girlish smile. This was getting worse, Tate thought. Maggie had snapped. She was flirting; she was using sex to manipulate the patriarchy that oppressed her. Next she'd be sporting high heels. Then Tate looked at the bartender again. Possibly, just possibly, things were getting better.

"We're looking for Janice," Tate said cautiously.

"That's me," the bartender said. "My sister send you in here? It's nice to see some family. I'm right, aren't I? Some family?"

Maggie tapped the pink triangle earring in her right ear.

"I thought so," Janice said. "So what can I do for you?"

"It's a woman," Vita whispered into Tate's ear.

*I know*, Tate mouthed.

"I thought she was a dude."

"Shh, Vita."

"Do you think she's trans?"

Tate shot Vita a look that said, *For the love of God, shut up!*

"We're trying to find a young woman who's run off with Frank Jackson," Tate said to the bartender. "Actually, we're trying to find his daughter, Krystal. She found out he got out of jail and came looking for him."

"That's sad," Janice said. She called over to the barback and invited Tate and her company to sit at a table in the corner. When they were all seated, she said, "We've had every kind of trouble with Frank. But I never seen anyone good come looking for him. Usually Frank does the looking."

"Does he come in here?" Maggie asked.

"Not since I threw him out on his scrawny ass, pardon my language."

Maggie beamed at Janice.

"You did that?"

"He's a bad man. There a lot of messed-up people out there, but most times, you can see the good person they used to be. It shines through. But if you think you've seen that in Frank, you've just seen his latest scam."

"Got any recommendations as to how we get in touch with Krystal?" Tate asked.

Janice took a sip of water and wiped the back of her mouth with her hand.

"First, I wouldn't go out there myself, not unless he got ahold of my sister or someone I really loved."

"He does," Maggie said. "Go out where?"

"He's living outside of town, off the old Logging Road 32. Supposedly. Some people says that he's out there with his sister. I don't know why a woman like that would spend a minute on him. She's Mennonite, you know. Not the kind of woman who comes in here, but a good person. Solid. Works as a nurse out in Newport."

"Can you show us where the logging road is?" Maggie asked.

"I can. But I wouldn't go out there if I was you."

"Do you think the police would go out with us?" Lill asked.

"Police? Who's hiring police around here?"

"They don't have police," Vita said in a stage whisper. "It's like the Wild West. They probably shoot people for poaching."

Janice laughed. "It's not that bad, but it's not that good neither. State police'll come if there's an incident, but there hasn't been an incident with Frank yet. We're all waiting. But so far, nothing."

"We could file a missing person report," Tate said.

"That's a fine idea, and that's what I would do too, if I could. But they're not gonna come out if she wrote her own note, saying she's wanting to be with him."

"But he's a murderer," Tate said.

"Well, what are you going to do about it?" Janice asked, putting her arm around Maggie's shoulders.

Lill, Maggie, Vita, and Janice all looked at Tate.

"You carry a gun?" Janice asked.

"Of course not," Tate said.

"But you want to talk to Frank Jackson?" Janice asked.

"Not really," Tate said.

"But we have to," Maggie added. "It's our responsibility as women, as the collective mothers and protectors of our community."

"Krystal's twenty, but she's a child." Tate sighed.

"Well…" Janice dragged the word out over three syllables. "I can take you up to Road 32, to the gate. That's an old logging road. You gotta walk the rest of the way. You sure you don't want to pick up a gun first? That's the language Frank understands."

Tate sighed and shook her head. That might be the language Frank understood, but it wasn't a language she spoke.

After lunch, they piled into Lill's van and followed Janice's faded, orange pickup truck deeper into the foothills than Tate thought one could possibly go. Finally, Janice stopped. Ahead, Tate saw a metal gate locked across the road.

Tate was starting to wish she had picked up a gun.

"Close as I know, Frank lives about a mile up and off on a side road," Janice said, pointing to the gate. "It's probably not marked, but there's only one road come off the main drag. You sure you want to do this?"

Tate was not sure. Everyone was looking at her. And suddenly it occurred to her that they weren't coming along. She had envisioned the whole gang trouping up to Frank Jackson's house. In her mind, she had stood at the front, the first to call out, the first to get killed. But they were in it together. Now she noticed that Vita was still wearing last night's stilettos. Lill had on flip-flops. And Maggie, for all her political fervor and her leftist battle cries, was an old woman. Her shoulders slouched, and she swayed when she stood up quickly. She was not going to clamber up the coastal foothills.

The forest crackled with life. To Tate it sounded like twigs snapping beneath the footsteps of the murderous Frank Jackson.

"You're frickin' crazy," Vita said.

Lill pressed the xeroxed court decisions into Tate's chest like a talisman.

"Remember," she said. "This man has killed."

Tate rolled her eyes.

"Thanks."

Tate set off up the hill. Each rocky step sent a crack of pain through her foot and up her leg. After a hundred meters, she broke off a sapling from the side of the trail to use as a cane. But the pain in her foot had kept her from focusing all of her brainpower on her own imminent death. The walking stick lessened the pain, but that freed up more brain space for Frank Jackson.

Eventually, she came to the footpath that led off the main logging road. For several meters, there was no sign of human habitation. But eventually, she thought she heard the shriek of a small child. She froze and listened, but there was only the creak of the forest as cool wind blew down the hill.

She took a few steps forward. Through the trees she made out the gray of weathered boards. She took a step forward, and another. Each time she paused, she leaned against the far side of a tree, hoping to conceal herself for as long as possible.

Eventually, she arrived at the edge of a clearing. In front of her, a single sheet flapped on a clothesline. Behind that stood a tall, weathered house. The paint was long gone. The windows were small squares.

She dropped her walking staff, so it would be evident she was unarmed, and stepped into the clearing.

The sheet flapped on the clothesline, obscuring the front

door. Behind the noise of its movement, she heard a sound she knew only from late-night TV drama: the sound of someone cocking a shotgun. And like a character from the same late-night drama, she saw her life flash before her eyes—not so much a story as a few fleeting images. Vita standing in front of a burning porch. Maggie handing her a plate of cookies. The lights dimming in a lecture hall at PSU. The espresso machine hissing at Out Coffee. Laura's face lit by the light of Palm Springs.

She heard another authoritative click as metal met metal.

# Chapter 31

Don't shoot!" Tate said.

The tip of a rifle appeared at the corner of the sheet and threw it back.

Standing before Tate was a woman of about fifty in a long dress, white sneakers, and white mesh cap over her hair.

"Who are you?" The woman's face was plain and clean, and her lips were set in a thin line.

"Tate Grafton, Portland barista." Tate raised her hands to show her good intentions. "I'm looking for Krystal Jackson. I'm a friend of hers. I just want to talk to her."

Slowly the muzzle of the rifle came away from Tate's chest. The woman eyed her from her boots to her labrys tattoo.

"You look like a friend of Krystal's." It did not sound like a compliment. "What's your business with her?"

*This must be Frank Jackson's Mennonite sister*, Tate thought. She was not sure how honest to be. Perhaps blood *was* thicker than water. Perhaps this godly woman would not appreciate the fact that Tate had come to rescue Krystal from her brother.

"I'm worried about her," Tate said.

"I asked Krystal if she left any loose ends in Portland. She said no. Would you call yourself loose ends?"

"Maybe."

"Meaning?"

"Krystal's been living with my friend, Maggie. We had a disagreement. Krystal left us a note, and said she'd gone to see her father."

"And you're worried 'bout what my brother might do to her now he's been released."

It wasn't a question, and Tate did not bother denying.

"You better come in," the woman added.

Tate approached the house slowly. Inside it was as quiet as the forest beyond. It took her a moment to realize what was missing: TV, radio, the hum of a refrigerator. There was only the slightly muffled sound of the wind.

"Sit," the woman said.

The woman took a seat at the table across from her. She was silent for a long time.

Finally, she said, "There are a lot of people lookin' for my brother, lot of people who aren't celebrating his homecoming."

"I'm sorry," Tate said.

"Ran into some men down in town said they was looking for Frank, said he owed them a debt. They said they'd come looking for him if he didn't get them their money. I told them the only debt Frank owes he paid to the state of Oregon. Rest is up to the Lord. But they'll be back. I know they will. That's why I have the shotgun. Didn't mean to scare you."

"You didn't," Tate said reflexively. "Well you did, but I understand."

"I'm not sure you do."

The silence stretched between them.

"No. You're probably right."

*She's killed him*, Tate thought. She's killed Frank and Krystal, and now she's going to kill me.

A pale-faced boy of about six appeared at the window in the back door, startling Tate with his ghostly appearance.

"It's okay. Come in, son," Frank's sister called. "My Zacharia won't leave my side, never does."

The boy pushed open the door and ran across the kitchen on bare feet. He buried his head in his mother's lap.

"She's not one of the bad men I told you about," the woman said to him.

"When are they coming?" the boy spoke into her skirts.

"We don't know when they're coming, but you know what to do when you hear someone."

"Hide," the boy said and began to cry.

The woman pushed him off her, rather roughly for Tate's taste.

"What did I tell you? I told you you could be a grown boy or you could stay with Miss Aster from church. Which'll it be?"

"I want to stay with you." The boy sniffed, the effort to hold back tears turning his face red.

"And what do you do if you hear someone who isn't Uncle Frank or New Sister?"

"Hide in the root cellar and don't come out 'til I hear someone I knowed."

The woman patted his head.

"Okay. Go bring in your toys." To Tate she said, "Miss
Grafton?"

"Yes."

"You came here to see Krystal. I think it's time you see
Frank too."

Tate followed Frank Jackson's sister up a flight of stairs as steep
as a ladder. The top of the stairs opened onto a narrow corri-
dor with two closed doors. The space was dark, except for a
small window at the end of the hallway. Tate noticed something else that was missing. Light fixtures. She scanned the
baseboards—no sockets. Above their heads only the stained
plaster. There was no electricity. She opened her mouth to
comment, then closed it.

"In here," the woman said, knocking gently on one door,
then pushing it open. The room hung heavy with the scent
of disinfectant, urine, and, over that, something like sage. As
Tate's eyes adjusted to the dark she saw a plain room, like an
Andrew Wyeth painting. Curtains were drawn over the window. In the middle of the room stood a bed. In it lay the
remains of a man, like someone who had starved or desiccated.

"Tate!"

A voice from the corner of the room startled her. It was
Krystal, dressed in a loose gown and wearing a handkerchief
over her hair. Tate rushed over. Krystal flew into her arms.

"Are you all right? We were so worried." Tate squeezed her.

"Shhh," the sister said. "He's resting quietly."

"I'm sorry, Sarah," Krystal said, falling out of Tate's embrace. "Sarah, you met my friend Tate." Krystal clasped her hands and looked down.

"You said no loose ends, Krystal," Sarah said. "You told me you'd made your peace with everyone you was leaving behind."

"I did," Krystal mumbled.

"Well, clearly you didn't because she's here. We got too many loose ends here already."

"I wrote a letter."

"Then you didn't say what needed saying."

"Yes, ma'am."

The transformation was shocking. Gone were the pink pigtails. Gone was the bubble-gum-pink lipstick, the Hello Kitty purse, and the eighteen-buckle boots.

"Are you okay?" Tate asked again, trying to catch Krystal's eye so Krystal could signal her unspoken distress. Krystal met her eyes, but there was no hidden message.

"This is my father," she said. "They let him out because he has liver cancer. They let him out because it was too expensive to take care of him in prison, and they wanted him to die." She looked at the bed, her face a mask of grief. "How could they do that, Tate?"

Sarah put her hand on Krystal's shoulder.

"He'll be with God soon."

"But I want him to be with me."

Sarah frowned.

The figure in the bed stirred. Tate jumped.

"Is he in pain?" Tate asked.

"No," Sarah said.

"Sarah's a hospice nurse. She takes care of people like him."

Tate heard pride in Krystal's voice.

"How long does he have?" Tate asked.

"Krystal-Anne, go downstairs and fetch a glass of water and make sure Brother Zacharia isn't playing with the chickens."

When Krystal had disappeared downstairs, Sarah sat wearily in a faded wingback armchair.

"About a week. Less probably. He's just using up the last of his air. That's what my gram used to say. It's one last, long sigh, this part of life is."

Gingerly, Tate lowered herself into a facing chair. In the dim light, Sarah looked older and less stern. She rubbed her hands together and gazed past Tate.

"I knew it would come down to this. Him dying and the rest of the family not knowing to grieve or to just thank the Lord for a safe passage. But I didn't figure on her." She glanced toward the door.

"Krystal was in foster care since she was ten," Tate said.

"Probably for the best. Frank had the devil in him," Sarah said, as though Tate were not in the room.

"Why are you taking care of him here?"

"He's my brother."

*Blood is thicker than water*, Tate thought and felt glad that she had picked her family. At the same time, she appreciated something in Sarah's plain speech. It was clear: In her world there were some things one had to do out of duty because honor called for it. Perhaps Sarah wasn't that different from Laura. Weren't these the same reasons Laura had pushed her into the closet? Wasn't it all because of her family's greater calling?

"You could put him in a hospital," Tate said.

"God brought him back to me for a reason."

Krystal appeared with the water.

"Maybe so I'd meet Krystal-Anne," Sarah added. "Set that water down for your father then come and talk to your Miss Grafton."

"Tate," Tate said.

Sarah gave her a closed smile and said nothing.

"Tell her what your plans are," Sarah said to Krystal.

"I'm going to stay here with my dad," Krystal said.

Tate hesitated.

"And after…?" she asked.

"I'm going to learn about my family."

"What about your GED?" Tate asked.

"We'll see to it she gets her education," Sarah said.

"I'm going to be a certified nursing assistant like my cousin Louisa."

"Are you sure this is what you want?" Tate held Krystal's gaze again. "Maggie is down at the foot of that logging road, and she's waiting to take you home if you want to go. No one cares about those videos."

"I didn't post those videos."

"No one cares if you did," Tate said.

"Well, I'm staying."

Tate looked from Krystal to Sarah.

"Back home there are people who care about you. Maggie thinks of you like a daughter."

"I'm his daughter!" Krystal pointed toward her father.

Tate stared at the man in the bed. There was so little left of him. It was hard to imagine that he was anyone's father, but Krystal sounded as certain as she had ever been about anything.

"He is my father," Krystal said.

Tate tried to picture Krystal's life. She could stay with Sarah and wear a modest dress in a house without electricity. She could be a CNA and tend to the sick with Christian devotion. Maybe she would marry a logger and have a brood of children. Or maybe she would walk back down the hill, dye her hair Crayola purple, and spend her twenties barhopping and taking anthropology classes at community college. Maybe she would start her own coffee shop or become an activist or meet a girl and join the Peace Corps. Tate thought, *This is the moment when you choose.*

What about the choices she had made? What would have happened if she had picked her studies over Maggie's coffee shop? What if she had waited in Laura's closet? For that matter, what if she had tolerated her stepbrother's abuse, stayed in the house, lived with her mother? There was no way to know. It seemed to Tate one simply had to walk blindly forward into the world, hoping for solid ground.

"I won't force you to come back," Tate said. "But please, will you at least write to Maggie and let her know you're okay? She's so worried."

"You can tell her," Krystal said. "I can't tell her. I know what she's done for me, but I can't be her daughter like that."

"She'll write," Sarah said. "I'll see to it she appreciates those that helped her when she needed helping. Now, Miss Grafton, I think you'd better go."

They were halfway down the stairs when Tate heard the sound of branches snapping and an engine roaring. A second later, the little boy flew into his mother's skirts.

"They're here," he said, his voice muffled. "They're here. The bad men who want to take Uncle Frank."

"Get back in the cellar," Sarah barked. "Krystal, you lock yourself in your father's room. Stay away from that window."

Tate followed Sarah down the stairs, but when she reached the bottom step her bad leg buckled beneath her and she sank to the ground. Cowering in the stairwell, unsure whether to fight or flee, and unsure how she would go about either one, she wished that she and Krystal were in the root cellar with the boy, but it was too late.

Through the brown lace of the front curtain she could see the grille of an enormous vehicle, the chrome like shining teeth. The engine growled to a stop. A car door slammed. Hard, angry footsteps marched up the wooden stairs outside. Sarah grabbed the shotgun and braced herself against the kitchen table, the rifle trained on the door. The door flew open.

At first, Tate thought she was hallucinating. Perhaps the sound she had taken for the door slamming against the wall was really a gunshot. She touched her chest. Perhaps she had been shot. This must be a last, fading dream, for it appeared to be Laura Enfield bursting through the door in high heels, a navy skirt suit, and too much gold jewelry.

"Laura!"

It did not make sense. She looked like a cutout from a magazine pasted on the Andrew Wyeth painting that was Sarah's house. And she was walking directly into the muzzle of Sarah's shotgun.

"This is unnecessary," Laura said, as though this was a business meeting she could control with a stern tone. "Put that thing down before you kill someone."

"Get back," Sarah said.

"Drop the gun."

Tate heard the ominous click of metal locking into place.

"Sarah, no!" Tate yelled. "I know her."

"I said put it down," Laura barked.

Tate watched the next seconds in slow motion. Laura reached for the shotgun. Sarah took a step back and stumbled against the table. A shot rang out. Instinctively Tate closed her eyes. One arm flew up to cover her face. She heard Laura yell "No!" Then a painful ringing silence followed the shot.

# Chapter 32

When Tate opened her eyes, Laura was standing in front of Sarah. Both women held the gun, its muzzle pointing toward the empty kitchen.

"Tate!" Laura called.

Tate staggered to her feet, grasping the banister for support.

"What have they done to you?" Laura ripped the shotgun from Sarah's hands and pushed her with the butt end. "If you hurt her, I'll kill you."

"Stop. She's my friend," Tate said, lurching forward. She wasn't sure who she was referring to. It really wasn't true of either one of them. "Sarah, she's not here to hurt you. Laura, put down the gun."

From the top of the stairs Krystal called out, "Oh my God! What happened?" She hurried down the stairs, her footsteps echoing in the sudden quiet. When she got to the bottom, she asked, "Is that Hillary Clinton? It is! What's she doing here?"

"Just leave us alone." Sarah sagged into a kitchen chair, her hands displayed in protest. Her eyes darted from Tate to Laura. "Please. Take whatever you want, just leave me and my family."

Laura looked around the room. "Take what? I only came for Tate."

"I knew you'd be back." Krystal bounded down the stairs. "Because of the videos."

"You said no loose ends," Sarah said.

Tate saw the Krystal she knew reassert herself. Krystal put her hands on the hips of her long dress.

"They're not *my* loose ends. It's not *my* fault those two can't figure it out. I told them. They're in love, and they won't admit it. No one ever listens to me. Sheesh!"

Sarah opened her mouth and closed it without a word.

Laura grabbed Tate's arm.

"We're getting out of here."

She still held the gun.

*Sorry*, Tate mouthed to Sarah, allowing Laura to pull her toward the door.

Outside, Laura hurried Tate to the door of an enormous black SUV.

"Quick. Get in." Laura glanced at the house as she closed the door behind Tate. Then she hurried over to the other side. "Is she going to come after us?"

Tate shook her head.

"Are you sure?"

"She's harmless."

Laura took the shotgun and tossed it, muzzle first, into the underbrush. Then in one incredibly graceful and authoritative movement, she swung up into the enormous vehicle, started the engine, and roared out of the clearing with a burst of speed that knocked Tate's head back against the headrest.

"My God, look at you," Laura said as the SUV bumped along, crushing the small saplings and blackberry vines that lined the narrow path. "What did they do to you? You're limping. Your face!" Laura reached tentatively toward Tate's face, but even the SUV's massive suspension system could not smooth over the rocky path Laura had cleared through the underbrush, and her hand bounced away before she could touch Tate.

"I'm fine," Tate said.

They reached the logging road, which was much closer when one reached it by crushing everything in the way with a vehicle the size of a tank.

Laura said, "How long have you been up there?"

"Twenty minutes."

"They beat you." Laura's voice was strained, and she looked at Tate so intently Tate pointed to the road to remind her of the trees they were coming close to hitting.

"They didn't beat me. I'm fine."

Eventually, they reached the bottom of the road, where Lill's van was still parked and Lill, Maggie, Vita, and Janice were still milling around like bystanders waiting for a traffic accident to clear.

Laura turned off the SUV. She made no move to get out or roll down the window. For a long time, she looked at Tate, then very tenderly she brushed her cheek.

"What happened, baby?"

The term of endearment and the tenderness in Laura's voice nearly broke Tate's heart. It would be so easy to fall into Laura's arms, to forget that they were entirely wrong for each other, to forget what she had known lying on the Hawthorne Bridge surrounded by the Portland Gay Men's Choir: that she might be able to steal another kiss, but in the end she was careering toward heartbreak. It was up to her to look, clear-eyed, into the future and protect herself from ruin.

And then she was in Laura's arms.

Her body betrayed her. Laura reached across the gap between the seats, and, a second later, Tate's head was cradled against her shoulder. Laura was stroking her hair with one hand, pulling her close with the other. The warmth of Laura's body and the comfort of her touch were too much. Tate heard a soft moan escape her own lips.

"Talk to me," Laura said. "What happened?"

Tate didn't trust her own voice. She felt exhausted, as though the weight of the past three days had crushed her.

"You're shaking." Laura held her tighter, and Tate winced. "How did you get this bruise? I need you to tell me."

"My bike. I lost control on the bridge. What are you doing here?"

Laura's fingertips grazed her side, lifting the hem of her shirt.

"Oh, God, you're bruised all over." She released Tate from her embrace as though suddenly afraid to break her. Then very gently she pulled her shirt up, exposing the whole blue-and-purple expanse of Tate's ribs. Laura drew in a sharp breath.

"What happened? Why didn't you call me? You shouldn't be up here. What did the doctors say?"

Tate pulled away, wiping the threat of tears from her eyes.

"I can't afford a doctor. You know that."

Tate pushed the car door open and stepped out. She was reeling, trying to take in the strange juxtaposition of people and events. Sarah waving a shotgun. Krystal standing over the bed of her murderous father, now reduced to a husk of a man. She turned back to Laura, who was getting out of the car too.

"Why are you here?" Tate asked.

She did not get to hear the answer. Maggie was at her side.

"Where is she?" Maggie asked. "What happened? Why didn't you get her? She's not there. She's dead, isn't she? This is all her fault." Maggie pointed at Laura.

Tate walked over to Lill's van. The sliding side door was open. She sat down on the running board of the van and rested her chin in her hands.

Vita was trying to explain something about Laura. Lill was talking very quickly. Tate caught a few snatches, like "carbon footprints" and "... rare species of trillium crushed into nothing!" Maggie leaned in close.

"What happened? Who's up there? Why didn't you get her?"

Tate did not know what else to do, so she started at the beginning.

When Tate was done with the story, Maggie said, "You have to go back."

"What?" Tate looked up.

"Krystal's alone up there, with some crazy woman and drug

dealers trying to kill her. Laura!" Maggie called out. "Laura, take her back up there."

Laura still had not explained how she came to be charging up a hill in a rented SUV, nor had she added anything to Tate's telling of the story. Now all eyes turned to her.

"Absolutely not," she said. "We have been here too long already."

"You have to!" Maggie pleaded.

"Honestly, I don't think she wants to come back," Tate said.

"She doesn't know what she wants," Maggie said.

Tate shrugged. "He's her father. He's dying. And he's here. She's desperate to have him in her life."

"She has us!"

"It's not the same." Tate felt very tired.

"But it's better," Maggie said. "This is the family we choose."

"I know." Tate dropped her head into her hands. Her foot throbbed, and she felt like she might faint. "But this is a gift. That's the whole point. You took her in when no one else would."

"So why would she leave?"

"She feels like she owes you. She'll always owe you, and even though you *never* would, you could take it all back. But these people..."—she shrugged weakly—"...for better or for worse, they will always be her family. No one can take that away, and she never has to pay that back."

Tate looked up. It was a miracle, that kind of gift. When she looked back on her own life, she saw it clearly. There was no getting out from underneath that kind of debt.

"She doesn't owe me anything," Maggie said.

"She owes you everything." She did not know if she was speaking for Krystal or for herself.

A second later, she felt Laura's hand on her shoulder. She stared down at the ground. In her peripheral vision she caught Laura's slender ankle and her gold-tipped heels.

"But what am I supposed to do?" Tate heard Maggie's voice as if from a great distance. "You're gone. Lill's gone. Out Coffee is gone. Krystal's all I've got. I'll be all alone. Tate, go back there."

Somewhere in the outer atmosphere, Vita said, "Maybe Maggie's right."

Tate stared at the ground again. She was very, very tired. For a second her vision went black. The conversation above her head blurred into a murmur from which she caught only phrases.

"Those people…"

"…if he's dying."

"Tate won't mind."

"I mind." That was Laura. She spoke again. "Look at her!"

It took Tate a moment to realize Laura meant her.

"She can barely walk. She has a black eye. *Look at her.*"

Tate rather wished they wouldn't.

"Oh, Tate." Maggie clasped her hands to her chest.

"What the hell did they do to you?" Vita asked. "Those bastards!"

"She had a black eye when you dragged her up here," Laura said. "You just didn't notice."

It wasn't really fair. The bruise on her face had faded to a pale yellow. It was just a shadow now.

"Tate, is that true?" Maggie asked.

Tate nodded wearily.

Laura said, "I'm taking her to the hospital, which is what *you* should have done before you came charging out here."

"I'm fine," Tate mumbled as Laura slipped a hand under her elbow and lifted her from the running board.

"Wait!" Maggie called after her.

But the doors to the SUV were already closed, and Laura's hand was on Tate's knee.

"I'm sorry, Tate. I'm so sorry."

Tate slept most of the way back from Eddyville, both because she was exhausted and because she feared that speaking might bring on a deluge of tears.

When Tate finally opened her eyes, they had pulled into the parking lot of a hospital off Highway 217.

"Laura, I can't afford a doctor, and I'm fine," Tate said.

"I'll take care of it."

"You don't have to."

"Yes, I do," Laura said.

Inside, the urgent care clinic was blessedly quiet. Tate let Laura lead her into the building and usher her into a seat like a child.

"Stay here," Laura said gently.

Tate tried to muster the energy to say something, but she could not think of anything.

At the front counter, the receptionist asked Laura, "What's the patient's name?"

Standing at the counter in her navy suit, clutch purse, and

gold-tipped heels, Laura looked more like a CEO than a woman bringing someone to the hospital. It occurred to Tate that if Vita had taken her to the clinic, or she had taken Maggie, or Maggie had taken Lill, the receptionist would have asked, *What's your friend's name?* But Laura did not have friends like Tate. Everyone could see that.

Laura said Tate's full name, and then spelled it.

"Amber Tatum Grafton. A-M-B…"

Tate wondered how Laura had learned her first name. For that matter, how did she know Tate's birth date and address?

"Insurance?" the receptionist asked.

Laura glanced over at Tate. Tate shook her head.

"I'll pay," Laura said.

"Just for the intake examination?"

"Whatever she needs." Laura placed a credit card on the counter.

The receptionist disappeared behind a cloth-covered cubicle divider.

Laura turned to face Tate, leaning her back against the counter.

Tate stared at her. She was so beautiful. Maybe, Tate thought, rich people were born prettier. They did not get stuck with archetypal noses. Or maybe they just bought the right features. Maybe Laura's mother had handed over the same credit card when Laura turned eighteen and had some surgeon smooth everything over. That was surely what Laura was doing now. Smoothing things over. Avoiding a scandal. Tate wanted to believe it was love in Laura's eyes. When Laura sat down beside her and gently put her arm around Tate's shoulders, Tate's body told her it was love. But her mind knew better. She knew from experience.

"Please don't," she said very quietly, pulling away from Laura's touch.

A few minutes later, she followed an orderly past a thin curtain, into the back of the clinic. He took her weight, her blood pressure, and a short version of her life story. Then a young man in scrubs x-rayed her foot and her chest. An hour later, a doctor in a yarmulke sat down across from her and explained that she had hairline fractures in three of the bones in her right foot.

"Nothing else. Just some bruising. You got off lucky. These things are more painful than they are dangerous," he said kindly. "Crutches for three weeks and you should be fine. Come back for a follow up x-ray just to be sure. I'll give you a painkiller for the next couple days."

"Thank you," Tate said, although she knew the pain in her heart would outlast any pill the doctor could give her.

Tate was relieved when they finally arrived at her apartment. It was after midnight, and even Pawel and Rose had given up their sentry post.

"Thank you," Tate said because it was the right thing to say. "For taking me to the hospital."

She opened the car door. The dome light threw a faint glow on the peeling-paint exterior of her apartment building. It was such a far cry from the desert mansion, just a box with windows and a spider-web-encrusted stairwell. There wasn't even a light fixture on the bare bulb that hung over the foyer. Still, it was home.

"Can I come up?" Laura asked.

Of course she wanted Laura to come up. She wanted Laura to carry her up the stairs, throw her on the bed like a romance heroine and say, *Tate, I love you. I've told my family everything.* But that would happen when Vita stopped womanizing and Maggie got a job investing stocks for Wells Fargo.

"Why?" Tate asked.

Laura released the death grip she had on the steering wheel.

"I need to talk to you about the videos."

*The videos.*

"Come up," Tate said reluctantly.

She wrestled the crutches out from the backseat of the SUV and swung herself out of the car on one leg. But when she reached the stairs, she tucked the crutches under one arm and headed up on two feet.

"Wait." Laura stood beneath the bare bulb and the cobwebs, as out of place as a marble sculpture. "You're not supposed to walk on that leg."

"It's a little late for that." Tate took the first step. She did not even wince. "I'm not going to hop upstairs."

"Just sit down and climb up. I'll hold your crutches."

Tate eyed Laura. Her perfect suit. Her perfect face.

"I don't think so."

"But you could make it worse."

"Hiking up a mountain so I could get shot at by some gun-wielding Mennonite made it worse." At the top of the stairs, Tate turned to Laura again. "And I'm not worried about my foot. I'm worried about my pride."

After everything Laura had put her through, it was still so

easy to be honest. She hoped her smile was as wry and un-touchable as Laura's.

Inside her apartment, Tate lowered herself onto the edge of the bed. Laura produced a bottle from her purse and handed it to Tate with a glass of water.

"The doctor said you should take one."

So it was going to be *that* kind of conversation, Tate thought, the kind that was better with narcotics. She did not feel like arguing. The water tasted metallic.

"I didn't post those videos," she said, as Laura settled into a chair on the opposite side of the room. "I'm sorry that some-one did. I'm sorry that happened to you. I think it was Krystal, but she swears it wasn't. I'll ask around, but I don't know if I can take them down."

The medication hit her faster than she expected. The world began to swim around her. The titles of her books blurred. Her photographs came in and out of focus.

"But you shouldn't have shut us down like that. You could have at least warned me. I didn't deserve any of this. I didn't do anything to you," she murmured. "Why did you even come back? How did you find me?"

Through the fog of fatigue and hydrocodone Tate saw Laura float toward her. Then her crutches were gone, her jacket lifted from her shoulders, and she was lying down. Laura leaned over her, her brow furrowed, her eyes in shadows. She seemed to be searching Tate's face for something.

*If I asked, she would stay*, Tate thought. Then she closed her eyes and was instantly asleep. In her dreams, Laura took off her suit. Her pantyhose pooled on the floor. Then her arms were around Tate, her legs across Tate's hip. They were both naked. *I love you.*

Tate startled awake. Laura was still dressed, still standing over her, staring at her with a look of consternation.

"Laura." Tate hated the tremor she heard in her own voice. She wanted to be commanding, aloof. "I care about you."

*I love you.*

"I care about you too," Laura said, kneeling beside the bed.

Tate closed her eyes.

"But," Tate began, "I'm tired. I don't feel well. I want to make the right decision this time. I don't...I can't...I need you to make this easy for me, and, please, just leave."

Speaking the words hurt more than hitting the metal rails of the steel bridge, but it was the right thing to do. Tate knew. This was the answer she should have given Laura the first night at the Mirage. *You won't even tell me your name?*

# Chapter 33

It took about twenty minutes for Laura to admit to herself that she had become a stalker. No...the stalking had been completed successfully. Now she was an intruder.

For the first seconds after Tate told her to leave, she simply stared at her, waiting for her to wake again. Then for several minutes she watched to make sure Tate was all right. The painkiller had hit her so quickly she had nearly collapsed, and Laura wondered if the dosage was too high or if she was having an allergic reaction. But after several minutes, Tate rolled over on her side and curled her body around a spare pillow. Clearly asleep. And all Laura wanted to do was stand over her and watch her stern face, worried even in sleep. So noble, so true. But something about hovering over the sleeping form of a woman to whom she had just administered drugs—even if they were prescribed—said "serial killer." Laura sat down at the kitchen table, which wasn't much better. *Go*, she told herself, but instead she rested her chin on her folded arms because she felt certain that if she left now, she left forever.

Laura was not sure how long she had been asleep with her head on the kitchen table. It could have been hours or just a fleeting second. It was still dark out. A moment later, she realized she had been awoken by the sound of Tate crutching the eight or so steps it took to reach the bathroom. Click, step. Click, step. Tate watched the floor carefully, but even on crutches there was something confidently athletic about her movements.

Laura watched the light come on in the bathroom. Tate had not closed the door. Why would she? She was alone in her own apartment. Supposedly. Laura worked through the scenario. If Tate turned the light off when she exited, she might not see Laura at the kitchen table. She might fall back in bed and back asleep before spotting Laura. But then, the apartment was considerably smaller than the smallest swimming pool Laura had ever bought, and her breathing sounded monstrously loud.

The toilet flushed. Tate washed her hands. The light stayed on. Tate was awake. In a second she was going to step from the bathroom, perhaps to sit quietly in her apartment and take stock of the life Laura Enfield had ruined. Only she would not have a chance to sit alone with a bottle of plum sake—or whatever Portlanders drank when they were depressed—because Laura was still in her kitchen.

"I'm sorry," Laura said as Tate emerged from the bathroom.

Tate jumped, dropping the crutches.

"You're here," she said. She limped over to her bed, where she sat down with a perplexed look. "You're still here."

At least it wasn't, *Why are you still here?*

"I was worried about you." It sounded lame.

Laura searched Tate's face in the blue darkness, but she looked only curious and slightly disapproving. *She doesn't need me*, Laura thought.

"You've been here the whole time." Tate hesitated. "Watching me sleep?"

Laura knew it didn't look good.

"I just…I needed to talk to you."

"Now?" Tate picked up a fold of the blanket and examined the stitching.

"I didn't want to leave, and I didn't want to wake you."

"So what did you want to talk to me about?" Tate did not look up.

"I know you didn't post those videos."

"I didn't," Tate concurred. "They were from Krystal's phone." She pulled at a thread in the blanket. "But I swear I'd never seen them before they showed up online."

"I know you didn't post them because I did."

Tate looked up. Laura hoped she would smile. She wanted to see Tate's face come to life with that wide, honest smile that was so much more precious because it was rare.

Instead, Tate said, "You can't do this to me." It was a fact, not a request.

"I posted them." Laura heard the desperation in her own voice. "I tagged them. It was me."

"I don't know what you're talking about." Tate frowned. "I don't...I *can't* care. You made it really clear that you couldn't live this kind of life, that you can't be out, and I can't be your dirty secret."

"But that's why I did it. I don't want you to be a secret. Please listen to me," Laura pleaded. "The thing is, I asked Krystal to take them and send them to me, but not for that. I was just so happy that night. I was happy with you. I realized I'd never be that happy again, and I wanted proof. I didn't want it to disappear. You. Me. That night. The dancing. This city. Then my family showed up, and I panicked. I should have taken your hand and introduced you as my lover...my love. I saw you walking away. We were in the middle of planning the next press conference in the living room, and I just threw it out there. 'I'm here with a woman.'"

The story poured out. She wasn't sure if it made any sense.

"They were pissed, and I went looking for you, but I couldn't find you. I saw that you had booked your return flight, and I was going to fly to Portland that afternoon and say I was sorry. Then my father had a heart attack. That's what my brother told me. He told me that he'd talked to my dad, told him I'd come out, and that my father had had a heart attack right there. I flew back to Alabama. I thought it was my fault."

"No one drops dead of a heart attack because they find out their daughter is gay," Tate said.

"Maybe in Alabama they do, but that's the thing. He hadn't. I was sitting in the hospital cafeteria. Alone. I was trying to figure out how it was that I had to choose between killing him and loving you. I was thinking about everything I was giving up. Then I ran into this guy I went to college with. He's a resident at the hospital. We were talking about my father, and he just let it slip, because he thought I knew. My dad didn't have a heart attack. He went in for a routine coronary angiogram. It's outpatient, but my dad asked the hospital to hold him for a few days, and they did because he's Stan Enfield."

Tate said nothing.

"It was all a scam. They wanted me to think I'd given him a heart attack. When I called them on it, they just laughed. They thought it was clever. They thought I'd be happy that they'd helped me see the light. It was just one more PR gambit, and they really thought they could just slap me on the back, and we'd keep on going. Business as usual. So I posted the videos, and I tagged myself in them, and I called the newspapers in Alabama, and I told them."

*A video.* It had felt like such a grand gesture at the time. Now, in the face of Tate's silence, it was nothing.

"I realized there was nothing I wanted more than you. There was no place I wanted to be except here."

"You don't have the right." Tate's voice was cold and quiet. She stared at the blanket in her lap, pulling angrily on the threads. "You didn't have the right to pick me up at the Mirage when you *knew* what you were going to do. You let me take you home, you let me love you…"

Laura's heart lifted at the words. *Love you…*

"And all that time you thought you could just play both sides." Tate's voice cracked. "We could be lovers for a week, while you were here, because it didn't count. Because I don't count. Because you could go back to your real life. But you put me out of work. You closed down a place that was home for me."

Tate shivered but did not look up.

*I'll buy you another coffee shop*, Laura wanted to say. *And a house, and a pension for Maggie. I'll take you to the hospital, always and forever. I will pay anything to make this right.*

The thread Tate had pulled from the blanket had begun a cascade of unraveling. It wasn't a blanket, Laura thought. It was an afghan. It was *knit*. Tate wrapped the yarn around her hand. She would probably reuse it. She would reknit it, maybe into a sweater or a handbag. It had probably been a handbag, and now it was an afghan, and then it would be a sweater. With stripes. Tate would wear it under her motorcycle jacket in the winter on her way to some ridiculously noble job. You could not buy that kind of integrity. It was so ludicrous and impossible and beautiful, and Laura's heart simply broke as she watched Tate sit there in silence pulling the blanket to yarn.

"You asked me to go," Laura said finally. "I'm sorry. I had no right to stay here." The space between them seemed to expand. Laura scanned the room, looking for some place to rest her eyes. Her hands were tight on the edge of the table. "Do you want me to go?"

She held her breath.

Tate touched the side of her face where the bruise was fading.

"I am so sorry, Tate."

Laura moved from the table and knelt on the floor beside Tate's bed because there was nothing she could do but kneel.

"I am so very, very sorry. I thought I could prove how much I loved you—because I love you so much—but it all went wrong. As soon as Clark-Vester found out about the videos, they wanted to put as much distance as they could between me and you and the whole scandal. They couldn't support Stan Enfield and own a building with 'Out in Portland' emblazoned in rainbow letters on the side."

"It is a little garish," Tate said.

"I had no idea they had evicted Out in Portland until I went there to find you. You were gone. I swear I decided I was going to drink myself into a stupor at that bar you like. I was just going to sit there until…I don't know. Then Abigail, with those freckles, told me you'd probably gone on some crazy mission to save Krystal from her father because you thought she had posted the videos. I thought, I've done it again. I lost you your job. I got Out in Portland evicted. And then I found out you were chasing after some murderer in the forest, and it was all my fault. Thank God Eddyville is the size of a postage stamp. Everyone knew who you were and where you'd gone, so I went after you."

Laura thought she saw the slightest intimation of a smile at the corner of Tate's mouth.

"That was rather spectacular," Tate said. "That SUV is a tank."

"I didn't know where I was going. I figured I should rent the best. At least the biggest."

"Thanks."

"You're the best lover and the only real friend I have in the whole world," Laura said.

Tate drew back and looked at Laura.

"You wrecked my life," she said. But Laura could tell she was trying not to smile. "You're worse than Krystal. I'm surprised you haven't set something on fire."

Tentatively, Laura rose and sat beside Tate. She put her arm around Tate's shoulder, then withdrew it quickly, afraid to hurt her and certain Tate would shrug off her embrace. But Tate did not pull away, only drew in a breath.

"Do you still want me to go?"

Tate lay back on the pillows.

"I never wanted you to go."

Laura felt like she would break in half, torn by so much passion and tenderness. She wanted to devour Tate, and she wanted to hold her as lightly as a butterfly in a gilded cage. She wanted to rip Tate's clothes from her body, mount her so forcefully the futon collapsed into the sum of its wooden parts, and she wanted to enshrine every object in the apartment, a testament to Tate's life. To her goodness.

Instead Laura unbuttoned the top two buttons of her shirt. She glanced at Tate.

"May I?" she asked.

Tate nodded.

Slowly Laura removed her shirt and her bra, her heels and her nylons. She did not even feel embarrassed as she dropped her skirt to reveal the flesh-colored infrastructure of her spandex body shaper.

"What are you wearing?" Tate asked. Her voice was gently teasing.

Laura laughed and leaned over and kissed Tate.

"This is something you should never know about," she said and wriggled out of the tight garment.

"That's better." Tate's eyes lingered on her body. "That's beautiful."

When she was naked, Laura slid into bed beside Tate and lifted Tate's shirt over her head. Tears welled up in her eyes when she saw the bruises along Tate's side.

"I don't want to hurt you," she whispered.

"Then don't."

Laura knew Tate was not talking about the bruises. She ran her hand along the curve of Tate's hip, so lightly she barely felt her skin. Outside, the first hint of dawn was turning the black sky navy.

"What time is it anyway?" Tate asked, glancing at the bedside alarm clock.

"Almost five," Laura said. She kissed Tate on the forehead. "Sleep. I'll be here in the morning."

*Every morning.*

Gently, Laura pulled Tate to her, nestling Tate's head on her chest, stroking Tate's short hair. Slowly, she felt Tate relax into the rhythmic touch.

"Sleep," Laura whispered. "I won't go anywhere."

Lying with Tate cocooned in her arms the night before, Laura had disavowed all earthly goods. She was ready to live in a studio apartment and eat brown rice and bike her compost to the community garden. But daylight came, and with it realism. People only changed so much in a lifetime, let alone a night, and she was not going to live in an apartment the size of a subway car.

She lay on her side, watching Tate, who was watching her with a look of concern. That was what poverty did to people, Laura thought. It made them worry. And that was why this life—the tiny apartment, the missing health insurance, the day-to-day labor—was simply not going to work for her.

# Chapter 34

Tate, I have to talk to you," Laura said.

Tate closed her eyes and fell back on the pillow, bracing herself.

Laura slid out of bed, donned Tate's robe, and went over to the counter, where she started a pot of coffee brewing.

"Cream? Sugar?" she asked.

"Just black," Tate said without opening her eyes.

She heard Laura moving around the tiny kitchen, opening a cupboard, stirring sugar into her own cup. Then she felt the futon sag as Laura sat on the edge of the bed.

"Look at me." Laura set both coffees down on the bedside table.

Tate opened her eyes.

Laura looked worried. She looked like a woman about to deliver bad news.

Tate felt anxiety rising in her chest. *I knew it.*

"Did I tell you I got fired?" Laura asked.

"No." Tate rose to a sitting position, wincing a little bit. She propped herself against the headboard. *Don't hope*, she thought. But her body was more optimistic. She had fallen asleep to the comfort of Laura's body easing away pain. Now she felt as though every nerve reached out for pleasure. Even the blue sky in the window seemed to caress her. *Don't be reasonable*, her body said. *She's right there. It's summer.* She reached out and stroked Laura's thigh. "What happened?"

"I should have seen it coming. Clark-Vester has been working with my father for years." Laura pursed her lips. "They're not keen on having his gay daughter on the payroll."

"They're bastards if they did that to you."

Laura did not look troubled.

"Oddly enough, they actually have a nondiscrimination policy that includes sexual orientation. Don't know what lawyer slipped that in. They probably figured no one would ever use it. You can see where I'm going."

"You want to sue them?" Tate asked.

"And a nasty lawsuit it would be too," Laura went on. "All sorts of interesting things would come out about Clark-Vester and my father. I'd probably lose, of course. No one wins discrimination cases. But it would be so awkward." The smile she gave Tate was not the wry, self-effacing smile that said, *Ah, such is life.* It was a grin. "They agreed to an attractive severance package."

"What do you mean?"

"You might say, they offered me the rainbow parachute."

Laura slid into bed and curled up against Tate's chest.

"I just made a lot of money."

Tate shook her head.

"You get fired and they pay you?"

"Of course."

Laura kissed Tate's chest on the side that had not been bruised. She cupped one of her breasts and gently stroked Tate's nipple, sending a shiver into parts of her body Tate thought were too deeply buried to feel an outside touch.

"So I was thinking of doing what I do best and buying something."

"Like a dress?"

Laura chuckled. "I was going to start with a house."

So that was the kind of "attractive severance" Laura was talking about.

"And then I was going to buy some space, maybe a small building with retail on the first floor and apartments up above. Maybe something with a restaurant or a bar or a coffee shop. I think you have a point about coffee shops. The ones people love aren't the clean brand names. Everyone likes Starbucks coffee, but no one loves them the way they love their dingy, local independent. Now if you could somehow get the Starbucks efficiency into the local shop or start a chain with the independent feel, there is money to be made. Portland is an emerging market even with the recession."

Laura looked so hopeful—her eyes wide and shy as she watched Tate, waiting for her response—Tate almost said yes just to see the smile spread across her face. But she had made that mistake before.

"I don't want to work in a coffee shop anymore," Tate said.

"Neither do I," Laura said casually. "It's too much work. But you could consult. You know the industry. You know the city."

"I want to go back to school and finish my degree, maybe *then* start my own place."

"Fine. Good." Laura was suddenly serious. "What I'm saying is this: As far as I can tell, you've spent your whole life taking care of other people, and I want to take care of you. I want to buy a house in Portland, and I want you to move in with me. I want to find a job for Maggie. I want to help you do whatever you want to do. And I *can* because I have a lot of money." She took Tate's hand in hers and kissed her knuckles. "I got lucky. And I know you're going to say no for all the right reasons. It's too soon. You're your own woman. Maggie doesn't want my charity. I know. And I love that about you. But I thought, maybe, this time, since you don't have anything else going on right now, you could just pretend that you weren't so noble. We could go drive around the city today and look at houses. We could find one with a garden, with room for a dog and a study for you if you want to go back to school."

The robe had fallen open around Laura's shapely body, and now she gathered it closed, hugging herself as though the room had suddenly gone cold.

"You could keep this apartment, and if I disappoint you, you could go back to this life, exactly like it is. You won't owe me anything. You *don't* owe me anything. I know what you think, and I'm so sorry I hurt you. I'm sorry you're afraid that I'm going to leave. You have every right to worry after the way I treated you in Palm Springs, but I'm not going anywhere."

Tate's eyes followed the curve of Laura's long, graceful neck as Laura looked down at the floor.

"I know it's too soon. It's crazy. It's not the way people do things. But what if we just pretend that we don't know that?"

*She actually thinks I might say no*, Tate thought.

"I've heard," Tate said, "you really haven't seen Portland until you've looked for houses."

Laura stared at Tate. For a moment, she could not make sense of her own good fortune. It was a ridiculous notion: the idea that she could just ask Tate to be happy with her, that they could just ignore all reasonable cautions and rush out into the world like kids running headlong into summer vacation. No one did that in real life. There were jobs and paperwork and schedules and recriminations. But Tate had just said yes. Tate was smiling. She was sliding her arm around Laura's waist.

"Come here," Tate said. She kissed Laura gently on the lips.

They kissed for a long time. Laura felt like she could go on kissing Tate like this forever. Then Tate slipped her hand between Laura's legs. Suddenly, Laura felt alive with happiness. It amplified every touch. She wanted to cry out for more, to press Tate's hand to her, but she whispered, "Your leg... are you sure you're okay? I don't want to go too quickly if you're hurt."

"I think..." Tate slowed her touch and made it lighter, rubbing a tiny spot below Laura's clit until Laura could not keep from squirming. "I'd be a failed lesbian if I let one little motorcycle accident..."—she removed her fingers, licked them quickly, and returned to her delicate ministrations—"...keep me from such a beautiful woman."

With a touch so light it could have been a dream except that

Laura's whole body arched toward her fingers, Tate stroked the opening of Laura's sex, drawing the moisture up to her clit.

"You're teasing me," Laura whispered.

Tate smiled. "You said you didn't want to go too quickly."

"For you. I didn't want…" Laura lost her voice in a cry of pleasure as Tate slid her fingers into Laura's body and then around every fold of Laura's sex.

With each caress, Laura felt her body respond, dampen, swell, until she did not know if Tate touched her clitoris or if every part of her sex was as sensitive as her clit.

"There," Laura cried, although she did not know where "there" was anymore, only that she needed Tate's touch everywhere.

"Here?" Tate asked gently.

"Yes."

"Or here?"

"Yes." Laura needed Tate to consume her, to take her, to touch all of her.

As if intuiting her desires, Tate leaned over, kissing her deeply. Then she rubbed harder, gathering all of Laura's sex—her clit, her labia—into her hand and massaging in deep, hard circles. Laura wanted to tell Tate that she felt like a teenager, that everything she had known about sex before had just become words on a page, that she finally understood why people could not sacrifice this—not just the sex but the love that swelled in her heart—for money or position. She wanted to tell Tate all of that, but the orgasm was mounting inside her, and a minute later she was coming uncontrollably.

When her breathing had slowed and her pulse had returned

to a steady beat, Laura opened her eyes. Tate was watching her, and nothing about her gaze made Laura self-conscious. Without looking away, Laura gently rolled Tate onto her back.

"I want to feel you come," Laura said quietly.

Tate stared at her, as if in amazement, and said nothing.

Carefully Laura eased her fingers inside Tate expecting to feel at least a hint of resistance as her body opened, but Tate's body was wet and hot. The walls of her vagina contracted as soon as Laura touched her, and she cried out softly. Laura knew from the tension inside Tate's body that she was already close to orgasm, and she was delighted that she knew. She *knew.* The first time they had had sex, her desire had warred with her fear that she would make some terrible mistake, that Tate would sit up and say, *You haven't done this before, have you?* Now she knew how to caress Tate, how to make her wait, how to strike that perfect balance between tenderness and force, how to touch all of her, then to circle Tate's clitoris until Tate fell silent, her mouth open in a silent moan, her hands grabbing the pillow behind her, her back arching, her hips thrusting into Laura's hand.

Laura felt the orgasm take Tate's body. She held Tate until the last spasm had subsided. Then she slowly withdrew her hand and wrapped her arms and legs around Tate. She could not see Tate's face nestled against her shoulder, but she could feel Tate smiling and hear her whisper, "You set me on fire, Laura Enfield."

# Epilogue

*One Year Later*

Tate stood on the second-story porch that jutted off the master bedroom. Below her, the graduation party—her graduation party—was in full swing.

Literally. Vita was swinging a woman across the lawn, waltzing to the Decemberists' "O Valencia!," which blared from the massive speakers Vita had borrowed from the Mirage. The girl she danced with was, Vita swore, the one. Tate had her doubts, but the girl did wear a lot of animal print. They looked terrific together in a performance-art-on-acid kind of way.

Krystal and her new girlfriend, a beatific, reedy girl with a modest black scarf tied over her hair, tried to tango through the interlacing circles of Vita's waltz. The couples collided, laughed, pretended to enact a kung fu vengeance on each other, and went back to dancing.

Maggie and Janice watched their antics from a set of reclining wicker armchairs and called "Whoa!" when the dancers got too close to their lemonades. Every few minutes, a customer from their new shop, Out in Southwest Portland, would stop by to thank them for the invitation. Janice would hand them a flyer for an upcoming open mike. Then Janice would lift Maggie's hand to her lips to kiss. Maggie's smile made her look a decade younger.

Lill passed around a plate of vegan chia-seed and hemp brownies. Meanwhile, Butch, the Rottweiler puppy Laura had given Tate at Christmas, followed the plate, doing the other party guests a vital service by eating the fibrous blocks behind Lill's back.

In the far corner of the yard, Lill's husband helped Bartholomew and Sobia set up a slip and slide.

Tate's closest friend from PSU, an Iraq veteran with a bicycle covered in Veterans for Peace stickers, took the first slide, going down gown, mortarboard, and all.

"I'm putting that on YouTube," Tate called to him.

He stood up and raised his arms in soggy victory.

Behind Tate, Laura emerged from the bedroom.

"What are you doing up here?" she asked, kissing Tate and leaning her cheek on Tate's shoulder. Tate put her arm around Laura's waist.

"Just watching. Waiting for you."

"That was my brother on the phone," Laura said.

"I guessed."

"Dad didn't get the nomination."

"I'm sorry. Was he mad?"

Laura shrugged.

"The other candidate worked it."

"You being gay?" Tate asked.

"Not exactly. It was everything that happened after that. Dad letting his business partner fire me because I was gay."

"Really?"

"The other guy, Todd Gaven, said my father didn't stand by his own." Laura sounded incredulous. "He said I'd been a faithful daughter who dedicated my whole life to my father's campaigns, and the minute he discovered my sexual orientation he denounced me."

"That's kind of what happened," Tate said.

"And the Republicans picked Gaven. My brother said there's a big push to get the centrist vote and the libertarians. Disowning your gay daughter and lying about it doesn't get you the capital it used to."

Tate shook her head.

"Who would have thought?"

Laura looked down at the garden party. Crown Princess Margarita and his boyfriend and a dozen other members of the Gay Men's Choir were filing in, shaking hands with Krystal's Mennonite relatives. One of the aunts and Jeff the baritone struck up a beautiful harmony, their "Amazing Grace" mingling with the Decemberists' declarations of love.

"You know, I used to think this whole place was an illusion," Laura said. She gestured to the skyline view, to the perfect snowcapped peak of Mount Hood, and then to the party below. Finally her hand rested on Tate's cheek. "And you..."

Laura stared at her with a look Tate recognized because she had seen it in her own eyes.

Tate had spent the first months of their relationship waiting for it to end, waiting to realize she'd played the fool again. But every morning she had woken in Laura's arms, in the beautiful house, with a pile of textbooks spilling out of her backpack and the new Harley parked in the garage. Every evening, she had returned from class to find Laura finalizing some paperwork for her latest project with Portland Green Developers or standing in the kitchen staring, with cocked head, at the contents of the refrigerator because she had the inclination to cook and absolutely no previous experience. And every night, Laura pulled her close and whispered declarations of love that Tate both returned and finally…believed.

Now she pulled Laura into her arms and kissed her temple, inhaling the scent of her orange-blossom perfume.

"It's all real, sweetheart," Tate whispered. "It's all absolutely real."

# About the Author

Karelia Stetz-Waters is an English professor by day and writer by night (and early morning). She has a BA from Smith College in comparative literature and an MA in English from the University of Oregon. Other formative experiences include a childhood spent roaming the Oregon woods and several years spent exploring Portland as a broke twentysomething, which is the only way to experience Oregon's strangest city.

Her other works include *The Admirer*, *The Purveyor*, and *Forgive Me if I've Told You This Before*. She lives with her wife, Fay, her pug dog, Lord Byron, and her cat, Cyrus the Disemboweler.

Karelia loves to hear from readers. You can find her at KareliaStetzWaters.com.

CPSIA information can be obtained at www.ICGtesting.com
Printed in the USA
BVOW08s0910151115

427108BV00001B/5/P